Praise for *Superwoman's Child*

"J. L. Woodson captures the heart and soul of teenagers today. This novel tells the story of a young man who draws on the wisdom of his loved ones as he struggles to get back on top. Recommended reading for parents and teenagers alike."

—Helen Stanton Hawkins, principal, Triumphant Charter School

"This teenage author has written a realistic story that speaks to issues plaguing our children today—overcoming obstacles and inner turmoil to obtain a greater level of success. J. L. Woodson has done it again."

—Ella Houston, Book Lovers Book Club, Chicago

Super
WOMAN'S
Child
Son of A Single Mother

Super WOMAN'S Child

Son of A Single Mother

J. L. WOODSON

SBI

STREBOR BOOKS

NEW YORK LONDON TORONTO SYDNEY

Strebor Books
P.O. Box 6505
Largo, MD 20792
http://www.streborbooks.com

ISBN-13 978-1-59309-059-3
ISBN-10   1-59309-059-5
LCCN 2006923549

Cover design: www.mariondesigns.com

Distributed by Simon & Schuster, Inc.
1230 Avenue of the Americas
New York, NY 10020
1-800-223-2336

First Strebor Books trade paperback edition June 2006

10 9 8 7 6 5 4 3

Manufactured and Printed in the United States of America

For information regarding special discounts for bulk purchases,
please contact Simon & Schuster Special Sales at 1-800-456-6798
or business@simonandschuster.com

Acknowledgments

First, I would like to thank: GOD, the ultimate **Supereverything** in my life, for blessing me with the ability to tell a story. To the **Superancestors/ guardian angels** Mildred E. Williams (my great-grandmother), Jean Woodson (my grandmother), Paul "Deno" Thomas (my karate instructor), Rev. J. B. Sims, Jr. and Rose Morris. I thank all the **Superwomen** in my life: My mom for sticking with me through it all. My grandmothers, Sandra "Sandy" Spears and Bettye Odom, for encouraging me; my god-mother, Linda C. Belton, and a warm thanks to Rev. Renee Sesvalah Cobb-Dishman for spiritual guidance, and Alyse—my best friend, Aunt Vinah and Mama Frankie Payne for teaching me so much; to Ms. Helen Hawkins for giving me a chance to prove myself. Mary B. Morrison, L.A. Banks, Judy Clarke, Leslie Esdaile, Zane ["**Superpublisher!**"], Kimberly Morton Cuthrell, Trevy McDonald, Ph.D., Pat Arnold, Aisha Lusk, Tee C. Royal, the teachers at Olive-Harvey Middle College ["super-cool!"], to my Aunt Monica, cousin Erica and the rest of my family from both sides of my heritage: African-American and Mexican (naming you all will still take too many pages!)

To Avalon Betts-Gaston, Esq., my agent, for lifting me up when I thought it was too hard, taking care of me on the business side, and for being a good person; to Marisa Murillo, my lawyer for coming through for me when I needed it most; to Ms. L. Peggy Hicks (**"super-publicist"**), and Ms. Tori Dickerson for giving me promotion and publicity advice. To the Payne Family—thank you for accepting me with open arms and even bigger hearts. To the (super-editors) Marilyn Weishaar (the fact-checking queen), Christine Meister, Susan Mary Malone, and Anita Doreen Diggs for such insightful advice and helping to develop my writing skills.

Now I'd like to thank the **Supermen** who have helped me through my hardest times. My brother Eric I. Spears, for being a great friend, and to Chris McKee—my "Big Brother;" to my uncles Donny Woodson and the late Eric Harold Spears. To Larry C. Tankson (one of my karate instructors). Thank you to Eric Cuthrell, and also to my original cover designer, Mr. Barron B. Steward, for coming up with such wonderful concepts. Thanks to Keith Saunders for the final cover for SWC—great job. I would like to thank my French teacher, Mr. Jason Robinson, for doing an outstanding job with my book and being a great mentor; my English teacher Mr. Reynolds for adding to my skill of writing. To my photographer, Mr. Pete Stenberg, for bringing out the best in my pictures. To my best friends that helped me through high school and made it fun: Aaron Hester, Chris Irving, Vince Carter, Curtis Meeks. Thanks, guys.

Now on to the **Superpeople**, a big thank you to Fisk University for supporting me through everything. A special thanks to Macro Publishing Group for giving me a start. I would like to thank my Spiritual family from Prayer, Praise and Faith Ministries; to Power Circle Congregation, and the teachers and fellow scholars at Olive-Harvey Middle College (OHMC) for supporting me in the process, giving me something to write about and getting me to college. I don't know where I would be without you guys. I also want to thank my Fisk advisors, Dr. Faulkner, Ms. Ogleton, and Ms. Parker.

To all of the Historically Black Colleges and Universities I visited during the OHMC/TCS college tour. That college tour is why I attended an HBCU. And all of the Fraternities and Sororities that have helped me out with a lot of information.

To the people who came to my book signings, workshops, and discussions.

I can't tell you how much I appreciate it. To all the words of wisdom which come from my mentors, teachers, church members, www.RAWSistaz.com, The Book Lovers Book Club, Dignified Divas, Black Women With Opinons and Attitudes, Different Shades of Black, and authors I have grown to love, you will see that I listened very closely.

peace,
—J. L. Woodson

Su-per wom-an—*n*.

1. A woman who takes on the roles of both mother and father. A woman who pushes her child to be the best they can be. 2. A woman who takes control of a negative situation and turns it into a positive one. 3. A woman who is active in her child's life. 4. A woman who can balance work, her child, her husband, and the workload of an entire household all at the same time. 5. A woman who is there to lift her child's head to the sky when the world brings it down. 6. A woman who doesn't mind embarrassing her son, to make him respect women. 7. A woman who protects her child from the cruelties of the world, but doesn't shelter them to where they become weak.

Chapter 1

Run!

That one word screamed through every corner of his mind, but Sean Morris was too afraid to move.

Run!

As much as his mind said, "nothing is as bad as it seems," if Sean's suspicions were correct, things were *worse* than they seemed.

His rapidly pounding heart slammed against his chest. Sweat poured down his face. Fear gripped him in its ugly jaws. Memories of last year came flooding back with full clarity. With every vision, his mind screamed…*Run!*

Although fright had kept his feet rooted to the floor of his bedroom, his legs finally had the right idea—*Run!*

Dashing out of his house into the icy winter night, the thirteen-year-old came to a frightening conclusion: His mother would kill him this time.

The last time she had whipped him so hard that the bath brush imprint stayed on his butt, arms, and thighs for days. Whenever he was within her reach, the brush landed on some part of his body. That time he had run from the house butt-naked, bare feet trampling through six-foot snowdrifts. He barely felt the wind on his butt. He didn't bother cupping a hand over his exposed genitals as he ran the eight blocks to safety— Kevin's house. Kevin's mother had called Cynthia Morris, Sean's mother, and after a short conversation, Sean had stayed with them overnight.

He had been so frightened that when he got to school the next day, he couldn't open his mouth. He was too upset to concentrate on his work.

It only took a few questions from the principal and Sean was spilling his guts: The one woman who had protected him from the effects of the cruel world had—somehow—scared the living daylights out of him.

He spent a few months at his Grandmother Cecilia's house while his mother calmed down and went through therapy. She hadn't put a hand on him since. Even before that, whippings weren't normal—a couple of taps with a belt once a year in the month before his birthday was all he could remember. Until last year.

Now, a year later, he was running again. At least this time he was wearing clothes. At least this time, she had given him a few seconds before she went off the deep end.

Run!

And the reason was simple. Sean had messed up in school again—easy to fix, if he knew how. Teachers were calling all the time about missing assignments, talking in class, walking out without permission, and fighting with the guys who kept messing with him.

Sean couldn't care less about school. What he did care about was that his mother said in that sad, flat tone: "I can't take this anymore." Sean knew those words by heart. He knew *exactly* what they meant. She was about to give him a serious whipping—no words in the dictionary or anywhere else could even begin to describe it. Especially since something a bit more extreme happened this time. Everyone in the house could have died.

Run!

The week before the Fourth of July, his father had given him fireworks. Not the cute little sparkly kind. No, Roberto gave him the stuff that could take off an arm or two, or rearrange a person's face. Big bang stuff. His mother was never supposed to know. But that all changed when his dad never showed. A sour smell hovered through the house. Three weeks of repairmen, several searches of the two-story house, and days of keeping the windows open even on the frosty fall mornings didn't turn up the source.

Earlier that morning while Sean was at school, Aunt Denise's quick trip to his room to scoop up overripe laundry solved the mystery. She dumped out his hamper, and the fireworks rolled onto the floor; anger lit a fuse under his aunt, then she lit a fuse under Cynthia.

How was he supposed to know that keeping the hamper near the radiator would activate those things? They started turning on the heat higher and he had forgotten all about them. Just like his dad had forgotten all about him—The Fourth had come and long gone with no sign of his father.

Then Cynthia received another phone call. And it was "that time of the month." Then the real fireworks began.

Run!

Sprinting up the street across Mrs. Allen's lawn, Sean almost tripped over the nativity scene. He paused a second, putting baby Jesus back in place, saying a prayer to the little guy, hoping he was watching Sean's back. Sean never looked back to see if his mother was coming. He couldn't afford the time. When Cynthia Morris was angry, that old girl could cover some serious ground—those extra fifty pounds didn't matter. He had seen her go from zero to twenty miles per hour in less than three seconds—and that was on a *slow* day.

Sean should have seen the signs. Normally, she would talk to him. Normally, she would give him a chance to explain. Normally, she would try to help him figure things out. But he remembered last year when she hit the roof. Then she hit him. And hurt him. That's what he couldn't take.

Whoever said PMS was a myth had never experienced his mother's anger. He knew when she would be reasonable. And like now, he knew when to get the hell out of Dodge. Usually he kept a calendar and spent the night with Grandma Cecilia, but somehow he'd slipped up.

Run!

Chapter 2

Run!

Wearing only gray jogging pants, black gym shoes, a white T-shirt, and a Chicago White Sox coat, Sean felt a deep shiver of fear stab his heart. His Godmother Beatrice's house was off limits this time because Sean had promised to get his act together.

Truthfully, Sean hadn't seen "together" in a year and his act—that was just the same scene with different actors, different teachers, and still no sign of the male lead, his father. If he could fix things, change things, he would. Frankly, he didn't know how.

The cold air stung his chest with every breath. Sean didn't know where he was going, but his legs seemed to guide him to Torrence Avenue. The long stretch of road would lead him out of the suburbs, into Chicago, and straight to his father's house. Since he was part of the problem, he should be part of the solution. It was his darn fireworks!

Roberto Maldonado had been the missing factor in Sean's life as long as he could remember. He made guest appearances now and then, but it was anybody's guess when. Then he would disappear again.

Cynthia had raised him with Grandma Cecelia's help. She wasn't Sean's biological grandmother, but she lived with them from time to time. and had helped raise Sean. Cecilia was actually a dear friend of his Grandma Linda. Cecilia was the go-between when Cynthia and Grandma Linda got into it. Sean had known her all of his life and loved her dearly. It was like they were best friends. To make sure there was no confusion when both grandmothers were around, she asked him to call her Cecilia. Instead, he gave her the nickname, Celie.

Aunt Denise, a flight attendant, touched down between international flights. But even she couldn't calm his mother down. Whenever Cynthia became this angry, she would turn into a Warner Brothers cartoon—smoke pouring from the ears and all.

As he ran through the wintry night, Sean knew that in a few more seconds, she would have self-ejected through the ceiling, then the roof, and shot straight into the star-filled sky.

Whether his father would take him in was anybody's guess, but it was worth a try. Sean didn't mind the cold, but he did mind the dark. It was scary on the nearly deserted road. He slowed, changing his mind as he scanned the dreary acres of land filled with God knew what. But the moment he thought about what would happen to him if he went home, his feet moved faster again.

Passing the Ford Auto Plant, reality kicked in.

Cry!

Sean began to cry. His side ached, his head throbbed, and his chest heaved, trying to filter the frosty air. He wanted to be home, he wanted his warm bed, his family. He wanted his momma. His *real* momma—not that alien who appeared in their house for seven days every month.

Cynthia only wanted what was best for him, but sucking it up and taking a whipping this time wasn't best. His heart said so. His backside agreed.

His mother was already stressed out from no money coming in, bills piling up, bill collectors calling every day. Sean knew he wasn't helping matters but for some reason, he couldn't change things, either.

From the moment Sean turned twelve, he kept getting into trouble. He went from being a straight A/B student to a student simply getting by.

At one point, Cynthia thought he was doing drugs. At least that would have been an explanation, because he certainly didn't have another one. She would tear up after every teacher's phone call. She would cry after every progress report and every report card. She became strangely silent when the teachers said, "He's a bright young man, but he's going to fail because he didn't turn in his work." She *knew* Sean had done the work. She sat up with him most nights and watched. Somehow those papers mysteriously disappeared the moment he reached into his book bag to turn them in. He had no excuse and didn't try to give one. Oddly enough, all bad news came about the same time—the wrong time.

Cry!

Now he had really done it. Maybe now his mother didn't love him anymore. He would soon find out if his own father ever had. Doubt crept into Sean's thoughts. Going farther felt hopeless. He wanted to turn back around and go home, but couldn't. He had gotten this far. He had to continue.

Walking slower now, he passed the Calumet Bridge, which meant he had gone about a mile and a half and was on Torrence Avenue. Sean realized he was now in Chicago, but far from real civilization. The only thing shining down on him was the yellowish moon. He gazed up at the midnight blue sky, filled with stars and a few airplanes, wondering why he wasn't on one of them. Yellow headlights abruptly brightened the dark, concrete road that stretched endlessly in front of him.

Hide!

Sean darted off to the side. He stood still. The only company he could find was an occasional rusted green lamppost and an eerie-looking steel plant. Acme Steel—like in the Road Runner cartoon. But this was real life, and right now it was no laughing matter.

An orange-red Chevrolet Cavalier slowed, then pulled up next to him. Sean inhaled deeply, pressing his body closer to the lamppost for cover.

Hide!

Someone rolled down the window. A white woman with reddish brown hair, brown eyes, and a friendly face looked out at him. "Do you need a lift?" she asked softly.

Every TV commercial about not taking rides from strangers, every reminder about not taking candy from strangers, every newscast about runaway children being killed, rolled through his mind. As Sean thought about whether he should take an offer from a total stranger, the warm air from the car washed over him and clouded his mind. His options: go back to the trouble waiting at home, or keep walking, get frostbite, and lose a toe before he made it to his father's house. The fear disappeared, replaced by pain and deep unhappiness. He was tired of walking, and it seemed like he had miles on top of miles to go.

"Sure, thanks," Sean answered, getting into the car with an uneasy feeling settling in his mind and gut.

"No problem."

His mother had once said, "*God watches over babies and fools.*" Hopefully, Mom was right about that.

Sean glanced over at the woman, who could be a cheerleader's mom or a serial killer, and wondered if things had gone from bad to worse.

God!

Help!

Me!

Chapter 3

The car smelled of stale cigarettes and car freshener. The ride would have been smooth if it weren't for the potholes every few feet. A layer of snow covered the road, making it hard to see, let alone avoid, the holes. The gas tank needle stood at half full. At least they wouldn't be stranded on the long stretch of road. But then again those "Chicago Craters" could flatten a tire or two. Then they'd be in real trouble.

A quick glance in the backseat showed leather upholstery patched up with duct tape. McDonald's bags littered the floor. There also was a baby seat. The woman was a mother! Maybe she *was* safe.

He relaxed a little, wiping away his tears. Now was not the time to cry. He had to keep his eyes peeled and his hand near the door handle.

"So where are you going?" the woman asked, startling him as she stopped at the 106th Street traffic light.

"Um…" Sean, totally unprepared for questions, cleared his throat. "My dad's house, on One-Hundred First and Crandon." Sean slid closer to the door. Although the woman was pretty and had a baby, she could still be dangerous. Killing could be her night job.

"Okay, I know where that is." The woman's hand gripped the wheel. "But what are you doing out here this late?"

Sean wasn't prepared to answer that question, either. He wasn't prepared for being in a car with a stranger. Her voice, soft and sincere, reminded him of his momma's.

"I ran away from home, Ma'am," Sean blurted out. Then he lowered his head, crying once again. This time he couldn't stop. He was angry, afraid, hungry, and tired.

The woman gently placed her hand on his shoulder. Sean winced at the contact, but sat still. She patted him gently. "Why would you do such a thing?"

"She…" Sean paused, gathering his thoughts. "She was going to whip me because I had bad grades on my report card and they gave me detention." He glanced at the woman. Somehow he couldn't mention the fireworks—the fireworks that wouldn't have been there if his father had kept his promise.

"No matter what she was about to do, you should never have left home," the driver said. Every few seconds, streetlights illuminated her pale face. "These streets are much worse than getting a whipping. Do you understand?"

Even though Sean wanted to block out what the woman said, he knew she was right. The news was always full of kids being kidnapped and killed, and then dumped in the garbage. Some disappeared from their own beds. Kids had to be careful in this world. It had become a dangerous place for them, but then, adults didn't have it all that great either if the news reports were right.

Warm air blowing from the front vents whisked away the cold in his long, thin fingers and dried his tears.

"Besides, I'm sure your mother cares about you a lot. She's just frustrated by the fact that you aren't getting the grades she knows you're capable of getting in school," she said solemnly. "Know this—without an education, you can't get anywhere in this world. You might as well be on the streets." She whipped into the turning lane of 103rd and Torrence.

Folding his arms over his chest, Sean thought about the things his mother had done for him. Being a single mom was hard, but every kid he knew had a single mother. Sean did notice how hard she struggled. His mother went without so he could have things. He had seen her miss a meal while putting a plate in front of him. She would laugh it off, pointing to her plus-size frame. "Does it look like I can't afford to miss just one?" Sean knew it was more than one. She wore the same clothes all the time, but Sean had new clothes every school year. He heard that she skipped paying some bills so he could have a saxophone for music class and go on class trips. Somehow, things became better when Grandma Cecilia and Aunt Denise moved in. But not much.

All those times when she did extra or did without so he could have—that's when his mother earned the title Superwoman. And yes, he had seen all of that, but something was still missing and hurting deep inside of him. He was angry. He didn't care about school and rules and homework and the kids who all seemed to hate him. He didn't care about anything anymore. And he couldn't put it into words for his mom or anybody else.

Slowing down, the woman turned on Crandon, where the beige stone and green painted Goldsmith Elementary School loomed on the corner. The woman's words echoed in his head. The more he listened, the more he knew he should be at home. Maybe he was wrong about what his mother planned to do. She had changed a lot since last year, and he had seen her walk away when she was angry—doing that count-to-ten or hold-your-breath thing. But she had never been this angry, so he had skipped out moments after she had turned and walked out of his room.

"It's right here," Sean said, pointing at a two-story brick house with yellow aluminum siding. "Thanks for the ride."

"No problem. Just remember things aren't always as bad as they seem," she said, putting the car in park. "If you do something, it's better to suffer the consequences than run away from them."

"Yes, Ma'am," Sean said, hesitating to get out of the car. He glanced back at the woman for a moment then at the house and swallowed. A light was on in the living room and another in an upstairs bedroom. Someone was there. He looked at the woman again.

She smiled. "Why don't we call your mother just to let her know that you're okay?"

The car purred and rumbled beneath him. Sean didn't answer. He was already at his father's house. What would a call to his mom matter now? Sean shook his head.

"If you're worried about me telling her where you are—don't," the woman replied. "But I'm a mother and I know I would worry about one of my children being out at one o'clock in the morning."

The wind whipped against the Chevy, causing it to shake. Sean held tight to the black door handle.

"Yes, Ma'am," Sean said. "You can call her."

The woman reached into her purse, pulled out a silver phone, and waited.

Sean didn't say a word.

A slow, unreadable smile spread on the woman's thin, curved lips. "I need the number."

"Oh, yeah, right." Sean swallowed again. A lump had formed in the base of his throat, making it hard to speak. He finally got his voice to work and gave the woman the number.

As Sean waited for the woman to call his mother, he noticed there was frost on the shoveled sidewalk from the quick drop in temperature. Though the yellow siding was somewhat new and the shutters had received a bright white coat of paint, the house looked unfriendly.

"What's her name?"

"Cynthia, Cynthia Morris."

"Mrs. Morris?" The woman perked up. "My name is…" Then she paused. "My name is not important. Your son is sitting next to me in my car and he's okay. He asked me not to tell you where he is, so—"

Sean turned around, wondering why the woman had fallen silent.

"Yes, I found him on Torrence around…One-Hundred Thirtieth, just past the Ford plant."

Sean felt an instant alarm and reached out to touch the woman's arm.

The woman shook her head, assuring him that she would say no more than that. Then she fell silent again.

"May I say something, Mrs. Morris? Your son was walking on a dark, lonely street at one o'clock in the morning. I almost didn't pick him up because it's so late and I'm alone. But as I got closer, I saw he was a little boy. I thought about my children, and I couldn't just drive past." The woman glanced over at Sean whose glistening eyes had filled with tears.

"I can tell he's very well mannered, and he seems like a great kid. But he doesn't need to be out here, no matter how disappointed you are in him right now. We just wanted you to know that he's safe."

Sean wondered how a complete stranger could tell all that about him in a short while. She had kept the engine running and the heater on. It was better than being outside in the cold.

Sean tugged on the woman's leather coat.

She covered the phone and turned to him.

"Tell my mom that I'll call her real soon. I really will. And that," he choked, "I love her."

She nodded slowly before putting the phone back up to her ear, a smile parting her thin lips. "He says to tell you he'll call real soon and that he loves you," she said somberly. "Okay. Yes, Mrs. Morris, I'll tell him."

The phone disappeared into her purse.

"Your mother says to tell you that she walked away to calm down. She didn't know you were gone until she came into your bedroom to say good-night," she said in a low voice. "She said that she loves you, too."

As Sean slowly got out of the car, tears flooded his eyes. He wanted to go back home right now. All this was for nothing. Now maybe he was in *real* trouble. He looked at the woman and asked, "What's your name?"

She hesitated a brief moment, "Just call me Mary Beth. I can't tell you more than that, because I can get into real trouble for what I did tonight."

Trouble? For helping him? That was sad. Sean thought for a moment before he said, "Thank you, Ma'am."

He closed the door and trudged to the gate. The Chevy sped away down Crandon, past the little park near the corner.

Walking up his dad's steps, Sean gazed at the old rusted doorbell outside the vestibule. Inching his finger toward the doorbell, he pressed it.

No one answered. He pressed it again and then went over to the living room window. He peeked through the gap in the sheer, white curtains. The television was on. Someone stood at the top of the stairs and cast a shadow against the wall. Someone was home. *Why wouldn't his dad open the door?*

Chapter 4

An hour later, Sean was still sitting on the steps. It was so cold, his fingers felt numb. He'd tried banging on the door and tapping on the windows. Sean went back to the door. Just as he raised his hand to knock again, he saw his dad look out the peephole. He then turned and walked back up the stairs, as though keeping silent would make Sean go away.

Sean didn't want to leave even if his mother wasn't mad anymore. He wanted his dad to know that he was there. He wanted some answers. *Why hadn't he shown up on the Fourth of July? Why hadn't he heard from him since then? Why couldn't his dad be more active in his life? Why did he tell him "I'll be there," and never show up?*

Getting angrier by the second, Sean again got up from the cold, concrete stairs. He would push the doorbell one last time before making the long walk home. He waited three more minutes. The door stayed shut.

Sean realized he would be frozen like a TV dinner if he didn't get moving soon. He started to walk away. Then he heard a creak and turned. Half of his father's face appeared in the shadows. From his father's scowl, Sean knew that he was either unwelcome or interrupting something. He hadn't expected his dad to roll out the welcome mat, but he didn't expect the cold shoulder either.

"What can I do for you, Sean?" Roberto asked harshly.

"Dad, can I stay with you?" Sean pushed himself to ask while he still had the courage. "Mom was about to whip me again, so I ran hoping you'd take me in."

Seconds ticked by before Sean's father growled, "Come in." He looked as if he meant *go away* instead.

Sean walked into the cozy house, took off his jacket, and laid it over the arm of the tan couch. Sean heard the TV coming from his father's room. He smelled tamales coming from the kitchen. Sean watched his father pat a green towel on his damp, dark brown, gray-streaked, wavy hair.

"Is someone here?" Sean asked, looking around and listening closely for footsteps. Maybe Grandma Lupe was home.

"That's none of your business, but no one's here. My mother's in Mexico."

"Then why didn't you answer the door?"

Roberto grimaced and didn't look Sean in the eyes. "I was taking a shower."

Sean's right eyebrow shot up, eyes narrowed to slits. "For more than an hour? There isn't that much clean in the world."

His dad just looked at him.

Sean looked back, waiting for him to say something.

"So what happened?" Roberto asked, sitting down in a wooden rocking chair, trying to sound concerned.

"I had some bad grades on my report card, and Mom got angry at me, so I ran out of the house and came over here." Sean was ashamed that he was only there for that reason. *Why couldn't it be to visit or go to Jesse Owens Park and walk around? Or maybe to toss a football, like he did one time when Sean was younger?*

"Everywhere you go, you're going to have rules," Roberto said. "I wouldn't tolerate bad grades, either."

Was there something on the carpet that Sean wasn't seeing? Why wouldn't his dad look at him?

"Well, Dad, *you're* the real reason I'm in trouble," Sean said, trying to control his anger.

"What are you talking about?" Roberto snapped, suddenly looking Sean in the eyes.

"Aunt Denise found those fireworks that you gave me," Sean said, speaking a little bit louder. "I didn't know I was going to get in trouble, because I got them from you."

"Well, what did you think when I said your mother wasn't supposed to see them?"

"Well, I wouldn't have had to hide them for so long if you'd shown up on the Fourth of July," he shot back without a moment's hesitation. "Instead, you stood me up like you do most of the time." *Wow! Did he say all that?*

"Sean, I apologize for that."

"That doesn't mean I'm going to forget. Especially since every time we've planned something lately you stood me up," Sean said in a somber tone. "I will never forget the three times you stood me up on Father's Day. The day that is supposed to be *your* day."

Roberto sighed heavily. "Sean, once again I'm sorry. There's nothing I can do about it now."

"I don't need your…apologies," Sean roared and almost cursed. *His mother would kill him!* "I need you to be in my life! Not part time, like I'm some mistake, but full time, like I'm your son. I *am* your son!!!"

Roberto turned beet red. He was hotter than a tamale.

Sean figured out by the the turn of the conversation that he wouldn't be staying there with his father and grandmother. He didn't even bother asking his father again.

Eyes brimming with anger, Sean broke the silence. "Can I please use your phone?"

"Sure, it's in the kitchen," his dad said, staring blankly at him.

Sean followed his father into the old-fashioned, yellow and brown kitchen. Sean glanced at the pictures that covered the refrigerator door. Pictures of Sean's cousins, aunts, and uncles. Pictures of everyone except him—his son. Nothing else really stood out other than the picture of Jesus praying to the heavens—something that Sean should be doing right now.

He had only punched two digits of his mother's phone number when the doorbell rang. Sean froze. His father jumped.

They walked to the door and looked through the peephole. Sean was shocked to find his momma and his Grandma Celie shivering on the porch. *How did they find him?*

Chapter 5

Cynthia looked like she just got out of bed. She was dressed in gray sweat pants, dark gray boots, and a zipped-up heavy black coat with fur around the hood. Celie was wearing navy stretch pants, a black leather coat, and had a black scarf wrapped around her head.

Aunt Denise always told Sean that having both of his parents in the same room was not a good thing. He was about to find out if that was true.

"You should have called me, Roberto."

"Cynthia, please don't start," Roberto said, closing the door behind the two women. He pulled his robe around him as the chill came in with them.

Grandma Celie gave Sean a quick hug before pulling him onto the love seat and away from his parents.

"Oh, Roberto, where should I start?" Cynthia asked, taking a seat on the couch. "First, why did you give Sean fireworks without telling me about them?"

"Because I knew you would freak out, like you're doing now. They're just fireworks," he said, standing by the window.

"Just fireworks! Those things could have killed someone. I almost went off on Sean today all because of you," Cynthia said, trying to stay calm and in her seat.

Roberto threw Sean a quick glance.

"Seeing how he ran to your house, he *obviously* trusts you," she said angrily. "But yet you tell him to keep something from me. Or were you deliberately using him to burn my house down?"

"Cynthia, I don't—"

"Save it," she said, tossing up her hand. "Maybe you should keep Sean, since you want him to go against me."

Sean looked up, elated with her suggestion. Maybe his dad would take him in and be in his life for good. He could also prove Cynthia and the rest of the family wrong, by showing them he cared for his son.

"Cynthia, what if I did?" he said meekly. Too meekly.

The punk!

Roberto continued, "Sean still would have to obey the same rules and probably even more."

Cynthia's full lips twitched. "Hopefully you'll be able to teach him how to be a man."

"What will he sleep on? I don't have anything for him."

"No problem. I'll give you his bed," Cynthia replied with a smirk. "And *I'll* pay child support."

His dad's face became blank. No more excuses.

He was going to live with his dad!

"Cynthia, I just can't do it, my mother won't let me…"

Sean's elation wore away as one excuse followed the other. The conversation was a waste of time. He knew why his mother gave Roberto the opportunity to prove he didn't want the responsibility of being a dad.

"Sean, get in the car," his mother said, tossing his father a look that would've scared the devil himself.

Mom did have the right to be angry. They did have that child-support thing going. A thirteen-year battle that was a sporting event all by itself. His father was the runningback, trying to make it to the goal line of "can't handle my responsibilities." His mother was a defensive tackle, trying to make sure he didn't cross that line without first taking him down on the Astroturf.

Tension crackled in the air. Sean waited for his father to say something. Anything.

His dad just looked at him with a grim expression.

Sean had spent a mere forty-five minutes with his dad. He really shouldn't have expected much from the man who didn't bother to call and had never come to a parents' day at school.

Tears welled in his eyes. He turned from his father and wiped them away. He didn't want to give the man the satisfaction of seeing him cry. All the things his mother said about his father were true. He chose not to be with Sean.

"Your grandmother wouldn't allow you to stay here anyway. It's her house," Sean's dad said defensively.

Sean knew better. Grandma Goose, as Lupe Maldonado liked to be called, *would* want him to stay—it's not like she hadn't said so. *Besides that, why didn't his father have his own place? He was forty-five years old. How long did a guy stay with his mother? Was he just hanging around because "he who is in the house when Grandma leaves wins?"* Roberto had never had his own apartment. That would mean keeping a job, which would mean paying child support, which would mean spending time with—yeah well, maybe not spending time with his son, since he was already paying anyway.

Sean threw an angry glance at his father as he walked past him and strolled out the door.

The glittering ice on the path lit his way to the car and away from the house. His mother and grandmother were right behind him. As Sean opened the car door for his grandmother, she hugged him firmly and whispered, "You could've died out here. I hope it was worth it."

It wasn't.

Sean felt a little sad as he rode toward 103rd and Torrence Avenue. Leaving home had been a waste of time. He was right back where he started.

"What possessed you to run away?" his mother asked, adjusting the rearview mirror so she could see him.

"I didn't want to get a whipping," Sean said, trembling.

"I wasn't going to whip you!" she said, her voice rising at the end. "And even if you were going to get a whipping, leaving wouldn't save you, only Jesus could do that. You should've never left home. You had me worried. Do you know how dangerous these streets are? Do you?"

Okay, here we go.

"They're dangerous enough to send you home in pieces. Is that how you want to end up?" Cynthia began to cry while speeding down Torrence Avenue.

Sean's heart leapt to his throat with every jump of the speedometer. "No, Ma'am," he answered, slouching in the seat.

Even his grandmother was keeping her distance, just in case his mother wanted to reach back and pop him one on the head. If Cynthia accidentally hit his grandmother, she would get a whipping of her own. Now *that* would have made sports television.

His mother was only getting wound up. "We wouldn't be in this situation if you were doing what you're supposed to do in school, and if you didn't allow your father to tell you to hide things in my house. Those weren't regular fireworks, and you know it! Oh," she said as she stared at Sean via the rearview mirror, "and you're still going to be grounded."

Sean looked toward his Grandma Celie, hoping she could get him out of trouble for running away. Celie remained silent.

Actually, he was glad to be going home no matter how long he was grounded. He knew the truth about his father—and that hurt worse than anything.

Cynthia was trying so hard to mold him into a "responsible and respectful man." All he was doing was making it hard on her. After listening to her and his father tonight, he knew why she was so angry. It was a father's role to teach his son how to be a man. Obviously his father hadn't learned that lesson himself, and it wasn't likely he ever would. Cynthia said he'd only be grounded. She had definitely changed and Sean was grateful.

One good thing would come from the night Sean ran away. But as usual, good things come at a price.

Chapter 6

One night in the middle of December, Sean's mom answered the door to find Roberto standing there. He was wearing a blue mechanic's jumpsuit and oil-stained work boots. Cynthia's eyes widened in surprise, then narrowed.

"Cynthia, can we talk?" he asked softly. "It's about Sean."

"Why now, all of a sudden?"

Roberto grimaced. "Well, when Sean showed up at my house two weeks ago, it really got me to thinking."

Sean's door was halfway open. He peered out at his parents. *It took Dad two whole weeks to think about what I said? Talk about your slow learner!*

"I realize that he needs a dad. He needs *me.*" Roberto looked at Cynthia with such intensity, Sean thought they were going to kiss. *Nah!*

"Okay, you have five minutes," Cynthia said grudgingly, allowing him in her house. He walked into the living room, where a remodeling project was underway. Cynthia was having stairs built and the workers were still laying the Pergo wood floor. There was a hole in the ceiling and two long wooden planks sat at an angle.

Roberto got right to the point. "I want to enroll him at Jayne Adamson. I checked into it, and he doesn't seem to be doing well at his school. I want this to be the first thing I do for him—put him in a school where he can do better."

Grandma Celie walked past them to the kitchen. She didn't acknowledge Roberto's presence, but Sean knew the kitchen was a better place to hear everything. *Dag. Why didn't he think of that?*

"Plus, it's time he knows he's not just African-American. He's also Hispanic," Roberto said, leaning against the wall. "There are mostly Hispanic and White students at Jayne Adamson. It's a great school, and his cousin Sara goes there. So he would already know somebody..."

"I'm all for you spending time, real *quality time*, with Sean," Cynthia said abruptly. She looked at him for a long time. "But why should I trust you with this? Putting Sean in a new school? One that's not even close by?" Cynthia shook her head, folding her fingers together, fighting the feelings of anger welling up inside.

Come on, Mom. I hate Gadson. Give Dad a try!

Roberto inhaled but kept his gaze steady. "He's not doing well, so what difference does it make? And how am I supposed to do *more* for Sean if you won't let me do *anything?*"

"I don't know. Try really *being in* his life for once. I'd really like to believe you, Roberto, but I'm not sure you can handle this." She paused, pressing her fingers to her temples. "Can you really deal with this kind of responsibility? Maybe you should just take it easy—one step at a time," Cynthia said. "How about child support? Child support would work for me."

Those words—"one step at a time"—seemed to shake Roberto, breaking the expressionless mask on his face, or perhaps it was the words "child support" that did him in. The silence in the room was overwhelming. Sean could see his dad trying to choose the right words.

"Just let me handle this. Please," he finally said, "I'll do what I'm supposed to do."

Sean couldn't stand it when his dad made a fool of himself. Everything Dad said gave Mom room to throw it back in his face. Neglect was a universal tool. Sean liked that his dad was taking a stab at being in his life, but something didn't feel right. How did Sean's running away cause this dramatic turnaround? Could he trust his dad again?

"You can watch every step I make if you want to, but just let me handle it," Roberto said.

Cynthia let those words settle in for a moment, looking at Roberto with renewed suspicion. "You're a grown man. I shouldn't have to watch over you. If you had really given this any thought, you'd realize that you're going to need him someday. You'd realize—"

"So are you," Roberto said.

"I already have him," she snapped. "I know my son. Do you?"

"I want to. That's what this is all about."

"I'll have to ask Sean—"

"Yes!!!" Sean yelled from the hallway. "Yes."

A long pause filled the living room. Finally Cynthia said, "Okay. Have him registered for school so he can start at the beginning of the semester. Maybe you'll realize that he's a good kid."

Chapter 7

Once everything was settled, Roberto moved quickly. By the second week in January, Sean's transfer to Jayne Adamson was set. Because Sean didn't live in Chicago, they used Roberto's address on the school paperwork. Superwoman was not about to let Sean *actually* live with his dad. But the school didn't have to know.

Sean thought that going to school on the east side of Chicago would be cool, but living more than five miles away in Calumet City meant relying on a suburban bus schedule, which made getting to school complicated.

The first day he woke up at five in the morning. He smacked the red snooze button on his Nickelodeon alarm clock. It was time to continue seventh grade at a brand-new school. Getting out of bed, he scanned the dark room. Not a speck of sunshine peeked through the white shades. *Man! Whose bright idea was it for him to go to a babysitter's this early in the morning?*

Cynthia didn't trust the bus to get Sean to school on time. She also didn't trust him to reach the bus on his own. He would never make it to school. Ever since he ditched school for a whole week in fifth grade, she kept a close eye on him to make sure he at least left the house.

That's where the Vega family came into play. They would look after Sean for an hour, then make sure he got to Jayne Adamson on time. Sean had met them last summer at his Aunt Monica's barbecue, which was the first time Sean's grandfather had heard of Sean. Cynthia and Sean talked about the shock which followed. The Vegas must have been extended family because Sean had never met them at any of Aunt Monica's earlier family get-togethers.

Sean grabbed the emerald-green towel and washcloth off the old wooden dresser. He plodded to the bathroom, dropped his towel and pajamas on the floor, set the shower temperature cooler than usual, and hopped in. As the water woke him up, Sean thought about no longer being at Gadson Elementary. He was kind of glad he was going to a new school, one where he could start fresh.

At Gadson, no one seemed to like him. For one thing, he dressed different, only khakis and polo shirts—no baggy clothes, no fake platinum chains. And he had good manners, he always said "please," "thank you," and "yes ma'am." Worst of all, he was constantly teased because he talked like a Preppie. Sean could manage more than one sentence using proper English.

Sean had tried to fit in but had only made one real friend—Kevin. His only other friends were the teachers and the janitor, Mr. Sharp. But Superwoman had always told him, "No matter where you go, the only time the other kids are going to get the best of you, is when you let them." Sean knew she was right, but he always let them get under his skin, arguing back when someone talked about him. Maybe this school would be different.

After showering, Sean brushed his teeth, put on some deodorant, and splashed on a little Polo Sport cologne. He gazed into the mirror, noticing that the peach fuzz above his lips was starting to get a little thick. *All right!* He returned to his dark room, turned on the light, and went to his dresser. He grabbed his underwear, walked over to his closet, and whipped out a white polo shirt and a pair of navy Dickies. He completed his school uniform with a pair of black dress shoes.

Struggling with his shirt, he ran into the wall. "Ouch!" he exclaimed as he bumped into the dresser and the door before regaining his balance. Why did that happen every day? Sean rubbed his forehead, then grabbed his black First Down coat and maroon book bag. It was fully loaded with pens, paper, notebooks, and a Walkman.

"Sean, here are the keys," Cynthia yelled from the top of the stairs. "Go start the car."

"Start the car? It's cold out there," he mumbled as the keys flew past him, hitting the metal front door and falling to the floor. "Yes Ma'am." Sean grabbed them and walked outside toward the silver Buick Century.

A light snowfall greeted Sean as he looked at the bright orange street-light. He realized he had never been outside this early before. He got in and started the car, hoping that the heat would get going before the sun rose.

Sean had never seen his mother this early either. Her "morning face" was one he didn't recognize until she got in the car. The bags under her eyes could've contained a cart full of groceries, with room for a few more. *Something major must happen during that extra hour she usually sleeps. Or was it the makeup that produced the final results? Why was she so tired these days?*

Twenty minutes later, the sun still hadn't appeared as they stopped at a red light in front of the Hegewisch train station. Sean listened to his Sony CD Walkman, and watched as the No. 30 bus pulled in. Students from St. Francis De Sales High School and Washington High School boarded the bus. At least he wasn't the only one riding the bus that early. The light stayed red so long, Sean's bus pulled off without him.

"Shoot! I'm going to have to take you down Burnham Avenue to catch it."

Gazing out the streaked window, Sean saw a number of morning joggers and bike riders around Wolf Lake. The sun finally peered just over the horizon, shining softly on the snow-covered grass, blue picnic tables, and water.

He snapped awake as his mother came to an abrupt halt. They were in an empty parking lot of a small plaza that had dollar stores and a health club.

"Okay, Sean, the bus should be pulling up in a minute," she said while he stretched. "You're close to their house. But I want you to know what it's like to do this on your own. From here, take this bus to One Hundred First and Ewing, then get on the One Hundredth Street bus and get off at Oreck Avenue. Walk over two blocks to this address," she said writing every-thing down on a napkin that she had pulled from the glove compartment.

"Yes, Ma'am," Sean said, knowing that if she didn't write it down, he'd be lost for sure. He opened the car door and put one foot on the ground.

"Oh, you don't know how to say bye?" She gazed at him with her brows raised and a light smile—the smile that belonged to Superwoman.

Sean stopped. "Bye, Momma, love you." He leaned over giving her a peck on the cheek.

Cynthia rolled her eyes, "Mmmm-hmmm, love you, too."

Sean closed the door as the bus pulled up.

The night they had rescued him from Dad's house, Cynthia told him, "A mother can still love her son but not like him for what he does." He believed her.

The bus doors opened and he boarded, sliding his wrinkled dollar in the machine before receiving a bus transfer. The bus pulled off so quickly, he almost fell into the blue and black seat. He was still tired from the early morning wake-up. His eyelids felt like they were holding three hundred-pound weights. He leaned against the window and, as Celie called it, "rested his eyes."

The roar of the bus engine snapped Sean out of his nap. Looking out the window, he saw them passing by the 101st Street sign. "Stop!" he yelled, running for the door.

"Boy, know where your stop is next time," the bus driver told him sternly.

Some people just shouldn't work in the morning. The bus driver didn't have to be so foul, but Superwoman had told Sean to respect his elders no matter what. Sometimes that was hard, especially when some of them weren't right.

"I'm sorry, Sir, I fell asleep."

"Be careful about falling asleep on the bus; you never know what kind of crazy people might be riding with you, son," the driver warned him.

Like crazy, maniac bus drivers, looking like they hit the bottle one time too many this morning. Sean really hated that he said "son" and wanted to say, "Unless my birth certificate has your name as my father, don't call me son."

Instead he said, "Yes, Sir," as the driver opened the door and let him out.

Chapter 8

S ean walked past the Cargill Oil Plant and down the sidewalk in Johnson Park. Though he felt cautious walking through a strange neighborhood, he knew he could handle himself if necessary.

When Sean was in Gadson Elementary, a lot of kids didn't like him because he carried himself like a gentleman. Fights after school became routine. Fights where it was three or four to his one. When Sean came home two days in a row with his shirt ripped and his nose and lips bloody, Superwoman gave him a piece of advice. "Sean, I know I've always told you to walk away from fights, but I was not talking about this kind of stuff— where a bunch of kids gang up on you. It's time to fight back. If one of those little cowards so much as even pushes you, hit him back," she said viciously.

That sounded like good advice, but knowing *how* to fight would sure help. She always packed two bottles of mace. Grandma Celie didn't fight, she took a belt or skillet to someone's behind. Aunt Denise always had her Smith & Wesson or a blade in her purse until she got a job with the airlines. Now she just swung a purse. As big as it was, whoever got hit with that thing was as good as dead. So who would teach him hand-to-hand combat?

Cynthia enrolled him in karate classes at Tankson's Martial Arts. At Shihan Tankson's dojo, Sean worked his way up to an orange belt, which is the second level. Soon he began to compete in tournaments. In the beginning, third place was his best finish. When they moved from Jeffery Manor to the 'burbs, he went to a partner school, Paul's Martial Arts.

He was tested at Shihan Deno's dojo, and kept his orange belt ranking. The first day of class, Sean got a serious workout. Shihan Deno was a beast when it came to discipline and karate—laps, push-ups, sit-ups, squats—all hard work. But it paid off. Within two weeks, Sean passed the yellow belt test. When he started competing in tournaments again, he began winning— sometimes second place, but usually first.

Shihan Deno was a large man, who could move like a jaguar and hit as hard as a lion. Sean soon looked up to him as a father figure. He didn't just teach him about karate, fighting, and flipping—but also about respect. He was the only male who was teaching him what it was to be a man. It sounded like the stuff Celie and Superwoman had been telling him, but it was somehow different when it came from a man.

As Sean walked to Paul's Martial Arts, he concentrated on his training efforts toward winning first place at the upcoming tournament. He would be competing in two events: a sparring match and kata—a series of choreographed movements where one fought an imaginary opponent.

As usual, his mother would be there to cheer him on and help out with equipment. She never missed his tournaments.

Sean stepped into the dojo wearing his all-black sparring karate *gi*—the uniform—with Paul's white martial arts logo on the back. The dojo had a sitting area in the front, showcasing the trophies the school had won. The dark gray carpet had a pink stripe which separated the sitting area from the class area. Every karate student had to bow at the dividing line, showing respect for the dojo.

"Hey, Sean, hurry and get warmed up for class," Shihan said. He wore a red-and-black karate gi with a black belt and five stripes. "We have a lot of work to do. You have one minute, starting now."

"Yes, Shihan," Sean responded as he ran to his locker, took his belt out, and stuffed his bag in the small space.

"Thirty seconds!"

Sean hurried to put on his belt. "Yes, Shihan."

If he wasn't ready in time, he would have to do fifty push-ups on top of the regular workout.

"Fifteen seconds," Shihan Deno yelled. Sean sprinted out and stopped in front of Shihan Deno to bow. Sean was crisp and clean, as Shihan wanted all of his students to look.

"Guess you learned your lesson from all of the other times," Shihan said with a chuckle, making a reference to the times when Superwoman had to rush home from work, yank Sean away from the dinner table, tear down the expressway leading into the city trying to get Sean to class on time. Sometimes they made it, but other times...

"Yes, Shihan, I have," Sean said, staring at his reflection in the large square mirrors that lined the back wall of the dojo.

"I want you to begin stretching and work on your kata forms. You will be teaching class for the day."

"Yes, Shihan," Sean said. He looked from side to side, letting that bit of shocking information settle in. It was a big responsibility, and Sean wasn't about to shorten up or slack off around Shihan Deno, because he would have to pay the consequences—the kind that would require him to schedule an appointment with Bengay, Icy Hot, and Aspercreme—his grandma's three pain reliever friends.

★★★

Shihan Deno had eyes in the back of his head and supersonic hearing. He may have not looked like it, but he was paying attention—other than the one time he was caught resting his eyes.

Shihan worked hard, not only in karate, but also distributing health products. Shihan also had narcolepsy—a sleeping disorder where he could fall asleep at any time.

In Sean's Wednesday karate classes at the St. Sabina Church gymnasium, Sean walked in to class, ready for the intensive workout.

"Get in line for class," Paul yelled. "You have ten seconds."

Sean sat in front, so he wouldn't be late. Walking the few feet to the line, Sean arrived seconds ahead of his classmates. Shihan placed a medium-sized, white bag on the table. It radiated a heavenly aroma that Sean hadn't smelled since they moved to the suburbs. Shihan opened the bag and pulled out a container, with mild sauce dripping on the side. He unfastened the container and the steam rose, revealing the famous Harold's Chicken, crinkled fries topped with mild sauce, and coleslaw.

"You guys took fifteen seconds to get ready for class. Seeing how only one of you was smart enough to sit closer to the class versus having to run," Shihan said as he ate in front of them, making them strain to understand what he was saying, "everyone has to run fifteen laps today."

As Sean began his last five laps he gazed at Shihan and noticed his closed eyes, his slouched body, and a chicken bone in his hand. He knew Shihan would wake by the time he returned to the line. Finishing his last lap, Sean ran to the line, standing in front of his snoring karate instructor. Soon everyone was back in line waiting for Shihan to give them their next exercise.

"I eat Harold's all the time, and I never fall asleep in the middle of eating," David said, laughing at the chicken bone still in Shihan's hand.

"I couldn't fall asleep eating at all," Sean replied. "Food's too good. Especially a six-piece. That *is* a six-piece, right." The kids craned their necks peering at the delicious food.

"Do you think he'll ever wake as loud as he's snoring?" David asked, making sure he kept it at a two-inch whisper. Shihan didn't like his students conversing in class. The other students stayed quiet.

"I don't know. Do you think he'd let go of that chicken bone if we tried to take it out of his hand?"

"Probably not. He could be testing us," David replied.

"A test for what?" Sean asked, raising an eyebrow.

"To see if we're going to stand here like we're supposed to."

David inched forward and reached out to take the piece of chicken from Shihan's hand. Suddenly their instructor shifted positions. David scurried back to place.

"Call his name," Sean suggested.

"I'm not doing it." David shook his light brown head, his glistening Afro spraying some oil on Sean's gi. "You do it."

"Wimp," Sean said to his friend. "Shihan," Sean whispered.

He didn't wake.

"Louder," David said. David was only a yellow belt; how could he order Sean around?

"Shihan," Sean whispered a little louder.

They gave up trying to wake him up, but they knew if they got out of the line and he saw them they would be as good as dead. A couple of times while Shihan slept, it looked like he was about to tumble out of the chair, but he always picked himself up before he fell.

Knowing parents would show up soon and wonder what happened, Sean took the lead and worked on kata forms with the class.

Twenty minutes later, Shihan, chicken bone still in hand, opened his bloodshot eyes. He saw his class standing at attention and awaiting his instructions.

"Did you guys finish your laps?" he asked, standing up, and placing the chicken back on the platter.

"Yes, Shihan. We finished them twenty minutes ago," Sean replied.

"Okay, do your push-ups, sit-ups, and suicides," he said, seeming to be awake, but the class knew he was going right back to sleep.

The students bowed out of class and within minutes had left to put away their fighting gear. "Great class today," Sean said to the other students, some younger, some older. As Sean took off his belt and began folding it, he heard someone clapping. "Great class, Sean," Shihan Deno said with a warm smile.

"Thank you, Shihan." Sean sighed with relief at the approval.

"Sean, you were very diligent with this class today and took initiative during the point that I—."

"*Rested* your eyes." Sean finished.

"Now where did you hear that?" Shihan asked, putting Sean in a playful headlock. "Now I want to see you apply that same diligence to the rest of your classes and to your education. I will not have any dummies in my school." He grasped Sean's shoulder. "You're improving here, and you have the ability to do better, to do great. We all saw that today, but I want to see the same improvement at school. I don't want to hear anything about being angry your dad isn't in your life. You have the ability to move on without him. Don't put that limitation on yourself. Do you understand?"

"Yes, Shihan," Sean replied.

Shihan Deno was hard on Sean because he believed in him. Shihan was a pleasant man to be around when he was happy, but when it was time to set things straight, he taught lessons the hard way. Shihan built up Sean so he would be ready to defend himself when it was time. "Karate is never to be used to start a fight; you're only supposed to use it in *self-defense*. It will help you be prepared for anything and everything."

★★★

And Shihan was right. Sean's long walk came to an end as he spotted Mr. Vega's big black van sitting in front of the light orange, brick house in the middle of the block. He picked up the pace. It would be a struggle to get to this house every morning, especially with as much sleep as he needed.

Sean gently knocked on the door and heard a small, sweet voice tell Mrs. Vega that someone was at the door.

Holding a rosy-cheeked girl about two years old, a short woman with dark hair and pinkish-white skin answered the door moments later.

"Come on in, Sean," Mrs. Vega said. "Are you hungry?"

"Yes, Ma'am," Sean said, dropping his book bag on the nearest chair and rubbing his stomach symbolically.

"I'll fix you some breakfast," she said, setting the little girl on the couch before walking into the banana-colored kitchen.

Baby toys, cradles, and playpens filled the living room and hallway making the house seem like a warm family home. A man with fair skin, thick eyebrows, and a wrestler's build came out of the bedroom, buttoning his shirt. "What's up, Sean?" Mr. Vega asked, before walking over to his wife and giving her a peck on the cheek.

"Nothing much. I just got here," Sean said, taking a seat on the plush black couch. *What a journey.*

Mr. Vega laughed. "So, I hear it's your first day at Jayne Adamson." He rubbed a beefy hand over his shiny, clean-shaven head. "Don't they have a school in your area?"

"I needed to change to another school. Too much drama at Gadson right now. My mother took one of the school board members to court and won. He was also the PTA president and had lived in the area a long time. Right now the school, his family, and people around our neighborhood are a little upset."

Actually they were more than upset; they were, well, piping hot. Cynthia Morris had exposed the mistreatment of Black boys at the school. Her efforts had landed them the first Black teacher to touch the doors of Gadson. Although the teacher was only for gym and coaching, it was a start.

Another door closed just to the right of the Vegas' kitchen. Mike Vega, who stood a couple inches taller than Sean, walked toward the dining room. He looked more awake than Sean. Mike's nonchalant, laid-back, positive bearing said he was popular with the ladies. He was smooth but tough at the same time, like his father. He went to Washington High School down the street and was on the football team. Sean hoped to be on the team someday, too. His father was into football and had played for St. Francis De Sales. Maybe if Sean played, his father would take more notice.

"What's up, y'all?" Mike asked, grabbing his keys off the table.

Mrs. Vega kissed him on the head as Mike hugged her.

Mr. Vega, who was absorbed with the *Chicago Sun-Times*, grunted a "Hey, Mike."

Sean nodded.

"I'm cutting out early to give Rochelle a ride to school." He turned to Sean. "Do you like to play football?" he asked as he picked up his blue Eddie Bauer book bag.

"Yeah, I'd love to play," Sean answered excitedly. His momma had put him in baseball because it was "safer." But after Sean was hit with the ball three times, and had a thumbnail ripped off, she didn't consider it so safe.

"I'll take you by my old coach's house after school. We'll see if you can try out," Mike said. "See you guys later."

"Bye, Mike," his folks said. The younger children crawling around on the floor didn't miss the big guy.

Mrs. Vega brought the plate to the glass table, which was almost covered completely with Mike's study guides. "Sean, come over and eat your breakfast."

"Thank you." Sean watched the family's interactions, wondering why he couldn't have a family that had a mother, father, and maybe a sister or brother. *Okay, well, maybe not the sister and brother part. Okay, yeah, well maybe a little sister.*

The Vega family was caring and humble. Sean glanced at the pictures the wall. There were photos of Mike and his parents. From family portraits to an outdoor trip, they seemed supportive of each other, as though they were a whole unit. They looked like they would be able to survive hard times, unlike families who had broken up over little things. The love they had for one another was something Sean wished his mother and father shared. But Sean's mother didn't want anything to do with his father. There seemed to be no love lost on his dad's side either. *How did those two ever get together long enough to…well…you know?*

"See you later," Mr. Vega said, grabbing the bag filled with his breakfast and lunch, then giving his wife a kiss. "Have a good day at school, Sean."

School. Sean realized it was almost time to go. He picked up the pace, shoveling the eggs with diced turkey ham into his mouth. He nearly missed, startled by a baby's loud shriek. Two of the little kids were going at it over a Kid Sister doll. Evidently, the younger one didn't take losing so well. Guess she felt like he did with his father—no attention. But there was also the smell of not so fresh baby booty. Mrs. Vega picked the baby up and headed for the changing table.

"Sean, do you want someone to show you a quick way to get to Jayne Adamson?" Mrs. Vega asked, as the smell of baby powder and wipes filled the air.

"Yes, please." Sean said, trying to finish the last of his breakfast.

"I'll call Manny. He lives across the street. You can walk with him," she said, coming back to the kitchen.

"Thank you for the breakfast," Sean said as he picked up his things. He walked across the street and rang the bell.

A heavyset boy with a golden complexion and black hair that lay tight on his scalp opened the door. He wore a school uniform almost identical to Sean's, but with a fresh pair of black Nikes instead of dress shoes. "What's up, man?" he asked as he walked out, closing and locking the carved wooden door. "I'm Manuel, but you can call me Manny."

"I'm Sean," he said, adjusting his book bag straps. They began walking up 104th Street until they came to Ewing. Across the way, Sean saw a supermarket with a Spanish name that he couldn't read. He would've preferred to learn it firsthand from his own relatives, but he hadn't seen them much. At least being around his Mexican side might help him with the language.

Chapter 9

As soon as traffic thinned, the boys crossed the street. Eight blocks down, only two more to go. Was this his dad's way of making sure Sean got some exercise?

Sean walked to the corner of the school and gazed up to a light brown building, which looked to be two or three stories high. The school grounds took up two blocks. It had a tall, red sign with the school name and announcements.

They walked to the front entrance where Sean's cousin Sara was talking with some of her friends. Even a few feet away, he heard her distinctive Hispanic accent. Her back was to him as she tried to pull her damp, wavy brown hair into a ponytail. As Manny stood off to the side talking with some of his friends, Sean crept up to his cousin. "Hey, Sara."

Startled, she turned to see who it was and a huge grin spread across her pale face. She had a few small brown freckles and light gray slanted eyes. "What's up, Sean? I haven't seen you in a long time," she said, giving him a big hug. "What are you doing here?"

"My dad put me in here with you," he said, shocked that Roberto hadn't mentioned it to Sara's mother. Aunt Monica and Sara tried to at least keep up with him on holidays and his birthday. Sara didn't care how the rest of the family felt about it—she loved her cousin.

"Wow, that's great! We can hang out now. Like I've always wanted." She hit him playfully in the arm. "So, how's your mom?"

"She's fine. She's probably at work by now."

"Tell her I said 'hi' and I hope she'll let you come over sometime," she said, pulling him in front of her. "Let me introduce you to some of my friends. This is Veronica, Eddie, and Rochelle," pointing to each as she said their name. "Guys, this is my cousin, Sean."

"Cousin?" they asked in unison, as they looked Sean up and down, before glancing suspiciously at each other.

"Is he your *blood* cousin?" Eddie asked, his left eyebrow raised, thin lips screwed up as though he had just eaten a lemon.

"Yeah. Is that so hard to believe?" Sara asked, folding her thin arms over her small chest. She stood close to Sean, who stared back at the other boy. Eddie had a "Rico Suave" look, with short, shiny black hair and a thin but muscular build. He wore a dark blue polo shirt and dark blue Dickies. He was obviously straying away from the preferred uniform.

"It's not hard to believe," Eddie replied, looking from Sean to Sara.

"I never knew you had Black people in your family," Veronica said cautiously. She had light skin and long, wavy brown hair with golden highlights and a slim figure. She wore thick, black retro glasses.

"I'm her Uncle Roberto's son, and my mother's *African-American.*" Sean hoped that would clear up everything. Hopefully it wouldn't be a problem.

Sean shook hands with Veronica and Eddie, who finally lightened up and smiled. Then he came to Rochelle who had a curvaceous body like the late Tejano singer Selena. Her straight auburn hair reached down to her lower back and her brown eyes glowed from the sun. She had thick, curved lips and a pert nose with a tiny nose ring. She didn't have to say a word. Her message was loud and clear.

Sean lifted an eyebrow, appreciating the view.

She winked back.

Yes, the day had gotten better already. Sean could have talked to her all day, but the bell rang. Time to go into the building.

Sean felt the stare of a Black female police officer who stood at the door. Sean smiled at her on his way in as she nodded, sending him into a tall hallway. It was probably only the third friendliest face he had seen at school. Three out of five hundred. That wasn't so bad. But that was before he realized his dad had lied.

When he reached the second floor, he stood at the door of his classroom, looked in, then gave the hall a quick scan. His heart sank. He was pretty much the only Black student. What happened to Hispanic, White *and* Black?

Everyone stood in the hallway in single file, listening to a girl speaking through the intercom. She welcomed the students before they said the Pledge of Allegiance and headed into their respective classrooms. Sean walked into his noisy homeroom, feeling like he was in fifth grade all over again. There were name tags taped on the desks and a colorful multiplication table chart on the wall. There were little desks that Sean knew were too small for him. A woman wearing a long-sleeved, peach shirt tucked into a khaki skirt pushed a cart of books into the room.

As Sean sat down, he felt one side of his behind slipping off the chair. Not the most comfortable position in the world.

He didn't like that he was possibly the only Black in the school. And he didn't like the way some of the other kids looked him up and down with disgust. At Gadson, the student body was mainly White, but there had been a heavy sprinkling of Black students. *All* of the teachers had been White, so that wasn't saying too much.

"Settle down, class," the woman said. "I'm Mrs. Nuevo, your homeroom teacher. Welcome to Jayne Adamson."

Sean tuned out the rest of what she said because he'd heard it all before at Gadson. As she let the class leave for the next period, Sean decided that she wasn't having a good morning. Her smile seemed sad and didn't brighten her pretty, lightly powdered face. She ran her fingers through her black hair all the way down to her neck, which she rubbed gently, as through she had a tension headache. He knew the signs. Mom did that on day one *and* day six of her cycle. On the days in between, it was cramps and bloating. Hopefully, she wasn't going to be grumpy like that all week.

Sean headed for his first class alone. Making friends here wasn't going to be any easier than it had been at Gadson. He stepped into his next classroom, which was reading. A man with pale skin and bright red spots on his cheeks sat at the teacher's desk. He was scowling, apparently aggravated that the new semester had begun. The man stood and stepped out in front of his desk. "Good morning, class. I'm Mr. Tyson, your reading teacher. If you *all* follow my directions and do all of your homework this semester, we'll get along just fine," he said, like it was a threat. No one could lay a threat like his momma. If you weren't her, you weren't going to threaten Sean Morris.

Sean looked at Mr. Tyson with a puzzled expression, thinking, *of course if we do our homework and follow directions we'll be fine.* That happens at any school.

His whole day was strange—the stares, the instructions—being alone. He thought he was starting out fresh, but it almost felt like Gadson all over again. He felt so out of place, so alone. Where were kids who looked like him? Were his parents the only ones who crossed the borders? But his father had put him in this school, so Sean would have to deal with it. He was glad when the school day was finally over. He would get to see his dad again.

When Sean turned the corner leading back to the Vegas' street, his father's blue, two-door Honda Civic was parked out front. He felt glad in one way, but sad in another. He wouldn't be trying out for football that day.

Sean walked into the house and saw his dad sitting in the front room, downing a Corona and talking with Mr. Vega. As soon as Roberto saw Sean, he got out of the chair and stretched, ready to take him home. No hug or anything? Wasn't he glad to see him?

As they drove south on Ewing Street, toward Sean's house, Roberto asked, "So, how was your day?" Sean's father had a slight tremble in his voice, as though he wasn't sure what he was doing. "You make any new friends?" he continued, still seeming insecure.

"It was okay, I guess."

Silence filled the car as they drove past the light green building that housed the driver's education center at Washington High School. They'd never had real conversations, only a couple of awkward ones on the phone. The questions were a start.

Chapter 10

B y March, Cynthia knew she'd been right. Sean was having problems at school again or at least with the teachers. This time he couldn't blame it on the school. He had started getting along with people and blending in, so that wasn't it either. Sean didn't feel like he had a template. Roberto let Sean do whatever he wanted: skip doing his homework and stay over at friends' homes until it was dark before returning to the Vegas' in time to be picked up. Sometimes his dad left him at the Vegas' for a lot longer than he should have.

Sean's grades *and* behavior dropped—all the way to the bottom of the slide. He wasn't really sure if he could reach the top again. He received detentions, but his mother never found out because his dad told him they had to keep it under wraps.

His father didn't want her to know because it indicated he couldn't handle the responsibility of taking care of his son. But actions spoke louder than words.

Sometimes Sean would sit in the office three days for an in-school suspension before his father would show up. Sean became a master at cover-ups, but the guilt at not telling Mom was tearing at Sean's mind. And it wouldn't go away.

A month later, Mrs. Esposita, the principal at Jayne Adamson, called Superwoman and requested a "family conference" with Cynthia, Roberto, *and* Sean. Her bright yellow office had oak bookshelves, filled with textbooks, and walls covered with paintings created by Mexican artists. Sean knew from the look on Mrs. Esposita's face that she wasn't going to lighten up.

Sean was going to complement her on how well she looked in her royal blue two-piece suit and orange silk blouse, but he knew that wouldn't work. Maybe telling her how beautifully the smell of strawberries and cinnamon flowed through her office. *Aaaaaaand* maybe not.

Mrs. Esposita was pretty and generally pleasant, but she could be strict when the job called for it. "I'm concerned about Sean and his performance in school." She looked at both parents. "Mrs. Morris, I know what you were trying to do. But you need to take Sean back from his father, because he isn't doing a good job raising him."

Apparently their lie about where Sean lived, remained undetected. But there was so much more to worry about. Sean could see his dad's jaw clench when the principal commented on his parenting skills. *She was right, so why was he even thinking about getting mad?*

"Sean has been in my office several times so that his dad could have a conference with me and his teachers."

Superwoman's infuriated brown eyes cut dead at Roberto without moving her head. Superwoman wanted to drag Sean and his father outside and teach them a quick lesson of responsibility, but the meeting wasn't over yet.

Mrs. Esposita continued, "We seem to also have another problem, Mrs. Morris. Apparently Sean likes to use profanity."

Sean choked. His father looked at the door like he was ready to bolt.

A wary expression crossed Superwoman's face. "What happened?"

"You don't know?"

"Know what?" Cynthia asked in a whisper, looking at Sean who sunk down in the seat.

Mrs. Esposita leaned back in her chair as she looked from one parent to another. "He called one of his classmates the 'B' word."

Superwoman's eyes grew as big as saucers. "Why would you say that, Sean?" Her voice had gone from alto to high soprano.

"Apparently, she called him a 'nigger'," Mrs. Esposita said. "That was three days ago. I sent a notice home for Mr. Maldonado."

Superwoman switched gears, shifting her burning stare to Roberto.

So did Mrs. Esposita as she continued. "And we called his job and the house."

Roberto sat there frowning. He knew he was going to get it, probably even worse than Sean.

"And he didn't come to the school to see about his son?"

"I couldn't take off work," Roberto said.

"Well if you thought like a parent, you wouldn't allow anything to stop you from going to a meeting that involved your son," Cynthia snapped. "I would have taken off work in a heartbeat."

Sean was relieved that his dad's troubles had taken the spotlight off him. Hopefully it would last a while.

"And you," Cynthia pointed in Sean's face. Hope flew out the window. "There's no reason to call a woman that word; you should not call *any* woman that." Cynthia's eyes blazed with anger. "Why wasn't I told about any of this?"

"Because I was going to handle it, Cynthia," Roberto said, looking ashamed and defeated. "I'm *going* to handle it."

Cynthia snapped, "I hope you do, because I don't want my son to grow up disrespecting women. He didn't curse when he was at Gadson, or any time when he was with me."

"I can't watch his every move while he's in school," Roberto said, finally defending himself.

"Obviously, you can't do it *outside* of school, either." She folded her arms. "They had to call *me* to get your attention. So much for you having things *under control*," she said. Then she directed her attention back to Sean, who was still slumped in his seat. "Now, tell me what happened."

Sean didn't want to explain but knew he had to. "I was in gym class…"

Chapter 11

Three days earlier, Sean had stepped outside to a beautiful sunny day, which had a foul, swampy smell misting the air. The pavement and grass glistened in the sunshine from melted snow. Dressed in his gym clothes—a white T-shirt and blue jogging pants—Sean ran across the street to play softball in the Carrasco Center. The bottom half of the building was made of dark brown brick and the top half was like the Georgia Dome. This building took up three blocks, probably because it had two basketball courts and a turf training facility for the local football and baseball teams. Sean had gotten so good at baseball that everyone started calling him Sammy Sosa.

Stephanie, one of Sean's classmates, was one of the shortest girls there, but she was also the prettiest. She wore a butterfly pin in her beautiful, light brown hair. Arched eyebrows accentuated her flashy brown eyes. Her eyebrows could either be drawn in for a mean look or lifted toward the sun. Her devilish smile often caught his eye. She wore gray jogging pants and a white T-shirt on her dangerously attractive shape.

Sean knew instantly that something was wrong. She usually wore tight black volleyball shorts and a navy blue shirt with a knot tied in the back. She was also acting distant.

As she stormed onto the field with a scowl on her face, she looked like she was ready to explode. She reminded him of his momma—when it was oil change time.

As they began the game, Sean's friend Joshua was up first. Robert, the pitcher, sailed three soft pitches past Joshua.

Joshua walked back to Sean, forcing a smile, but everyone could tell he was angry. He normally talked a lot of crap about hitting the ball out of the park. His mouth was closed now.

When it was Sean's turn at the plate, he picked up the wooden bat and took a deep stance, aiming high. He wanted to hit the ball past the gate this time.

Robert, a Puerto Rican kid with a dark complexion like Sean, looked like he was going to launch the softball at Sean. That would have cheated Sean out of a home run. Sean got even deeper, bending his knees as the ball came his way. He swung the bat and made contact. The ball didn't go high but straight up the middle, at a pace that could cause someone to lose a body part or two.

He ran to first and stopped. Usually the ball would be further in the outfield putting him on third base, but someone had thrown the ball to second base already. Shoot!

"What is your problem, Puta?" Sean heard someone yell from behind him as he squatted for a breather. He knew without a doubt it was Stephanie, and she was definitely red, seconds from exploding. Why was she mad at him?

"What did I do, Stephanie?" Sean asked.

"You almost hit me with the ball," she yelled as she punched him hard in the chest as if he had done it on purpose. It was definitely that time of the month for her.

"I'm sorry," Sean said.

"Watch where you're hitting next time, *dumb-ass nigga!*" Stephanie yelled in his face. Her remark echoed like a bad movie while the other kids laughed.

As much as he wanted to say something back, he knew he couldn't call her a wetback or a spic. Then he would be talking about himself. Instead, he responded, "Next time learn how to move quicker or duck—*bitch.*"

The anger he felt was almost instantly replaced by guilt. Just his luck that the gym teacher was standing close by, only close enough to hear Sean's reply. The teacher grabbed them both and headed to the principal's office.

Chapter 12

"And that's what happened," Sean said, lowering his head to his knees, avoiding Mrs. Esposita's stare and his mother's gaze of shame.

"This is the kind of behavior that my son displays while he's under your care?" Cynthia asked Roberto.

"I never heard him talk like that before," he replied, trying to brush it off.

"Sean, where did you get that word? You certainly didn't hear it from me."

He sank further in his seat. Sean made sure he stayed out of the way, just in case Superwoman decided to blast him out of the office. Sean knew women had power, but power that left his dad speechless for long periods of time? Wow!

"Well, Dad sometimes—um—calls you a, well, you *know*," Sean said, trying to shift the spotlight away from himself. He looked quickly to his left and caught his dad's face with an expression that said "you little devil."

Superwoman snapped at Roberto. "Oh, so you like to call people a bitch? Not only that, you're trying to turn my son against me."

Sean sat up. *Oh yeah! It's on now!*

"Mrs. Morris," Mrs. Esposita said, placing a hand on her desk.

"No, I'm not trying to do that." Roberto squirmed in his seat, throwing an angry look at Sean.

"Well, obviously you allow him to say that kind of thing whenever you two talk," she said, folding her broad arms across her chest.

"He's a boy. He should speak his mind. So can I and sometimes you are…" Roberto let the thought drift.

Sean swallowed, watching his dad struggle to say the word to Cynthia's face.

Wimp!

Superwoman's eyes sparked with anger, but thank God she kept her hands down. "When he's with me, he knows not to curse, even if it's a joke—"

"Mrs. Morris," the principal said a second time, looking from parent to parent, not knowing whether to wait and see what happened or to call security. Sean's vote was for—SECURITY!

"But Cynthia—" Roberto tried to interject.

"No Roberto! You can't curse when you have conversations with Sean. And you can't allow him to use vulgar language. That is not how you win your son's respect, trust, and love. You have to set an example. You're supposed to be the parent and you have to have rules. Am I clear?"

"Yes, Cynthia." Sean's father let out a sigh of defeat and slumped down in the chair like a little kid.

"Mrs. Morris, please—" Mrs. Esposita started.

"Mrs. Esposita," Cynthia said, turning her gaze away from Roberto. "Is it okay if Sean goes to get the young lady and bring her here? I believe he has something to say." She glared at Sean.

"Sure," the principal said with a sigh, then directed Sean out the door. No one had to tell him twice!

Sean walked up the stairs feeling ashamed. He'd allowed his dad's example to affect his behavior. He had betrayed his upbringing—no matter how bad his grades were—he had always been known for his manners. He walked into his homeroom, where math problems were displayed on the projection screen. "Mrs. Lopez, Mrs. Esposita would like to see Stephanie Cordova."

"Oooooh," echoed in the classroom.

Mrs. Lopez allowed Stephanie to leave.

Sean escorted her down the stairs in silence. But he could tell that she was still mad at him for what he had said. *She'd started it!*

As they walked into the office, Sean wondered what had happened while he was gone.

"First, Roberto, I would like for you to show your son a good example of an apology," Superwoman ordered, resting on the arm of the chair.

"Apology," he snapped, glaring at her. "For *what?*"

"For disrespecting me. Not only that, but in front of my son."

"I am not apologizing for speaking what I believe."

Roberto obviously wanted his head taken off. You never disagree with a woman. You'll never win.

"I guess you want your child to be as stubborn as you. But I'm not having it. Maybe you can learn something from your son." Superwoman fixed her eyes on Stephanie. "Sean, don't you have something to say?"

Sean folded his fingers, twirling his thumbs nervously. "Stephanie, I apologize for calling you out of your name. I shouldn't have done that. I was raised better than that, and you are a beautiful and respectable young woman."

"And I apologize for calling you that name, too. I didn't mean what I said. I was just having a bad day," she said, hugging him as tears slid down her cheeks. *Romance may have a chance.*

"Stephanie, you can go back to class," Mrs. Esposita said, handing her some Kleenex from the box on her desk. "I'll speak with your parents later."

Leaving the room, she closed the oak door behind her.

"Good," Superwoman said, gripping Sean by the arm. "Now, I want you to apologize to Mrs. Esposita."

Sean's eyes shifted in confusion wondering why he was apologizing to her. But Cynthia was mad. There was no time for questions. "I apologize for disrespecting you as a woman."

"You'll keep apologizing to your female relatives and to any other woman we see, until I say you can stop. When you disrespect one woman, you disrespect *all* women."

Mrs. Esposita gave Cynthia a little nod.

Roberto groaned.

Sean thought she was kidding.

By Friday, Sean was pulled out of Jayne Adamson. As soon as they were done with the paperwork, they went to River Oaks Mall. While they were walking toward Auntie Anne's, the buttery, cinnamon aroma of pretzels filled the air. Sean was happy because he was getting through to the good stuff, even though he was still on punishment.

Out of nowhere, Superwoman said to the women working behind the counter, "Ladies, will you please come here?"

Wondering what this was all about, they moved to the front.

"My son has something to say to you."

Sean's smile quickly faded. "I apologize for calling all of you out of your names and disrespecting you. I shouldn't have done that because that's not the way I was raised, and because you are beautiful and respectable women."

The women stood confused, looking to one another. "My son called a girl at his school the 'B' word, so I'm teaching him how to be respectful to women."

"All right, Girl," one of the workers said, giving Superwoman a high-five.

Then Cynthia pulled him into the center of the mall. "Ladies in the mall! I have someone who wants to say something to *all of you!*" Superwoman yelled so loud Sean wouldn't have been surprised if the whole mall heard it.

"Momma!" Sean said as he yanked on her yellow shirt, trying to convince his mother to stop. "Momma, please."

He turned to make a fast escape, but she grabbed him by the collar, yanking him back. A large group of women—some big, some petite, some old, some young, some who were probably too young to even understand the word—formed a frightening circle around him.

"My son, Sean Morris, called a girl in his class the 'B' word the other day."

Embarrassed, Sean covered his face.

Some of the women gasped, covering their mouths and shaking their heads. Then, one older woman, who was leaning on a cane, piped up, "Shame on you, young man!"

"What makes it worse is that he got it from his *father*," Superwoman said with a big smile on her face and a movie star twinkle in her eye. The crowd gasped as though none of them had ever heard of a father saying that word. "But he has something to say."

Sean lowered his head, mumbling, "I'm sorry for calling you—"

"Lift your head up so they can hear you," Superwoman instructed.

Looking up at all of those women, who looked like giants hovering over his little body, Sean painstakingly expressed, "I'm sorry for calling you all...," he hesitated, "the 'B' word. I shouldn't have done that because I was raised better than that, and because you are beautiful and respectable women."

The women applauded. "It's okay, Baby; just don't do it again," said a light-skinned woman, kneeling down to hug him. *Finally a little bit of sympathy from somebody.*

"Now ladies, if you would excuse us, we have to get to the *rest* of the mall," his mom said, pulling him away from the clapping crowd.

Sean's face, lips drooping but eyes wide enough to hold golf balls, reflected his alarm. He was trapped in a horrifying nightmare.

Dad wasn't getting it all that bad. He should've been right here getting it with me.

Man! That Superwoman—always using her super powers. But one thing was certain: the "B" word was out of his vocabulary.

Chapter 13

Two days after the conference with the principal, Sean was working on fractions when he heard his mother yelling in the living room. "I'm not talking to you until you apologize!" Sean peeked out the door and saw Roberto, with Cynthia blocking the entrance.

"Cynthia, I was just speaking my mind."

"Roberto, you still disrespected me in front of our son. Imagine how many women he will disrespect if he has the same mentality you have." She held her ground, ready to slam the door in his face.

Minutes crept by. Sean held his breath.

"Cynthia, I apologize for disrespecting you in front of our son. It will never happen again," Roberto said softly.

"Go home, Roberto," she said, trying to close the door.

"Cynthia, wait." Roberto blocked the door. "Let me talk to you, please."

Cynthia rolled her eyes and huffed. "You have six minutes," she said, letting him in. "What do you want?"

"Please put him back in Jayne Adamson." Roberto folded his fingers in hope.

"You heard what Mrs. Esposita said," Cynthia reminded him. "Take him back in *my* control."

"Sean will do better. I will see to it, but you have to—"

"I have to do what?" She tapped her feet lightly on the wooden floor.

"Trust me," he said quietly.

"I did, and you messed that up. Now all I *have* to do is take care of my son and myself."

Would Dad have a comeback for that? How could he?

Sean didn't believe a word Roberto said; maybe if he went through the humiliation Sean endured, he would've had a shot. Now Sean couldn't go anywhere without some woman remembering him. He wanted to be famous one day but not because of using the "B" word.

Sean's faith kept wearing away with every broken promise. Failing to go out for Father's Day, forgetting to spend time with him on the Fourth of July—it had added up to a mountain of lies. Sean's faith in him went out the door when his mother snapped on him in the principal's office.

"There's no way you're having complete control again," Cynthia said, picking up a potato chip bag off the floor.

"Why not?"

"I don't trust your judgment. You allowed him to sit in the office for days, without coming to see about him. He's missed so many classes because of that, he probably won't pass to the eighth grade. And you lied—he was the only Black student at Jayne Adamson. And even as racist as some of those people were, no one ever called him a nigger at Gadson."

"But everywhere you go, someone will be racist," Roberto replied.

"The answer is no, Roberto," she said, opening the door.

"But Cynthia—"

"No, Roberto!"

Roberto took the smart route and walked out. If old habits stayed the same, he'd also walked out of Sean's life.

Chapter 14

A week after Superwoman pulled him out of Jayne Adamson school, she was still searching. No one wanted to take a new student so far into the school year. If there were a school that could help them, Superwoman would find it. This would be nothing compared to all the other miracles she worked. But she wouldn't grant one for Dad.

Sean woke to his alarm clock's loud, bugle call. It was six forty-five a.m. Before he could wipe the crust from the corner of his eye, or put his feet on the floor, his mother yelled, "Sean, are you up?"

"Yes, Ma'am," he answered as he got out of bed. He was grateful that the whole five a.m. thing was over.

Today was his interview at a new school in downtown Chicago. After showering, he went in his closet and picked out a pair of black Izod pants and a yellow, long-sleeved Polo shirt. Boy, he would've saved money if the uniform was the same as Jayne Adamson's. The Dickies Company was making a mint off him. Three schools in three months must be a world record.

Slipping on his shoes, he grabbed his coat out of the closet, his book bag and went to the living room. He sat on the big, cream-colored sofa and patiently waited for his mother. He could hear the water running.

She was washing up, since she usually took showers at night. She told him his pores wouldn't be open if he did the same. *What did open pores have to do with waking up?* Sean *needed* his shower in the morning.

While Sean waited, he had a bowl of Honey Nut Cheerios. He finished just as she came downstairs. Sean picked up his coat and umbrella because there was a chance of rain. Cynthia pulled her long braided hair into a blue scrunchie. She adjusted her dark blue slacks and purple shirt, making sure she was "sharper than a tack." She had a forest-green jacket folded over her arm as she walked into the kitchen.

"Now, when we go in today, we want to make a good impression," she said, smiling as she put on her jacket.

Roberto and Superwoman weren't on speaking terms, but she couldn't care less, as long as he still spent time with Sean *and* paid tuition.

"Yes, Ma'am," he said, putting on his coat. "I'll be okay."

"Now, your dad is going to help out with tuition because I won't be able to do it alone," she said, grabbing her keys off the wooden coffee table.

"Yeah, and how long will that last?" Sean mumbled under his breath.

"Did you say something, Sean?"

"No, Ma'am," Sean replied. *Did she have supersonic hearing, too?*

They walked swiftly to their new, navy Oldsmobile Ninety-Eight and climbed in to escape the sting of the cold air.

"Did you brush your teeth?" she asked before putting the car in drive.

"Ma, you *know* I brushed my teeth. I want to have all my teeth when I get old," he said, chuckling. Sean already felt grown up, even though he was only thirteen.

"Yeah! So that must be toothpaste on the side of your mouth," Superwoman said, licking her thumb, aiming to wipe it off.

"Ma, stop! I can do that!" he said, pulling away.

His mother always wanted him to look presentable. He could hear her now: *First impressions are everything. Yeah, but wiping things off with a slobbered thumb wasn't part of that.*

Arriving at the Hegewisch train station, Superwoman scanned the parking lot. "Man, you'd think at this time of morning we could find a parking space," she said, driving slowly down the rows of parked cars for the third time.

"People have to go to work the same time you do. That's why it's called rush hour," he said, peering out his window, hoping to spot a space. "Everybody's in one place, and nobody's getting anywhere."

"Don't be a smart ass," Cynthia said, rolling her eyes.

"I'm your child!" he shot back with a grin.

"Don't remind me."

Cynthia found a spot, two-and-a-half blocks from the station. Getting out of the car, Sean grabbed the money from his mother and ran over to the yellow pay box. He looked for the space number where she parked, folded the dollar bill, dropped it in, and ran to catch up to his mother. She could *move!*

The railroad crossing lights came on. They were just in time. Sean and his mother joined the rest of the passengers headed toward downtown Chicago on the long silver and orange train. Sean and Cynthia walked through the aisles. The seats were cushioned in orange and brown. They could not find a single empty seat and stood up for the entire ride.

"Now Sean," Superwoman said, "we're paying too much money for you to mess up in this school."

"Yes, Ma'am," he said. Day one, and he was already getting the lecture.

"We have to pay tuition for this school. Even though your father is paying part of it, my share is still ninety dollars a week. We don't have that kind of money to waste. I could always put it toward the light, gas, and telephone bills," she said, hoping the information would seep into his brain.

"Why do you have to pay for me to go to school? We never had to pay at any of my other schools."

"The others were public schools. This is a *lab* school, which is a *private* school. It's not funded by the state. It's funded by the parents," she said, looking out the window. "But I don't want you to worry about that. I only told you, so you would know how important it is for you to get good grades. You concentrate on that."

After getting off at the Van Buren stop, they walked to Adams Street and turned. Then they stopped at a tall black building with a lot of glass windows and a bank on the first floor. They went in and headed straight toward the elderly security guard in the lobby.

"Good morning, Sir. Which floor is the Chicago Loop Lab School on?" Sean asked politely.

"Well, young man," the dark brown security guard said, grinning as he looked over the top of his brass-framed bifocals and showing his pearly whites, "it's on the fourth floor. Take the elevators to your right."

"Thank you," Sean replied, walking toward the silver elevators.

Sean and Cynthia got off the elevator and walked down the white hallway. They came to a set of double doors. Two younger kids walked in their direction wearing black pants and yellow shirts. Through the doors was a lunchroom. All the students looked like a bunch of bumblebees. A tall Black man approached.

"Yes, Ma'am. How may I help you?" he asked, his wavy blackish-gray hair shining under the bright halogen lights.

"Today is my son's interview. I'm wondering where we go," Cynthia said, scanning the room's picture-covered walls and rows of vending machines.

"I'm Mr. Willard. I believe *I'll* be doing that interview, Ma'am," he replied, shaking her hand. "And this young man is?"

"I'm Sean Morris, Sir." He extended his hand to Mr. Willard.

"Wow, what a grown-up young man he is," Mr. Willard said. "Follow me."

Superwoman grinned. "I have to go to work," she said, fixing Sean's hair. "You're going to spend the school day here. Then I want you to come to my job."

She fixed his tie as he inched away. *The whole day? Man, this better be good!*

"Do you remember where my job is?"

"Sears Tower, eighty-second floor," he groaned. *Miles away.*

"Right," she said, smiling.

Sean gave his mother a hug and followed Mr. Willard down a different hallway. This one had gum-stained, brown carpet and beige walls.

The school was small, but that could be a good thing. He wouldn't have to worry about getting a teacher's attention when he needed help.

"Most of the classes are two grades together," Mr. Willard explained, noticing Sean peeking into each room they passed.

Since Sean was in seventh grade, he would be in with the eighth-graders. He felt important already.

Following the interview, Mr. Willard escorted Sean to meet with Mrs. Holmes, the principal. *Three schools, three female principals. Must be the in thing.* "Mrs. Holmes, this young man is Sean Morris."

Sean stepped in front of the elderly woman's cluttered desk. Why did he have to meet with the principal?

"Nice to meet you, Mrs. Holmes," Sean said to the gray-haired woman. She had a light-brown complexion. Her black-framed glasses resting on her nose almost hid the shiny, golden tint on her eyelids. Combined with the yellow jogging suit she wore, her outfit classified her as head bumblebee.

"It's a pleasure, Sean," she said. She smiled and gestured for him to take a seat. "Well, do you like the school so far?"

"Yes, Mrs. Holmes," he replied. The only things he had seen were Mr. Willard's office, the lunchroom, and her office. Not much material to form an opinion.

"Good. We'll make sure it stays that way," she said, tapping her pencil on the desk. "I'm sorry. I don't have a lot of time to speak with you today, but you seem like a nice young man. We'll talk again soon."

Mr. Willard escorted him to a classroom down the hall. Sean peered through the window and watched the beautiful, young woman in front of the classroom. Tyrese's song "Sweet Lady," played in his head. The young woman could've been a student who had forgotten her uniform. The students all looked like bumblebees, but the teacher wore a pair of dark blue, form-fitting jeans and a red Gap shirt. The ideal woman for every boy, especially the ones hitting puberty.

He walked in and stood between Mr. Willard and the young woman.

"Sean, this is your new teacher, Mrs. Tucker," Mr. Willard said.

Teacher. The song playing in his head screeched to a halt and his smile faded.

The man eyed the woman's figure as Sean had done earlier. *Shame on him!* Sean cleared his throat and Mr. Willard collected himself, straightening his mustache.

"Hello, Mrs. Tucker," Sean said. He was ashamed of himself for thinking of his teacher in *that* way. But hey, everyone had crushes on their teachers. Normally the teachers Sean had were older, probably around forty-five. And at thirteen with the normal raging hormones, it doesn't help to have to stare at the front and backside of a beautiful woman—not a single bit. Sean felt a little tug below the waist, and shifted from one leg to the other. Watching this woman all year was going to be hard.

"Hello, Sean," she said, pushing her red hair back. Her voice was deep and sexy, like Alicia Keys.

Since he knew he couldn't date Mrs. Tucker, he had the choice of either dreaming or checking out someone in his own age range. Getting a girlfriend would be the least of his problems. Keeping his little crush under wraps would be a problem, especially since he couldn't help staring at Mrs. Tucker.

Sean's year at Loop Lab School was his best academic performance in a while. Mrs. Tucker stayed on him and, under Superwoman's watchful eyes, his grades except for math were not lower than a B.

There were days that Sean's father would stop by and take him out for lunch. Every positive report made him smile. They usually went to Taco Fresco, a Mexican food place that Sean passed every day on his way to school. For the first time in his life, Roberto even brought a cake to school to celebrate Sean's birthday. It was their time together, Roberto trying to be a father and Sean enjoying it. Although their conversations were still uneasy, some things had improved.

One day, Mrs. Holmes pulled Sean out of class and into her office. He sat in the soft yellow chair, wondering what he had done wrong. He had really done well in school this year and couldn't think of any reason he should be sitting across from the principal.

"Sean, have you been in touch with your father lately?"

Sean shook his head slowly. He hadn't heard from him in a few days. "No, Ma'am, he hasn't returned my phone calls." He felt his father slipping away from him, and he didn't know what to do about it.

"Well, we need to talk with him," she said, looking at his file.

Sean snuck a peek and saw the words "balance due" before Mrs. Holmes shut the folder. Lowering his head, he wondered why this was happening. Why couldn't his dad do the right thing? Why was it too much for him?

"Hmmm," she said, gazing at him. "You're kind of in a mixed-up situation then. We've tried to reach him, too. If he calls, ask him to come see me."

"Yes, Ma'am," Sean said, trying hard to hold in his pain and tears. He knew what Mrs. Holmes wasn't saying. Money was a problem again. His dad wasn't paying child support. Now he wasn't paying tuition either.

Removing a post-it note from the folder, she said, "I'll have a memo drawn up for your mother. Make sure you give it to her." She jotted down a note.

He didn't say anything. He couldn't say anything.

"Sean, are you okay?" the principal asked, taking off her glasses.

"No, Mrs. Holmes, I need to go to the bathroom," Sean said, standing. "Go ahead."

Sean ran to the bathroom and cried so hard he threw up every ounce of lunch. He knew his dad wouldn't come back. He knew there wasn't a reasonable explanation for it, either. He thought his dad had changed.

Sinking to the gray-tiled floor, Sean held his knees to his chest and rocked back and forth.

Why would Dad try to hurt him? Or even make him cry? His father wasn't ready for responsibility. How many times had his mom said that Sean would have to see for himself? People like his father gave men a bad name. Sean knew he wouldn't be like his father. He wouldn't hurt *his* kids. He couldn't do that.

Some people just don't want to change. Roberto was one of them.

Chapter 15

Sean finished seventh-grade on an up note—good grades, no calls, no detentions, even with the complications from his father. But it had been a bumpy ride.

When Roberto stopped paying his part of Sean's tuition, Mom had taken his butt back to court for child support.

Many people understood Sean's pain. But it still hurt. Unfortunately he took his frustration out on the woman who had been both mother and father from the beginning—Superwoman. He wondered, with all of the arguments his parents had, was it something *she* said that turned his father away? Did she *push* his father away?

That anger spilled over into school work. Rather, it spilled over into not doing his school work.

Cynthia took him to their new pastor, Sesvalah, who was also a therapist and a clinical social worker. Sesvalah was the woman who had helped Superwoman get back to "normal." That was back when the stress of parenting and dealing with her own childhood abuse came out.

Sean walked into her two-story house, not wanting to be there. Sesvalah walked down the peach-carpeted stairs to greet him, wrapping her long, light brown hair in a tropical print headscarf.

"Well, good morning, Sean," she said, smiling and leaning to give him a hug. "How are you doing?"

"I'm fine," he said, hugging her back. He enjoyed her warmth and inhaling the aroma of strawberry oil in her hair.

"Well, let's go downstairs and get started," she said, walking toward the basement. She turned on the lights. Two white plastic lawn chairs with blue cushions were in the center of the room. He sat, waiting for her as she turned on the stereo, put in a CD, and let the relaxing sounds of music over ocean waves fill the air.

"So, Sean, I hear that you've been having some interesting times with your mother and at school," she said, sitting down, still smiling.

"Yes, Ma'am," Sean replied simply, not too sure what else to say.

After a brief pause, she asked softly, "Why have you been giving your mother attitude all the time?"

"Because she's always on my back!" Sean snapped. He looked away, realizing his tone might have been disrespectful. But he was angry. Just when things were going all right, they started going all wrong again.

"But she should help manage your life a little," she said, folding her slender fingers in her lap. "I hear that you're getting bad conduct grades on your report card again. And you don't do your chores like you used to. That's not the Sean I know. The Sean I know is one of the most wonderful young men I've ever met. And he's still wonderful. We just have to figure out what's going on with him. That's all."

Sean rested his head on his hand. "I've just been going through a lot of things."

"Like what?"

"My dad. He's decided I'm invisible," Sean said, going over possible reasons in his mind for the hundredth time. He was angry with the man, but he was angry with his mom, too. And angry with himself. Maybe if he had done what he was supposed to do at Jayne Adamson, Dad would still be around.

"Well, that's *his* problem. He's missing out on your life. You can't put your life on pause and wait for him to change. You have to move on and make your own life work. Do you think your dad has tried to stop what he's doing, because you're angry with him?" she asked, tapping Sean's knee softly.

"But I'm his *son*. He wouldn't leave like that. Mom *had* to have said something to him to push him away from me." Sean covered his face, trying not to cry. Trying not to hurt. "They argue all the time about stupid stuff like child support. He's a man. He has to realize *he* needs to take responsibility."

"Yes, he does. But that might not happen until you're out of high school, or when you're an adult," she said. "But you have to remember, it's his decision not to be around. That has *nothing* to do with you. He probably has his own issues."

"Like what?" Sean asked, gritting his teeth. "Mom knows how to be a *mom*, and her issues don't get in the way."

"That's right," she replied with a smile. "Yet you still believe that your mother tries to push him away. You should know that your mother would never do something like that. Isn't she the one who suggested that your father spend more time with you? Isn't she the one who's always taken you to see him and his family?"

"How do you know?" Sean said angrily.

"I've spoken to her," she said forcefully. "One day you'll realize that your mother is not keeping your father from you, that nothing you've done is keeping him from you. "

Sean poured his heart out to Sesvalah. He went to talk to her a few more times, sometimes with his mother and sometimes alone. His anger faded when he realized the truth. His dad couldn't keep him from succeeding.

Sean definitely saw the truth a couple of weeks later. He sat in child support court with both parents. His father, dressed in a tan sweater and black dress pants with square-toed dress shoes, stood before the judge and said, "Sean Morris *is not* my child. I want a paternity test."

Roberto had waited until after he had he helped put Sean through school? After they had spent time and done things together? Thirteen years later, and *now* he wanted a paternity test? Get real!

Chapter 16

The day after that ridiculous court appearance, Sean woke from a deep sleep. He walked into the lilac kitchen with its pearl ceramic tile. Grandma Cecilia was busy preparing breakfast and dancing a bit to "Running Away" by Roy Ayers.

"Hey, Celie," Sean said with a scratchy throat.

"Well, good morning, Mr. Morris. How are you?" she asked, grinning as she tied the strings of the white, jambalaya apron behind her back. He had bought her that apron in New Orleans. That little red crab had seen all sorts of cooking since Celie wrapped it around her heavyset frame. Celie could cook anything and everything.

"I'm feeling *terrible*," Sean said, grabbing his throat.

Celie poured pancake mix on the sizzling griddle. "What's the matter?"

"My throat hurts," Sean whined like a six-year-old. He felt like one, too.

"Awwww, go over to the seasoning cabinet and get me the salt. Gargle with some warm salt water. It'll make that sore throat go away," she said, setting the bowl down. She used a paper towel to wipe the sweat from her light-brown forehead. Celie had freckles on her plump cheeks and always had the same hairdo—a shiny, Jheri-curl shag. Either she was getting shorter or Sean was getting taller. He didn't feel so tall at the moment. His dad's statement in court yesterday had chopped him off at the knees.

"Salt water!" Sean exclaimed, thinking how nasty that would taste.

"It's either salt water or one of your Grandma Linda's home remedies. Maybe she'll crush some aspirin, mix it with Vaseline, and rub it on your chest. Or mix grape juice and vitamins with that brown stuff and make you drink it. Take your pick."

Sean cringed at the thought of the brown stuff that "the witch doctor" could put together. "She won't have to know I'm sick. I won't tell if you won't."

"She has ways of finding out," Grandma Cecilia said, smiling slyly.

Sean made a quick decision. "Salt water, it is."

He gargled the bitter salt water three times and the scratchiness was gone.

Cecilia Williams was a woman of wisdom, Sean thought, as he watched her cook. She had also helped raise Sean's mother. She was always happy, a church-going woman. But she was also a big woman who didn't take any mess. She was quick with a belt, too. The only time Sean saw her mad was when he was a little kid. She spanked his behind for jumping on her bed and knocking down the painting of Grandpa Clinton. She didn't make him take off his light-blue Super Mario pajamas, she just got straight down to business—hand to backside.

Sean looked forward to seeing her and eating some of her cooking, especially now that he left home at a *normal time*. And when he got out of school, he looked forward to seeing her then, too. Dinner was right around the corner.

When Sean was much younger, they had lived in Jeffery Manor. Then, there were always a lot of kids around the house. Cecilia "Celie" Williams took care of them from the time school let out until their parents got home from work. She had watched practically every kid on Merrion, Merrill, and Paxton avenues grow up.

Of course, she knew how to cure any and everything. Whether it was a cold or a sad face. She was the hero coming to the rescue in a child's nightmare. And at fifty, she was another Superwoman raising her grandson, Rick, alone.

Rick was Celie's biological grandson. When Rick was a baby, he'd been abused and severely injured. When the courts removed him from his mother's custody, Cecilia had stepped in.

She didn't allow anything but smiles and laughter around her. She said,

"Life's too short to sit and wait for somebody else to get their life together." Sean learned so much from her, things about girls and women and how he should respect them and how "certain" things at certain times can affect their behavior—*that* alone was a million-dollar piece of advice. He liked it when Celie told stories about the old days. They even came up with their own dance; it was like the Cabbage Patch dance. but with a little more head bobbing and a lot more neck movement.

"Sean, go finish your chores from last night," Celie said, flipping over the last of her pancakes.

"What did I miss?" Sean groaned.

"You didn't finish sweeping the hallway. I know you didn't make your bed this morning. Now you have these dishes to wash," she said, pointing at the sink.

Sean went to his room. The sun was trying hard to shine through the gray clouds that only dripped a few drops. He made up his full-size bed, changing to blue baseball sheets. He took a few seconds to fix his shoes and picked his dirty clothes off the floor before sweeping the hallway.

As he neared the kitchen, Celie heard Sean singing along. "What do you know about this ol' school, lil' boy?"

"I'm your grandson, Celie," Sean said, doing the Twist.

"That's right," she said, rubbing his uncombed, curly head. "You may be my grandson, but you don't know nothing about old school. Now this," she said, switching to the Temptations on the CD player, "is old school."

"Celie, those are dusties. And I got *these last two dollars*," Sean sang, "by Johnnie Taylor, and that 'Love and Happiness,' from Al Green, because old school is my first, my last, my everything."

"Get down with yo bad self," she said.

Sean finished sweeping, as Celie walked back into the kitchen, throwing her little dance into the song.

Sean could feel her gaze following him.

Celie knew the whole deal with his father. She could notice a change in anyone and would give advice, but as she always said, "They have to see it for themselves."

Sean was seeing a great deal he didn't *want* to see. He was a good kid, didn't do drugs, and didn't hang out all night and stuff. Why wouldn't Roberto want to be with him?

"So, are you feeling okay?"

"Yeah, that salt water helped," Sean replied, still trying to get the salty taste out of his mouth. Hopefully the pancakes would help, too. *Was she going to cook those things all day?*

She turned off the stove and moved the skillets off the burners. "No, I'm talking about your father."

There was an uncomfortable pause. "I still think about what happened. I talk to the rest of his family more than to him," Sean said. He had tried to think of ways to get back at his father, but how do you hurt a man who doesn't care?

"Sean, you can't hang on to this forever. For a minute, your mom was ready to ship you off to boarding school somewhere. But I realize you're just mad right now and I think talking about how you feel will help. You're a good person and I know you're wondering why he doesn't do the right thing. But if you let this anger rule your life, you'll miss out on the good things. You'll be too angry to see it, or you'll push people away. Just like your father's doing to you. You have to be the better person and raise your own children the right way." She looked at him and chuckled. "And I don't mean you should go out and have some *now*."

"Yes, Ma'am," he said, laughing. In some ways, Celie was also a grand-father. She had taught him about some "manly" things. She was the one to teach Sean how to put on a condom, using a lotion bottle as an example. Then she explained, "A lot of people aren't using them these days, and that's scary. It's important that *you* always do."

She was also the one to teach him how to treat a lady with respect. Even though Sean didn't have many men around the hosue to look up to, he felt Celie and Superwoman were doing a good job filling in. His best male role models were women.

"Where's Aunt Denise?" he asked, looking around:

"She left early. Her flight's leaving for Hawaii," Celie said, walking over to the stove. You know how those suburban buses and trains are."

"Man! She's gone all the time now. Everyone has a job. What time is Rick getting home? He's been working those late shifts like crazy. I don't see him, either. They're like ghosts."

"He should be home shortly. I don't see how he does that and school, but he's working it out," she said, checking her silver watch. "Just like you will."

Rick had been Sean's "play brother," ever since Sean was two. They said they were blood brothers, but hadn't actually gone through the trouble of pricking their fingers and letting their blood mix. Sean wouldn't tell if Rick wouldn't, since it didn't keep them from being close.

Rick had overcome six broken ribs and had endured serious head trauma and healing in order to lead a normal life.

When the doctors said he wouldn't walk or talk, the "witch doctor" as the family called Grandma Linda, stepped in. She had vitamins, brown stuff, herbs, ointments, and other concoctions. Sean had been subjected to some of them. Sometimes he ended up spitting it out in the kitchen sink.

Rick was now her best patient, and a walking miracle illustrating the power of love. Rick attended Chicago Vocational High School and worked at the Checkers fast-food restaurant on 87th and Stony Island. Rick kept his grades up, even though he worked late hours. In his spare time, he designed, wrote, and drew pictures for his own comic books.

Sean could hear Rick's hard footsteps as he walked through the door. It was rare that Sean saw Rick these days, because he was either busy or asleep. And the whole world knew when he slept. That boy could snore loud enough to wake the whole block.

"What's up Rick?" Sean said, standing at the kitchen door, letting the sweet smell of breakfast soak into his senses.

"Nothing much," Rick said, setting his bags down on the floor.

Sean followed him to the living room, where the bright walls wore a fresh coat of lavender paint. Momma and Aunt Denise had finally finished installing the wooden floor, light fixtures, and inside stairs. Sean's sixty karate trophies were displayed under them.

"Work getting to be too much for you?" Sean was surprised that he didn't turn on the big-screen wooden television in the corner by the window. Sean noticed a little light shining in. The rain clouds had finally moved elsewhere.

"Nope, just trying to concentrate on getting through high school and work at the same time," Rick said, stretching out on the couch. He was still in his work uniform. Rick must've been working hard, he looked rugged. His normally lined sideburns had grown into a full beard covering his fleshy medium-brown face, and his hair looked like rough black cotton.

"Is it really that hard?" Sean asked, sitting in the chair across from him.

"Yeah, it's hard work. Which is why you don't want to do this kind of stuff when you're in high school. It's hard for me to stay awake in class and at work sometimes. You need to keep your head in those books and get a scholarship or something. Saving for college is rough."

Sean had seen a serious change in Rick during the last two years. Aside from the comic books and school, he used to play video games and watch television a lot.

"So what's going on?" Rick asked, glancing at the food piling up on the table. Suddenly he did not look sleepy anymore.

"Nothing much, just helping Celie out in the kitchen and finishing my chores."

"Oh yeah, and she's been throwin' down in the kitchen again," Rick said. He got off the couch and walked toward the food. "Hey, Celie."

"Hey, junior, I thought you forgot about me," she said.

"Now how could I forget about my grandma?" Rick said, giving her a hug and getting cooking residue on his uniform. Wasn't like it didn't need to hit the washer.

"Yeah right, you know I'll whoop your behind," she responded, waving the steel spatula. "You ain't that grown."

"I know, Celie," he said as she turned the breakfast sausages over.

"I may be *older*, but I can still get the upper hand," she said.

"So, what else is on the menu for this morning?" Rick asked, reaching for one of the sausages on the plate covered with paper towel.

"Ask before you grab," Celie said, smacking his stubby hand.

Sean cracked up laughing.

"My bad, Grandma," Rick said smiling faintly and massaging his hand.

You don't mess with a woman who's been washing dishes in her household since she was six. Those are rough hands.

"Did you even wash your hands?" she asked.

"No, Ma'am," he answered.

Celie didn't like germs and Rick was probably covered with them. Sean was surprised she didn't take the Lysol to him.

"Both of you, go wash your hands, before I pop y'all upside the head," she ordered. "Knuckleheads!"

Walking to the bathroom, Sean asked, "Rick, how do you feel about your dad?"

"What do you mean?" Rick asked, reaching for the soap.

"I mean you rarely see him, so how do you feel about him?" Sean asked and waited for his turn at the sink.

"Well, I talk to him, he visits, and I've had plenty of times to see him. I just couldn't take off school," Rick replied, rinsing his hands. "Like now, my dad wants me to visit him in Tennessee to meet his new wife."

Rick Senior or "Ricky" as they called him, lived in Memphis, where he worked in a lamination plant. But unlike Sean's father, Ricky came back to see him whenever he could, not because Celie said he had to, but because he *wanted* to. And he sent money to help with Rick. No one had to take him to court either.

"At least your dad wants you to visit, and he stays in another state. My dad stays up the street and he couldn't keep me if his life depended on it.

"I'm going to college soon, so there's no reason for me to live with my dad. I'm more upset about my mom than my dad being in my life." They dried their hands and headed back to the kitchen. "After seventeen years, she finally wants to be in my life. I see her at every family funeral or she'll just show up here, expecting me to welcome her with open arms. How can I love a woman I don't know? You have your mom, I have Celie, and I'm fine with—"

"People aren't always perfect; some people aren't ready for parenthood," Celie said before Rick could finish. "It's a job helping someone become an adult. Sean, your father isn't mentally ready. Rick, your mother wasn't ready, either. But you can't let that tear away at your soul."

"Yes, Ma'am," they said.

"Some fathers leave the duty to the mother. Some mothers end up stressed out. They take it out on the people around them. It's a vicious cycle, but only God can judge parents who aren't around when we need them. The both of you need to change that cycle when you become fathers. Keep that in mind."

"Yes, Ma'am," they both said gazing at her, soaking up every bit of wisdom she had to offer. As they walked away, Sean thought, *It's incredible how most women can give guidelines for being a man, but a father and can't stick around to teach it.* Thank God for Celie. Thank God women don't just give up and say, "I don't feel like being a momma anymore." If they *all* walked, the world would be one ugly place.

"Now let me see your hands," she said as they sat down at the table. "Gotta make sure they're clean so we can eat. You little rascals always try to fool me," she said, kissing each of them on the cheek. Sean reached for one of the pancakes, but before he could grab it, a big smack popped his hands.

"Sean, say grace," Celie said, drawing her hand back. "Boy, you act like your mama, and Rick you act like your daddy."

Even his mother's brother, Mack, was no help. He was doing his own little child support dance.

Mack was best friends with Sean's dad, which was how Sean's parents got together in the first place. But Roberto had picked up some of Mack's bad habits. *Did being around an irresponsible man rub off on another? Was it a virus or something?*

Every single time Sean needed to bring a parent to school, his mother would have to take off work early, even on father-son days. They'd weave in and out of classrooms, between men proudly standing by their sons. Sean had only his mother, Superwoman. She would always be there for him. She'd been the one to come up with a plan to get Sean involved in something that would expose him to more positive men. Hopefully, it would make a difference and have an effect on his life. Karate helped to discipline people; it could help Sean push his anger away.

Chapter 17

Practicing karate and leading Shihan's classes boosted Sean's confidence, which carried over into his schoolwork.

Sean received his yellow and blue belts one right after the other. When he first started in the dojo, Shihan Deno had Sean sparring against the higher ranks. The people he had feared the most were Sensei Sherri (a black belt) and her husband, Donald (a green belt).

Sean would get smacked around like a volleyball, but he learned to be quick on his feet, and smart about his attacks. As his ranking advanced, he became more confident when sparring against them. He protected himself well, but still got his butt kicked from time to time. Thank God for padded equipment and rules only allowing hits in designated areas. Otherwise Sean would've been in serious trouble.

Sean rushed into the gym at St. Sabina Church on Racine. He looked at all the trophies to be awarded at the tournament and knew two of those first-place trophies would be his. There were numerous divisions; rings of colored tape covered the polished, wooden basketball floor. A number of people were already there, including some students from other dojos who, like Sean, arrived early to stretch and practice. The rest were parents and karate instructors, there to coach and support the students. There were more fathers there than he could count. And for a moment, sadness slipped into his soul. Where was the man who would cheer him on? Sean shrugged and sighed.

Then he felt a tap on his shoulder, turned around, and bowed to his instructor.

"Sean, I'll be spending more time with the other students today. We both know that you will do great, right?"

"Yes, Shihan, I'll do my best," he said with a confident smile.

"Great. Of course, I'll be there to see your kata and sparring match," Shihan said, slapping him on the arm. "So practice."

Because his skill level was higher than that of the other students in his age group, Sean joined the adults for kata. Sean had confidence—his techniques were crisp and he consistently performed to the best of his ability. Because of his agility, he often beat higher-ranked opponents to take first place.

"You need to look like you're really fighting. You need to have the right facial expressions, sounds, and movements. That's the same for everything in life. If you're going to do something, don't do it halfway," Shihan Deno had told him.

When Sean performed his kata, he demonstrated the imaginary fight so well, he beat out three adults for first place.

In the fighting division of the tournament, thirteen-year-old Sean was placed in the division with other competitors of his ranking—the fifteen-to-seventeen-year-old "beginners" division. Most of them towered over him, and Sean's mother really thought it was unfair.

Five points won a match. Each kick to a "legal" area on the body was worth two points, punches were worth one. Sean looked down the line. It was going to be a long night. He felt like it was a rematch between David and Goliath, Ali and Foreman.

Sean's first opponent was disqualified when he threw a kick to the groin area, which was illegal. The powerful kick sent Sean flying into the chairs outside the ring. Sean got up and stood ready to fight his next opponent.

During the second fight, Sean followed Shihan's instruction, no less than five karate techniques to the opponent each time. He won with a score of five to three.

Cynthia always got scared when he competed against students who were taller, but she always said, "You did great," even when he didn't win. The last fight was for first place and his opponent was a giant. He was so tall that Sean had to tilt his head up to look at him.

"Bow to me, bow to each other, and tap gloves," Sensei Sherri said as she adjusted her peach-tinted glasses.

They did, and she yelled, "Fighting stances!"

Both boys put up their hands for protection.

As soon as Sensei Sherri said, "Go," his opponent's long legs landed a swift kick to Sean's stomach. Sean, trying to catch his breath, kneeled on the ground. Out of the corner of his eye, he saw Grandma Celie holding Superwoman back. He knew she wanted to give a swift beating to his opponent. Momma didn't need karate classes for a good old Chicago butt whipping.

"Sean, get up, Baby," his mother cried out from the bleachers. Her voice encouraged him and his confidence grew. He thought about not disappointing Shihan Deno, who was sitting outside of the ring watching quietly.

Sean stood and resumed his fighting stance. Sensei Sherri gave Sean's opponent two points for the kick. If he wanted to win, he needed to catch up fast.

Sensei Sherri lifted her hand from between them. "Go."

Cautious with every move, Sean studied his opponent.

As soon as his opponent went for the kick, Sean blocked it and countered with a punch to the kidney. Sean earned a point.

After that hit, his opponent got mad, hitting his fist against his headgear three times. Sensei Sherri said, "Go," and Sean's opponent went at Sean, furiously punching and kicking, causing Sean to back up. Just before Sean backed totally out of the ring, he noticed that his opponent's chest was wide open for a shot, so he jumped up and double kicked him. He gained two points, but his back paid a price. The kick had pushed him off his opponent's chest, out of the ring, and into the bleachers. Sean, holding his back, let out loud grunts of pain. Right now, he would take baseball or football.

Sean got up slowly and re-entered the ring. The spectators clapped and cheered, which gave him an instant confidence boost. The underdog had his own cheerleading section!

Sensei Sherri looked at him. "Are you good to fight?" she asked.

"Yes, Sensei," he said, standing straight, forgetting the pain. Sensei Sherri gave two points to Sean for the kick. Two more points to go for the win.

Sean got in his fighting stance and as soon as Sensei Sherri said, "Go," he started to bounce around the ring in hopes of catching his opponent off guard. No luck. Sean went in blocking, trying to aim a punch for the stomach, but his opponent blocked it and countered with a kick and a punch, which Sean blocked.

The clash lasted until Sean backed out of a seven-hit combo. Sean continued to study his opponent, trying to figure out what he would come at him with next. Meanwhile time was running out. First place seemed so far away.

Sean bounced around the ring looking for an opening. His opponent gave him an open shot, but Sean saw instantly that it was a fake. Sean waited for the right time and went in with a back fist, but his opponent blocked it. Sean continued with punches and kicks. As Sean circled the ring, he noticed that his opponent was beginning to tire and leaving his side open.

Bingo! As soon as Sean had the opportunity, he threw a roundhouse kick to his opponent's side, grabbing the points and first place.

Sean bowed out of the ring with a busted lip, sore back, and a smile on his face. He shook hands with his opponent, who was holding his side, and went to the trophy table.

Two first-place trophies in a day, one for kata forms and one for sparring, was known as scoring an ace.

Shihan Deno was waiting by the wall for Sean, who ran over to him with his trophy, took out his mouthpiece, and bowed.

"Congratulations, Sean, that was some fight," Shihan Deno said, extending his beefy hand.

Still catching his breath, Sean said, "Thank you, Shihan," and shook his hand.

"Sean, I'm really proud of you."

"Thank you, Shihan," Sean replied, overwhelmed with emotion.

Although Shihan had a grown son, he accepted Sean as one of his own. Sean would do whatever it took to keep Shihan proud of him. Sean went many places with the school, even traveling to different cities for tournaments. That year had ended with Sean winning first place for fighting and fifth place for kata at the national level of the American Karate Association.

★★★

Sean's stay at Loop Lab School was cut short by lack of money. Sean's mother wasn't able to pay for tuition by herself. Roberto always ended up quitting his job, making it impossible for him to pay support. So Sean was back at the place where he didn't want to be, Gadson, and the people didn't let him forget that Cynthia Morris had messed up things in their town.

Their hatred even came out in their kids. Eighth grade was going to be hell for Sean.

One day after school, Sean was walking home from the corner of 140th and Saginaw when five boys from his class and some upper classmen from River North blocked his path. They were looking for trouble.

Trying to avoid a fight, Sean crossed the street and continued toward home.

They came after him, surrounded him, and pushed him into a blue garage.

Sean dropped his book bag and got in a fighting stance.

The boy wearing the Michael Jordan jersey jumped toward Sean.

Sean threw a sidekick to his stomach, then a fast back-fist to one of the other boys nearby. He followed that with a spinning kick to the one standing in front of him.

The two boys who were still standing looked at Sean with wide eyes. "You know karate?" one of them asked.

Neither boy moved an inch.

"I do now," Sean said, moving back into a fighting stance. "I'm ready when you are."

"Naw, man I'm cool." They quickly helped their friends up off the ground and ran to the other side of Torrence Bridge.

Sean picked up his book bag and continued home.

"Thank you, Shihan," Sean said, proud that Shihan had taught him how to stand up for himself.

Chapter 18

At the beginning of Sean's eighth-grade year, he was on the verge of a set-back. During another ugly court battle, he found out that his father was still trying to terminate his parental rights.

The rage came back and Sean once again began to have trouble focusing in school. He stopped turning in his schoolwork. A straight-A student and a karate champion, and his dad didn't want him? If Shihan Deno could love him, why couldn't his own father?

This time, Cynthia took steps to get Sean another male role model, by calling the Big Brothers and Big Sisters of Metropolitan Chicago.

One day, Sean came home after playing basketball at the park down the street. He saw an unfamiliar red Ford Mustang in front of the house. He walked into the living room and found his mother sitting on the couch. A tall, white man with light brown hair and a short beard sat in one of the comfortable chairs. When he saw Sean, the man stood, wearing a pair of black dress pants, a forest-green, long-sleeved dress shirt, and a shiny black tie. The flashy car and the man's clothes were total opposites.

Superwoman turned to him with a smile. "Sean, this is Chris McCray, your Big Brother."

When The Big Brothers/Big Sisters asked his mother if she felt strongly about Sean having only a Black male for a Big Brother, she said, "No. As long as he's not a pedophile, stands up to pee, and is a *responsible* man, I'm game."

"Nice to meet you, Sir," Sean said, extending his hand.

"Nice to meet you, too, Sean," Chris said as he shook his hand. Chris looked like Russell Crowe, with a pinker complexion and a bulkier frame.

"Boy, what will people think when they see I have a white 'Big Brother'?" Sean whispered to his mother, "or even when I say he's my Big Brother?"

Superwoman chuckled. "There's a lot I haven't been telling people. So I think they might even believe it."

Grandma Celie woke up from her midday nap and walked into the living room. "Oh, hello, everyone," she said.

"Hey, Celie, this is Sean's new Big Brother Chris," Superwoman said.

"Wow! You're rather tall," Celie said as she stood up straight.

"Thank you," Chris said, laughing.

"You're welcome, Handsome," Celie said, walking past him to the kitchen.

Sean didn't think he would have anything in common with a man who dressed up to the fullest every day, but maybe it was worth a try. Especially if Grandma Celie already liked him.

Chris looked Sean in the eye and asked, "So, are you up for spending some time together this weekend?"

Sean looked at his mother; she nodded.

"Sure, when?"

"Around ten, Saturday," Chris replied.

"So what do you like to do?" Chris asked as they sat down to talk.

"Well, I like to play football, watch movies, go bike riding, go carting, and other things that are fun," Sean replied, wondering if Chris would still be interested.

Chris didn't bat an eye, "Cool, we'll think of something to do this weekend."

Caught off guard at the positive response, Sean's eyes shifted to his mother. Chris looked like the kind of guy who concerned himself with work, 24/7. How could he possibly say *cool*? Although Chris was still young, he carried himself like a much older man. Sean found out soon enough the suit-and-tie look was just a cover-up.

Sean woke up at nine o' clock Saturday morning. He wondered what they were going to do and hoped it wouldn't be boring. Didn't white people like to be extreme? Rock-climbing, bungee-jumping, parachuting. Not for Sean! Ten o'clock rolled around and Sean heard a loud engine rumbling down the street. He looked through the beige horizontal blinds and saw Chris getting off a black motorcycle. He was wearing blue jeans and a black T-shirt and had a bunch of tattoos on his arm. He also wore a black helmet painted with a waving British flag. He looked completely different!

"Bye, Mom," Sean said, practically running out the door.

Chris met him halfway up the path. "What's up, Sean? You ready to go?" He handed Sean a helmet.

"Yeah," Sean said anxiously, hoping to get out of there before Superwoman saw what Chris looked like today. He was afraid she would call the whole thing off if she saw him looking like an X-Game biker guy. Chris looked promising as a mentor and Big Brother. And a whole lot of fun.

Chris started the motorcycle; the rumble underneath made Sean jump.

"There's a baseball game today—Cubs versus Giants—I thought we could go check that out," Chris said, as he grabbed the extra helmet strapped onto the back of his motorcycle. "But first we have to get something to eat."

Sean's eyes lit up as if he had won a prize. Baseball was a great start. "Cool, we can do that," Sean said, watching the way Chris put his helmet on and doing the same. Rick had hooked him on watching baseball when Rick used to be the family remote hog, centuries before he got off his tail, found a job, and registered for school.

Chris hopped on the motorcycle, then told Sean how to get on. Sean grabbed Chris' waist tightly and they sped off.

About forty-five minutes later, Chris parked the bike at El Famous Burrito, a Mexican restaurant known for its football-size burritos. The place was near Chris' condo in Palos Heights. Feeling a little rush from the bike's speed, Sean almost fell down when he got off the motorcycle. Chris laughed as Sean took off his helmet and peeked in the little round mirror on the side of the bike. Sean's hair was a mess, but then, so was Chris'. Sean pulled out a comb, quickly fixing his hair.

They sat down at a green booth. A beautiful young Mexican girl, with her hair pulled into a bun under her sombrero, took their order and soon brought them two huge steak burritos. They weren't lying about the burritos. As they ate, Sean found out a lot about Chris.

"So, why did you get all of those tattoos?" Sean asked.

"When I was in the Marine Corps, I got the first one. I just didn't stop getting them when I got out," Chris said, pointing out and explaining the significance of some of them.

"So, did you grow up in Chicago?" Sean asked before taking another bite of the burrito. He had to open really wide to get it in.

"Well, I'm originally from southern Illinois. I lived with my aunt."

"What's up with your mom and dad?" Sean asked cautiously, immediately sensing there was more to the story.

"Mom wasn't too good of a parent, and dad just wasn't there."

Surprised, Sean stopped asking questions for a moment, digesting that tidbit of information. He'd thought Chris had the perfect life, but it turned out he was somewhat like Sean. Guess it didn't matter about race, people were people. Chris looked like he had turned out great. So Sean didn't have an excuse.

Chris was also extremely smart and politically aware. He spent most of the remaining time at lunch explaining to Sean many of the things he thought needed changing in the United States.

They hopped on the bike, rode through the parking lot and into the garage of a beige, brick building. As Sean followed Chris into the building, he heard loud rock music. It wasn't until they stopped at the door where the music was coming from, that Sean realized it was Chris' condo. One more thing that didn't jibe with Sean's first impression. *Wow, very cool.* He followed Chris through the door and past a white laundry room on the way to the gray-walled living room. A man, holding a plate of spaghetti and garlic bread, sat on the couch. He shoveled the food in his mouth like a bulldozer.

"Leroy, this is Sean. Sean, this is my roommate," Chris said.

Sean and Leroy shook hands. Leroy was watching a motorcycle race on television. He looked a lot like Chris, except he was a little thinner, with long, light brown hair, blue eyes, and pale skin.

"Sean, I'm going to change my clothes real quick and then we can go," Chris said, standing in the hallway leading to his bedroom.

"Okay, cool," Sean replied, as he took a seat in one of the black living room chairs. He noticed the framed motorcycle posters lining the walls. The assortment of South Park, Spawn, and motorcycle figurines sitting on the shelves of a glass cabinet next to the large black entertainment center, caught his attention as well.

"Cool, aren't they?" Leroy asked, following Sean's gaze.

"Yeah, this is a little different from what I thought Chris' house would look like," Sean said, still taking everything in. He felt more at ease.

"That's what everybody says about Chris, but he's cool. We've been friends for a long time."

"How long?" Sean asked.

"Since high school."

"Man, that's—" Something flickered in the corner of his eye. He turned and saw a ball of fur prance by with its back in the air. His mouth went dry and an eyebrow rose.

"What the hell is that?" *Not cool.* If his mother heard that word, he was in big trouble. At least it wasn't the "B" word.

"That's Stewart, one of our pets. He's a ferret," Leroy explained, getting up from the couch. He picked up a long gray and white animal. Sean thought it looked like a stretched-out mouse.

"Whew, I thought you guys had a serious rodent problem," Sean said as Chris came out of his room wearing a red, white, and blue Sammy Sosa jersey.

"What's wrong?" Chris asked, buttoning up the jersey.

"Sean just met the *other* part of the family," Leroy said as he played with Stewart.

Chris chuckled and grabbed his keys off the end table. "Okay, are you ready to go?"

"Yeah." Sean stood, but took another look at Stewart. *Whatever happened to dogs, cats, fish, or birds? Now people had ferrets?*

They hopped back on the motorcycle, hit the expressway, and headed for the ballpark.

Sitting in the first level by the foul pole, Sean was anxious for the game to begin. He had had Chris all wrong. He was an outgoing person with a serious need for adrenaline rushes. Sean knew that Chris would be a great dad and husband, and would never treat his son the way Roberto treated him. Any guy who would spend time with someone else's child was okay in Sean's book.

Chris was open about a lot of things with Sean. Already Sean felt comfortable enough with Chris to express his own opinions.

They pulled up to Sean's house later that day, turned off the motorcycle, and took off their helmets, happy that the Cubs had won—finally. Sean didn't want to be home. They had done things that Sean only could wish he had done with his father. On top of that, Chris was so cool that if he had a slight tan, Sean would consider him a Black person.

Well, Sean thought, checking out the pink tint on Chris' face, maybe more than a *slight* tan.

"Hey, Man, I had a great time. Thanks," Sean said, handing Chris the helmet and hopping off the bike.

"I'm glad you enjoyed yourself." Chris put the spare helmet on the back seat and strapped it down. "I'll talk to you later this week. Let's see if we can hook up again next weekend."

"Next weekend? Cool! See you later," Sean said. They shook hands, then hugged and patted each other on the back. He unlocked the front door just before Chris pulled off. Sean closed the door behind him. It looked like the testosterone factor was up another level in his life. That day Sean secretly adopted Chris into his small family.

Chapter 19

"Boy, how do you get two detentions in the *same* class in the *same* day?" his mother yelled.

Sean scratched his head, which was almost bald after a bad haircut, and wondered the same thing. If there was an answer, *she* must have it, because he was drawing a serious blank. Chris was still around, and karate class was still in session, but suddenly Sean was back on the losing end of a good education.

Entering his freshman year at River North High School, Sean had a hard time adjusting to the culture. His mother called it *second-stage puberty*, but he knew that wasn't the problem. Sean hadn't enjoyed school in a long time, and the crazy transition to high school wasn't helping.

River North was undergoing serious changes. With an increasing Black student body, more and more teachers found they had little or no experience with the different types of students faced every day. The teachers weren't ready for serious diversity. Two days into his freshman year, Sean wished he were still in eighth grade. Better yet, he wished he was back in *third* grade.

The new people and the constant changing of classes and locations were all so confusing. The physical structure of the school made it even worse. Part of the third floor was actually on the *second* floor, and part of the second floor was on the first. Then there was a fourth floor, but he still hadn't figured out why. Sean didn't even know where he was half the time, and was late to almost every class.

The high school teachers were so much tougher than his previous educators. They cracked down on students who were late. In grammar school, he could get away with being late for class if he had a note. Now, even if he *did* have a note from the dean or principal, a Saturday detention would follow.

Fortunately, Sean had a few teachers who showed mercy. His three best teachers were Mr. Carson, his band teacher; Mrs. Vincennes, his keyboarding teacher; and Mr. Brantz, his English teacher. The rest sucked.

Sean's mother always said, "When you step out into the world, it's just waiting to kick your behind." Sean thought the teachers were probably so tough on the students for the same reason. But school was for learning, not a place to be treated as a prisoner.

Sean arrived ten minutes early for a Saturday detention. He waited outside the four-story brown brick building in the cool November weather with about fifty other students. Someone tapped his shoulder. When Sean turned around, he saw his friend Roger, a guy he knew from church.

"What's up, Roger?" Sean asked, slapping him on the arm.

"Nothing much, just waiting for this part of the day to go by." Roger checked his watch and then looked for Sean's book bag. A book bag that wasn't where it was supposed to be. "Where's your homework?

"I don't have time for homework," Sean replied, putting his hands inside his blue jacket to keep warm.

"Sean, you've got plenty of time to do stuff today." Roger pointed at the building where they would spend the better part of the day. "Especially now."

Roger O'Neal was the only person who Sean really knew at River North. For a while *both* of them ended up in detention because of the strict rules about tardiness. Weekday detention was like a little tap on the hand, Saturday was pure torture. The school had a computer call his mom to inform her that he had detention—detention which he had so often that even when he *didn't* have it, the computer called anyway.

There were quite a few times when his mother went to the school to check and found that Sean had told the truth—he *didn't* have detention— at least not that day.

Parents fumed as they dropped off their kids, probably because it caused them to lose sleep. Superwoman refused to take him, and Saturday buses were a joke. If he missed Saturday, he would be suspended—so he had to get up at four a.m. and walk two miles in the cold. He had complained, but Superwoman said, "It's not like you've never braved the cold."

The group of students dreaded walking into the building, all feeling that it was too early. Sean wouldn't smell the fresh cut grass from the field outside for hours. Trying to be the last one in, Sean saw his friends Corey and Vivica attempting to do the same.

"What's up, y'all?" Sean asked, popping up behind them.

Neither flinched. "Nothing much, just waiting for today to pass," Corey said, struggling to keep his overloaded book bag on his shoulder. Corey had skin so dark, it glowed. People always raved about how dark he was, but one thing he never had was bad acne or zits.

"Today can't go fast enough," Vivica said with her hair wrapped in a cheetah print scarf. Her caramel face wasn't its usual glowing color. Lip gloss, eyebrow liner, and the little bit of makeup that she never went without were amiss. And she was wearing green plaid pajama bottoms, with a white sweater hanging loose on her beautiful, normally showcased body.

"All day? That's the truth," Sean said as he helped Corey with his book bag. "Why do you carry so many books?"

"Because I have to do homework, unlike *someone* I know," he replied.

"Well, at least I won't have back problems later on. Carrying all those books is going to make your sex life horrible."

"What sex life? I'm grounded for like the next six months."

"Ooooh, that sucks." Sean cringed.

They walked into the long, yellow lunchroom and received instructions. Sean and Roger were at the back of the line. Some people had to double or triple at a table. A new record, without a doubt.

"I want you to find someone in your classes that you can get your homework from," Roger told Sean. "And I want you to work on it while you're here."

"But Roger. I—"

"No buts, Sean! Do the work. My mom tells me whatever she talks about with your mom, and I'm tired of hearing that you're not doing your work."

"I used to hear the same things about you, so you can't talk," Sean replied.

"But I'm not here because of it. You are. If you don't starting doing your homework and make it to class on time, I'll *make* you do it, and you don't want that," Roger threatened. "Do the work."

"All right I'll do it," Sean said, not wanting to anger Roger any more than he already had. Being in Saturday detention could drive a man crazy. Last time Sean didn't show up for class and received a Saturday detention for it. Roger locked him in the janitor's closet and put two heavy desks in front of the door.

"Vivica, can I get the homework assignments from our classes?" Sean asked, leaning over her back.

"I only have the math homework," she said.

"I'll take that, and I need the book," Sean said.

"Where is your book?" Vivica asked, holding her math book away from him.

Sean's eyes shifted from side to side. "At home."

"Boy, if I don't get my book back, one of these books will go flying upside your head." She pointed at the huge World History book.

"Yeah, sure." Sean grabbed the math book, definitely not taking her seriously.

Though Sean got the homework assignment, he didn't know how to do it. He spent the entire detention struggling on the work. *How did I graduate from elementary school?*

But that was only half the problem. Mom had taken a few more trips to child support court. She didn't allow him to go anymore, just told him about the end results. Money or no money—show or no show. All this because Roberto was pissed off. All this because mom "won," and got to decide where Sean went to school. He had done well, but did it matter, really? All Sean wanted was his father—but how long would that feeling last? Slowly, the anger was going away, but it was a take-two-steps-forward-and-one-back kind of thing.

Sean used music to soothe his anger. He played the tenor sax and made the marching, pep, and concert bands in his freshman year. Music was the best thing that ever happened to Sean, but it was also the worst. He would skip homework to practice in the garage. Music was everything. That and *girls*. But he wasn't doing too well in that department, either.

Just last week he told his mom, "I'll be in the garage," as he walked out carrying a little portable heater that had become his best friend.

"Did you finish your homework?"

"Yes, Momma," Sean lied, tipping over the vase of fake tulips. Whenever Sean lied, he'd trip over something or knock over something.

"Okay, don't stay out there too long!"

Sean plugged in the heater to warm his saxophone…and stayed out until ten, sometimes eleven o' clock if everyone else fell asleep early.

"Good morning, musicians," Mr. Carson had said that first afternoon in music class. "Most of you know me, but for those that don't, I'm Mr. Carson." He wrote his name on the blackboard, and four letters underneath: P—A—S—E. "Does any new student know what these four letters mean?"

The room fell silent.

"Old members, help them out," Mr. Carson said.

"Positive Attitude—Superior Effort!" they said in unison.

Mr. Carson taught him how to appreciate different types of music, from R&B to jazz, and even rock. Sean loved music—he gave it his all, leaving everything else to chance.

As the weeks went by, one low, pitiful grade after another, no one at the school seemed to care. They didn't even inform Cynthia of his progress. Summer school and groundings were inevitable. Soon music would be all Sean could do for a living.

And she couldn't pull him out of band. It was the only grade on his report card above a D. Like the A in band really made a difference to a 1.0 GPA! At Loop Lab School and at Gadson last year, Sean had given everything he had and gotten great grades. But at River North he had no inspiration to do well. And the teachers didn't have time to give it to him. If you didn't have your own, you were out of luck.

During the third quarter of his freshman year, Sean's mother came to school for the first of many parent/teacher conferences. She was enraged. "Ds" and "Fs" weren't allowed in her house. A—At the top of your game, B—Better than average, C—Caught sleeping and tripping, D—Didn't Do Diddly Squat, and F—Frankly, you didn't give a darn. Based on her standards, he was only passing two classes—band and *lunch*. He went home every night to his mother asking, "Did you finish your homework?"

He would reply with a bald-faced lie, "Yes, Momma." He didn't even know where his homework was.

The truth was bound to come out.

Cynthia kept hearing bad things about her only son. "That's not like Sean," she would reply.

She found out the band teacher had pulled Sean and other band members out of classes for games and extra practices almost every other day. When Sean's mother walked into the band room, she marched right past the other parents. She wanted to tear Mr. Carson's head off and beat him to a pulp

In his office, Mom chewed him out. "Mr. Carson, I've talked to the other teachers, and they said that you excused Sean for band-related stuff at times when he should've stayed in class, especially with these grades." She put Sean's report card on the desk. Mr. Carson glanced at it. A look of disbelief crossed his face.

"Mrs. Morris, if Sean was having a problem with his school work, he should have come to me. I make allowances for everyone. He isn't the only one with grade troubles," Mr. Carson explained, his blue eyes staring right into her brown ones. "I know about the students who are having grade problems because they came and told me."

"Well, Mr. Carson, maybe you should check in with your students instead of waiting for them to come to you. If you don't, you're going to lose other band members, just like you're going to lose Sean since he can't get his act together."

She threatened to take away band? Sean couldn't live with that.

"Momma, don't take it away, please," Sean pleaded.

Tapping at his report card, she said, "You have to get your grades up. If you don't, you won't have to worry about band *next* year either."

"Momma, please, I'll do better." Sean was so sincere in his plea that she believed him, and allowed him to stay.

For the remainder of his freshman year he tried to pull his grades up, but he was so far behind, it was impossible. The harder Sean tried to catch up, the further away his goal seemed. Sean eventually gave up; it didn't make any sense to try. Every report card was the same old rap: *I'm going to do better.* But he figured that during the last quarter, another "F" wouldn't make any difference. Cynthia didn't agree. She had had enough. She ripped Sean's band right from his heart. There was no way Mr. Carson or Sean could sweet-talk her into changing her mind.

Sean went to summer school, squandering his mother's time and money on an education he could have had free. He walked past his mother's room and heard her crying. Listening to his mother's cry to God on his behalf was the worst thing he could've imagined.

"Mom, I'm sorry for making you cry, but it seems like I just can't do anything right," Sean said as he turned on the light in her room.

"No, Sean, it's more like you don't *want* to do anything, period," she replied, looking at him with eyes irritated from tears. "You started out with an 'A' in your summer school course. But then you slipped up, and ended up right back where you started. It seems like I want you to do better, more than you want to do better for yourself, and that's not fair. Sometimes I don't know what to do but to pray to God that he helps you."

"Well, maybe God's on vacation," Sean said jokingly, trying to get Superwoman to cheer up. He couldn't stand to see her like this. No one should want more for him than he wanted for himself. The only way he could prove to her that he could make it was through action. But how was Sean going to do that? Failing was easier than achieving. But, oh, the consequences were unbearable.

"Sean, I know your father isn't in your life like he should be, but—"

"It's not about him," Sean interrupted angrily. He didn't want to talk about his father.

"Then what is it, Sean? Please tell me. I know you can do better. Most of your life, you've been an 'A' and 'B' student, with maybe a couple of 'Cs,' but now this." She held the report card in his face. "No one's going to go for this at all. No college will accept you based on these grades, if you even get to apply to a college. Based on what's happening right now, you won't even graduate from high school. So you have to think about whether school is really for you."

Sean knew all he could do was try.

Sophomore year came faster than expected, and his situation got even harder. A huge chunk of kryptonite hit him—he was not going to be allowed in band at all. At least not until second quarter, and only if he had turned things around. Trying hard to do his best just wasn't enough. No one even noticed his struggle or offered to give him any help.

Detecting very little progress, his mother began looking for alternatives. Especially when she heard that it wasn't only her son who had a problem.

One of the teachers at River North said something to Sean that he would never forget. While talking to his history teacher, Mr. Phillips, about his history grades and how to bring them up, the teacher told him, "I get paid whether you pass or not. It doesn't matter to me." Sean's view of school and learning suddenly changed. *What am I doing here? What good is school if the teachers have that kind of attitude?* At least at Loop Lab and Gadson, the teachers cared.

The first-quarter midterm tests of his sophomore year were over. Sean and his mother went in for another parent/teacher conference. Picking up his report card, Sean's mother took a deep breath, as if she was hoping to win the lottery. But her high hopes were crushed again.

Sean had straight Fs. There was no band class on the list to provide the only A he had become accustomed to seeing. The "A" in lunch didn't move Cynthia—that was a computer glitch. Sean looked around at the other families and noticed how happy they were about their children's grades. *What is so different about me?* He'd stayed up late, got tutoring, and studied with friends during lunchtime and still failed.

Superwoman didn't even want to speak to the teachers or to Sean. He was ashamed to look his own mother in the eyes. But she had to speak to at least one of them because the report card required a signature. She had a feeling that something wasn't right. They went to see Mr. Phillips, his history teacher.

"Mr. Phillips, aside from the fact Sean doesn't turn in his work on time, what else do you think is wrong?" she asked.

"Well, Mrs. Morris, he just doesn't listen. He doesn't pay attention to anything I say," Mr. Phillips replied, running his fingers through an army buzz haircut.

"According to some of Sean's friends, you're not exactly attentive to the students either. You don't like to answer questions. How do you expect them to pay attention to you if you don't pay attention to them?" she asked in a surprisingly mild tone.

"But there is one difference—*they* do their homework. I'm just there to tell them what they need to learn, Mrs. Morris," he said. "These kids are going to have to learn most of these things on their own. I get paid whether they learn or not, and Sean knows that. I told him that the first time we talked."

There was an uncomfortable silence in the room. Superwoman couldn't believe her ears. "So, what you're telling me is that you don't *care* whether your students learn, because you still get a paycheck?"

Mr. Phillips backpedaled. "No, Ma'am. What I said is that if the students fall behind, they're going to have to learn on their own. I have to move on with the students that are ready."

"But you also said that you get paid whether they learn or not. Does that mean that if you got paid based on how many kids learned, you would still have that attitude?"

"Well, um..."

Superwoman stormed off. She talked with three more teachers—all young white males. Each one of them had the same attitude. She knew what was going on and it was wrong. Sean's laziness was part of the problem, but the teachers' lack of caring was the other.

That night he could hear his mother talking on the phone to his Grandmother Celie. "What am I going to do with him? It seems like it's no use. I took band away, and everything else I thought that was keeping him from getting good grades, but it only gets worse. And the worst part is that he's not a bad kid. He's very smart. He just doesn't apply himself." She sighed and uttered the deadliest words ever spoken. "Maybe he should get a GED or I should ship him off to Job Corps."

Sean backed away from the door. GED? Job Corps? Why would he want what kids called a "Good Enough Diploma?" And what was Job Corps? Pretty much the same thing.

Sean didn't know what to do. He finished the first quarter of his sophomore year struggling and frustrated. Then things hit rock bottom. For the first time, he was taken to jail for fighting a group of kids who had jumped him. He promised himself that he would never go back. Jail wasn't a place he wanted to be, but it seemed like school wasn't the place either, at least not while he was at River North High.

Cynthia dreaded going to the next parent/teacher conference. So did Sean. But as soon as they walked into the school, they noticed changes in some of the other parents. Most of them weren't smiling either. Few were bragging about their son's or daughter's grades. Actually, most of them looked disappointed. Ninety percent of the students who had dissatisfied parents were African-American. And eighty percent of the students who failed at least two classes were boys. Strangely enough, Sean kept up with *those* numbers, but it was easy—he was part of that eighty percent. So he wasn't alone. Sean let out a sigh of relief. Eighty percent. Mostly Black boys.

But there was something else at work in Sean's case. The counselor secretly had Sean tested twice by a teacher, without his mother's knowledge. The counselor told him he was on a sixth-grade reading level and fourth-grade math level. That was devastating news to someone who'd had those same test scores in *third grade*. Sean's confidence sank to a new low. He felt dumb—maybe a GED *was* all he was able to manage.

As soon as Superwoman found out about the counselor and his behind-the-scene activities, she went off. He was trying to put the dummy label on her son. Not only was he being sneaky, he had been dishonest about the test scores.

Sean followed his mom to the counselor's office. "How is he at low math and reading levels on one test and not the other?"

Get 'em, Momma. Sean was elated that *he* wasn't getting yelled at.

His counselor looked like he'd seen a ghost. "Mrs. Morris, calm down," he said as he cleaned off his big bifocals.

"And who gave you permission to test my son *without* my knowledge?" Superwoman was bulging at the neck, mind flowing with the anger of a lioness.

The counselor was beet red. "We had to test him to see if we should put him in the remedial courses. With his low grades, I felt he needed to be tested."

"You are supposed to at least inform a parent or guardian. How do I know to make sure he got the proper amount of rest? Or if he had a good breakfast?"

"Yes, Ma'am, but—"

"Where are his test scores?" she snapped.

"We…we can't show you his scores. We aren't allowed to give those out," he said, trying to use his legal boundaries as a crutch.

An uncomfortable pause followed. Superwoman's face wore a blank look of disbelief. Then she exploded. "You mean to tell me, that you made him take two tests—one harder than the other because you didn't like the results—without my consent, and without notifying me *after* he took them? You're going to stick him remedial classes because of it and you can't show *me*, the *parent*, his test scores?"

"Yes…yes, Mrs. Morris."

"Mr. Heinz, give me my son's test scores. I have a feeling the dean doesn't know about this. Maybe he should find out." Superwoman got up and signaled Sean to do the same.

"Wait, Mrs. Morris. Okay, here are the scores." Mr. Heinz scurried to find them in a pile on his desk.

Looking over the scores, she said, "You lied. It clearly states that he's reading at a twelfth-grade level, and has a tenth-grade math level." Superwoman tossed the file back at him and stormed out, sending papers flying everywhere. Sean began to follow, but turned back, bumped into the chair in his usually clumsy manner, picked up the papers, and slipped his test scores out. He scanned the sheet as he ran to catch up with his mother. He had scored higher on the hardest test. *He was no dummy! Then what's wrong with me? What's wrong with me?*

With the note and the scores, Superwoman went to the dean's office. Then the district's main office. Superwoman soon learned that the counselor had done the same thing to other Black boys. All of them ended up in remedial classes. Some didn't deserve to be there. Superwoman joined with the other mothers, their superwomen powers combined in protest with the constant phone calls and trips to the school and an article in the *Sun-Times*.

Mr. Heinz was fired within the month.

Once again Superwoman had led the way.

Chapter 20

The beginning of Sean's junior year at River North differed slightly from what he expected. The school had shaken things up and the teachers who remained had rediscovered their excitement for instruction again. A few Black teachers had been hired. However, even with these changes at the school, Sean knew that if he stayed at River North, he wouldn't graduate on time.

Superwoman wasn't sure whether they would try to sabotage Sean again. She wanted Sean to have a new start in a different school, but didn't know which one. It would be the same problem when Sean was in seventh grade. Finding one that would accept him in the middle of the school year. Looking for an alternative to River North, she heard about Olive-Harvey Middle College High School. The only downside was that they would have to move into the city for him to attend. Superwoman was more than willing to make the sacrifice.

"Sean, come here," Superwoman yelled from the bottom of the creaky, wooden stairs.

"Yes, Ma'am," he said, running from his room.

"We need to have a talk. Have a seat," she said as he plunked down in the plush oversized chair. "I believe you should go to OHMC to finish high school."

"Momma, I don't want to get a GED. I can't go for that—just put me in another regular high school," he replied. "I'll be fine."

"I *can't* put you in a regular high school. You messed that up, Sean. So you would rather go to the Job Corps or military school instead?"

"No." Sean slumped in his seat. Things were not looking good for the home team.

"Well, you don't exactly have a lot of options. Actually, you don't have any."

There was a long pause as Sean collected his thoughts, and weighed his options—which had become fewer by the year. He wanted to graduate on time—but how? "I'll just go to Olive-Harvey."

"Good. You'll be happy to know that I got the information wrong; it's *not* a GED program, it's an advanced alternative high school, so you'll be able—"

"I'll be able to get—"

"Yes, you'll be able to get your diploma—*on time*. But—and I'm only going to tell you this once—you mess up at this school, and it's over for you. You'll be at Job Corps on the first plane smoking. Am I clear?"

"Yes, Ma'am," he said, looking into her eyes, his face lighting up like a Christmas tree.

"We can't switch you to another school. There *is* no other school. You already messed up at a public school. This is a fresh, new start—your last chance to get your mind right. Do what you're supposed to do and we'll be fine. It's just me and you. No Grandma Celie and no Aunt Denise. A new school, a new house, and I have a new job. That means the household chores will fall to you. Just hold up your end, all right?"

"Yes Ma'am," Sean replied solemnly, thinking hard about what she had just said.

"Okay—I love you," she said, smiling slightly, arms open wide for a hug.

Sean got out of his seat. "Love you, too, Momma," he managed to say over the lump in his throat as he gave her a big hug.

Cynthia decided to leave the house to Grandma Celie, Aunt Denise, and Rick. They definitely wouldn't survive in the new house, with only two bedrooms and one bathroom.

"What's up, Grandson?" Celie asked, flashing a wide smile as she walked into the kitchen where Sean was packing boxes for the new house.

"Nothing much, just finishing up this last box of dishes," Sean said, struggling to fold the wings of the box and trying to groove to Earth, Wind and Fire's "Serpentine Fire" at the same time.

"Boy! You're folding the box all wrong," she said, stepping in to do it for him.

"Always showing off, Grandma," he said as he watched so she wouldn't have to show him again.

"Well, I can do that because *I'm all that,*" she said, switching her hips. "Don't get in the city and act like you can't visit anybody, with your forgetful self."

Sean smiled up at her. "Grandma, you act like I'm leaving the state."

"The city and the suburbs are worlds apart." She put a kung-fu grip on his ear. "And don't get smart. Before I moved in, you rarely called."

He gave her a kiss on the cheek. "I promise I will call and visit."

"You better, you may be older, but you're still—"

"I know, not too old for a butt whooping," Sean said, rolling his eyes.

"You're about to get it," Celie said and popped him on the butt. "I can finish my own sentences."

"And while you're talking about me forgetting about you, don't you forget about me. I know you're going to throw a party here every weekend," Sean said. He moved the box on top of a blue crate. "And I better be invited."

"For what? It would be a grown folks party, with *grown folks'* Kool-Aid."

"I am *grown,*" Sean said, poking his chest out.

"Boy, please, you haven't even grown your first gray hair yet."

"Yeah, but I've got a mustache," Sean said, chuckling and wiping the sweat from his forehead.

"Hey, when you have your own place and you can drink something stronger than soda *legally,* talk to me then," Celie said, as she reached over to squeeze his cheeks.

"Okay, Grandma."

"Oh yeah, don't forget what I taught you about cooking. You know it's against your mom's religion to cook."

"I won't, Celie," he promised as the song changed to Peabo Bryson's "I'm So Into You."

"Oh that's my song," she said with a snap of her hands and a swivel of her hips. "You know this song is probably how you got here—"

"Grandma!"

"Or with your dad, it was probably that Tito Puente song, 'Oye Como Va.'"

"Grandma!"

"I'm just saying that Peabo knows how to put it down," she said, drifting off into a vision as she looked up at the ceiling.

"Grandma!"

"What?"

"I don't need to hear that with my *virgin* ears," he said as he covered them.

"Virgin! Boy, stop hallucinating!" She popped Sean on the arm. "The way your mama talks, your ears are porn stars."

"Grandma! Stop."

Celie was so silly sometimes but it kept his spirits up. He'd miss the in-person everyday conversations—and the out-of-this-world home cooking—but he knew the move was something that had to be done so he could graduate on time.

Olive-Harvey was a high school within a college. It was started by Ms. Stanton, a woman with vision who understood that teaching was the key to success.

They moved to 93rd and Wentworth, close to the Dan Ryan bus and train terminal. It was the inner city of Chicago.

Their new place in Princeton Park was almost like the Jeffery Manor section of Chicago—a maze of streets where it was easy to get lost. It was a better jump from the boring life of the suburbs, though living near the terminal made it a lot easier to get around, and a lot more was happening everywhere.

Superwoman had whipped out her cape, swept him away from the big bad River North, racism, and rushed him into the heart of the ghetto—a section where they had never lived but they hopefully could learn to adjust.

Chapter 21

"Sean, time to get up for school!" his mother yelled, standing in the doorway of his new room.

Sean hadn't lived in the city in a long time. After three months of living there, he still wasn't accustomed to the gunshots that sent him to the floor in panic. The block was loud with people bumping their cars' sound system, drunks screaming and singing, and dogs howling. On top of that, somebody was always fighting next door. It was usually some girl who didn't like another girl. Those fights were rough. Slapping-on-the-grease and taking-off-the-heels-and-earrings rough, girls-pulling-out-each-other's-ten-dollar-weaves rough. They were amazing to watch, but only when it didn't keep Sean from his much needed sleep.

"Mom, it's six o' clock, I don't have to get up until six-thirty," he mumbled.

"Sean, get up," she said, yanking the covers off his half-clothed body. He instantly balled into a fetal position, protecting his prize package. He certainly didn't want her to see that!

"Get up! I told you I was going to wake you up early."

Turning over on his side and rubbing his cold arms, Sean begged, "C'mon, Mom, let me have thirty minutes, please."

"No, you're the one who falls asleep in the shower."

"All right, I'm up." He groaned. She had discovered the secret shower naps that were part of his morning routine. Those silver bars kept him propped up and he could get at least ten minutes of extra sleep. Water? He didn't feel a thing.

After showering, he went back to his room to dry off. He put his Old School Mix CD in his computer and played Frankie Smith's "Double Dutch Bus."

Dancing to his closet, Sean almost tripped over the floor mat. He whipped out his Old Navy khaki pants and a red and blue-striped, long-sleeved Polo shirt, along with his underclothes. No uniforms for this school, thank God. He wore them enough in elementary school.

While he got dressed, Tom Browne's "Funkin' For Jamaica" began playing. Pop-locking in front of his closet mirror, Sean was energized for the day. He liked current music, but sometimes he needed to take it back to what his mom called "the good old days." Celie considered that music just okay. Grandma Celie's "back in the day" was, Smokey, Barry White, The Temptations, The Dells, and The Chi-lites. And that was all good, too.

Once, at a family barbecue, Sean, who was in charge of the music, put on Kool and the Gang's "Jungle Boogie," and Aunt Denise asked, "How does a young man like Sean know about old school?"

"Don't be alarmed," Grandma Celie had replied. "He'll break you off with some Kool and the Gang's 'Get Down on It,' or some of Roy Ayers' 'Don't Stop the Feeling,' and he can get down with a little Barry, too."

Strutting to the beat of the old-school song still running through his head, Sean left the Princeton Park townhouse. The sun shone brilliantly, causing him to shield his face. As he strolled down the walkway to the sidewalk, Sean was startled by his next-door neighbor Sheila yelling at her oldest daughter.

"Lauren, what is this boy doing in your room?" she shouted as the guy, the do-rag over his cornrows untied and his jeans near his ankles, burst through the front door.

Pulling up his faded black jeans, the guy ran past Sean and asked, "What's up, man?" as though running out of a house half-dressed was normal.

"Get your ass up and go to school, before I knock you into the middle of next week," Sheila said. A door slammed.

"You don't have to slam my door!" Lauren snapped.

Sean knew he'd best get off the block as quickly as possible. As the fight escalated, some of their possessions would be flying out her open window. Last time he didn't leave—or duck—fast enough. Now he knew how Stephanie felt that day at Jayne Adamson.

"I swear people don't know how to act," his other neighbor Doris said, coming in from walking her dog, Jazzy. Doris was an older woman who had a good heart but was nosy, nosy, nosy. She had short, dark hair with small patches of gray, a raspy voice from smoking too much, and a very bad gambling problem. Almost every weekend he would hear her talking to Cynthia about losing money at the gambling boat, basically trying to sweet talk Cynthia into giving her some money.

"I know, but they both go at it every morning," Sean said.

"Well, if her daughter would stop acting so fast, maybe life would be better for everyone on this street," she said as she opened the screen door and held Jazzy back to keep him from running toward Sean. "They scream so much that my husband thinks he doesn't have a hearing problem anymore."

Sean laughed, but it was true. These two went at it all night and all day and the walls were thin. "Well, I'll see you later."

"Okay, tell your mama I said hey," she said.

He didn't have to tell Momma anything. The woman would beat him to it. She hadn't realized that Momma didn't care about neighborhood gossip. And if the woman tried to get any more money out of Cynthia, the bank was closed. Soon as Doris let it slip she was a gambler with a maxed-out guest card from the casino, the handouts ended.

Sean turned at the corner of 95th and Wentworth. That argument between Lauren and Sheila would probably be the same one he'd have with his mother if he ever brought a girl into the house, just to chill or for anything else. When they first moved to Princeton Park, Sean had made a friend, Whitney Sears. A beautiful girl, a few inches shorter than he and with a body so smooth and curvy she could be a waterslide. He wanted her to visit. He told Momma it was to study, but Sean knew it was for something else. Sean was sixteen. It was uncommon for someone his age to be a virgin; it was partially his fault for wanting to wait, but it was also his mother's for being such a Superwoman.

"No, you can't bring her here," Cynthia snapped. "Not in my house, when I won't be here. No!"

"Mama, it's just to study," Sean whined.

"Then the both of you can wait until I get home," she said, flipping through the TV channels.

"Mama, why?" He looked at her with puppy dog eyes.

She muted the TV. "Because, there won't be a parent or guardian around, and I don't want this girl saying that you raped her or did anything bad to her. With me around she can't say that. I'm going to keep you right where I can see you."

"She won't say that. We're just *studying.*"

"Sean, I know you. Sex will not go on in my house. And if you're ever going to have sex, I want you to take that young lady to dinner, a movie and a hotel. A nice hotel, not one of those hotels around the corner. If you're going to do it, do it right. And you better use a condom, 'cause I don't want no grandkids, or a call from the doctor saying you have an STD or that it's about to fall off because you put it in the wrong place. So, once again the answer is no."

"Yes, Ma'am." Sean lowered his head and turned to the door.

"I love you, I just want the best for you," she said as he touched the knob.

"I love you, too," he said, closing the door. "I'm never going to lose my virginity."

"Yes you will," she shouted after him. "Just not in *my* house!"

Laughing as he remembered that conversation, Sean stopped at the red light on the corner of 95th and Lafayette. The Dan Ryan terminal was filled with buses, people going to work and school, and a few begging for change. Everyone always stopped at the Dunkin' Donuts inside the terminal or the McDonald's across the street for their usual coffee, breakfast sandwiches, and doughnuts.

Walking into the terminal Sean joined the crowd and loud-talking security guards with their muzzled K-9 patrol dogs. As he walked past the convenience store, he felt a tug on the bottom of his coat.

Turning around, he saw a little kid, who only came to his hip. He looked to be about seven or eight. He wore a blue coat with a ripped hood, had dried snot around his nose, and was missing a patch from his blue jeans.

"Excuse me, Sir. Do you have a dollar?" the little boy asked, his eyes glistening, as he stared up at Sean.

Sean wanted to give him more than a dollar, but he only had three. He looked around for an adult, a mother or someone. "Where's your mom?"

"She died," he said, looking at his feet.

"What about your dad?"

The little boy's eyes filled with tears. "He doesn't want me anymore. He left me here."

"When?"

"I don't know, twenty minutes ago." He looked around at everyone flying by, hoping to see his dad.

"I'll tell you what," Sean said, dropping to his knees and reaching into his pocket. "I'll give you two dollars, under one condition."

"Sure," he said. His frown turned into to a huge smile, showing his little white teeth.

"After I give you this, you must go to Bethel Temple on the corner of 94th and Wentworth. You can't miss it. I want you to see if they'll take you in." Sean wrote the address on the back of an old paper bus card.

While Sean waited for his reply, he felt a tap on the shoulder. "Is this kid bothering you?" a guard asked. Sean stood to acknowledge her and the boy hid behind him.

"No, Ma'am," he said. She looked like she was in her late thirties. Under all of that protection, she more than likely looked younger. Was it a rule that security guards couldn't look pretty on the job?

"I've been watching the kid for the past ten minutes. He was walking with a man, but he left before I looked up again."

"I was writing down an address to a church close to my house. Would you make sure he gets there? It's only up the street," Sean said, holding the card out to her.

She looked around making sure no one heard. "I get off in an hour, but I'll take care of him. And I'll take him to the church," she said as she discreetly took the card.

"Thank you so much, Ma'am," he said as he shook her hand.

"It's Maxine. If there were more miracle workers like you, more little guys like this one would be off the streets," she said, patting the boy on the shoulder after he finally poked his head out from behind Sean's leg.

"Yeah, I bet," Sean said, looking at his watch and making sure he was on time for his bus. They ran every ten minutes. "I wish I could talk more, but I have to get to school. It was nice meeting you, Maxine, and thanks again."

The little guy slowly reached out and took Maxine's hand, then looked at Sean and said, "Thanks, Sir."

"It's Sean Morris, and you're welcome," he said before walking away.

Before Sean got too far he heard, "Hey, what about those two dollars?"

Sean ran back to him, laughing. "I said I would give him two dollars if he went to the church," he explained to Maxine as he gave the boy the two crinkled singles. Maxine looked like she was about to tell him to keep his money. "I insist," Sean said. *That little guy is already having it rough. But he might be a future businessman or millionaire.*

Chapter 22

Getting off the No. 106 bus at Olive-Harvey Middle College, Sean walked toward the entrance of the large black building with its hundreds of smoke-tinted windows. As he followed behind all the college students, he felt taller and more confident. It gave him a new attitude about school. His new attitude, new casual dressing style, and new personality could've made the sun shine on him that morning.

Passing by the security guard at the front desk, he flipped open his wallet to flash his ID. Sean went to the bathroom and looked in the mirror. "I'm a changed man who takes care of his responsibilities. I am a leader. I am a scholar."

Pep talk over, he wiped off his black leather Stacy Adams boots with a paper towel. He had a new look, the *Scholar* look. Instead of being students, they were scholars and that made him feel important.

As he walked into the hallway, he ran into four people he had met the day they took the entrance exam: Vince Hester, James Meeks, Aaron Irving, and Curtis Carter.

"What's up, fellas?" Sean asked.

"What's up, Sean?" Vince replied, as the group walked into the white lunchroom filled with round gray tables and vending machines. Other new students gathered around the tables. The grillroom smelled of hash browns, eggs, bacon, and sausage. His stomach rumbled.

"Still wondering why we always get here twenty minutes early," Sean said.

"Well, you remember what Mr. Rinauld said during orientation?" Vince asked, letting his locks fall loose from a blue skullcap.

"If you're early, you're on time. If you're on time, you're late," they said in unison and then chuckled.

"Man, when are we supposed to have that meeting for the college tour?" James asked, dropping his red book bag on the floor.

James was six feet tall, heavyset, kept his hair cut low, and sported a trimmed beard. He was from the Hyde Park area of Chicago, and he always complained about how far he had to come to school. James was a computer genius; he could fix them and he could build them. In fact, Sean thought James was good enough to possibly put Dell out of business. Sean was surprised James hadn't come up with an illegal way to get high-speed Internet.

Curtis was a clean-cut guy from Mississippi. He worked at The Gap and had brown, naturally curly hair. He was often late for school because he had to have perfectly lined creases in his shirts' sleeves and pants.

Vince was the mysterious one. No one could get a secret out of him. He was five feet eleven inches, had a dark-brown complexion, thick locks, and pointed fingernails. He also had something in common with Sean—karate. Vince studied the art of ninjitsu.

Aaron unzipped his black leather jacket. "I think the college tour meeting is supposed to be next Monday." He was the basketball player of the group, standing at six feet two inches tall. He wore his hair in a mini afro, and oozed charm that got the ladies all the way from 75th and Coles Avenue—"Coles Mob" as he called it. Aaron worked security in the downtown area—top-flight security. As the rapper of the group, he could come up with lyrics off the top of his head.

"How many of us are even going on the college tour?" Curtis asked, putting away his Palm Pilot.

Sean and the other three raised their hands. Curtis didn't.

"You're not going?" Sean asked with a raised eyebrow, taking his math homework out to check it over one last time.

"I don't think so. I don't need to waste my time or my money," Curtis replied confidently, taking out his notebook. "I already know where I'm going."

"Oh yeah? Where's that, bigshot?" Aaron asked, folding his arms over his broad chest.

"Southern Illinois University, Mr. Irving," Curtis responded, imitating Aaron's opinionated pose. Curtis was graduating early. He had been attending the Kennedy-King College program, before it closed and he transferred into OHMC so he could graduate. The rest of them still had another year to go.

"Yeah right. You know your girl Sherri isn't going to let you go. Especially since you're in the dog house because we went to that poetry slam without her last week," Sean said.

"Her name is Marry, and I'm a grown—"

"So why does she run your life?" James asked.

"She's a big girl. Look at her size. She'll break you in half," Curtis said.

"Man, the girl is a size twelve. How in the world is that a big girl?" Sean asked, chuckling.

"Well, Sean, you date big girls," Aaron said.

"Sure, and I'm not ashamed of it. Those toothpicks you date got the nerve to wear pants that say, *Bootylicious* or *Do not touch*. They don't have any *booty* back there, so somebody needs to explain what I'm *touching*."

They all busted up laughing. "You got jokes, fool," Aaron replied. "What are you laughing at, James? You date toothpicks, too."

James's laughter died down. "Don't even bring it over here," he said, holding his hands up.

"He should, as much as you brag, believing in your mind that they're thick," Vince said.

Curtis called Vince out. "Vince, you can't say anything. You don't even have a girl."

"And my life is perfectly fine," he responded.

"Get off Vince," Sean said. "You're the one that changes girls as much as you change your drawers. I'm surprised you're still with Carey."

"It's Marry! *Jesus*," Curtis snapped as he stood up. A few people from other tables looked his way.

The others recoiled and looked at each other. "Okay, Man, calm down, it was a joke. Sit on down before you bust a vein," Vince said, still a little cautious.

"I'm sorry. You don't know what I've been through with that girl," Curtis said as he sat. "It's been so hard. She always calls to check on me, I always have to be with her. She blows up my cell phone to make sure I'm at work, and I feel if I dump her…" he whispered and leaned in.

"Go on," Sean said as he and the other fellas bent forward.

"… she'll throw a brick through my car window, and probably bang it up with a crow bar or something," he said, lowering his head into his arms. "I'm sorry, Sean. If I ever said your mom was strict, this girl takes the gold."

"Don't worry, we'll figure a way out of this," Aaron said, patting him on the back. "And if you have an issue, grab a tissue; you don't want her to see you cry."

"Thanks, guys," Curtis said, letting out a sigh of relief. "For a minute, I thought it was only God and a restraining order that could help me."

They all fell out laughing—even Curtis chuckled lightly. That's what made them friends. They stuck together no matter how big the problem was, and no matter where they came from. All of them were smart young men who had relocated to a better school, most of them for the same reason as Sean—smart as hell but poor performers.

Although OHMC was an alternative school, the principal believed *alternative* meant *superior.*

Sean agreed. When Momma asked him what made this school different, Sean's response had come quickly and easily. "The teachers believe I can learn. They teach me like they expect me to succeed, instead of teaching me like they're just passing time getting paid until I fail."

Sean got along with his teachers, did his work, and made it on time to class for a change.

The work was much harder at the college level. The instructors encouraged Sean to think, express his thoughts, research answers, and confer with his group on projects, just like businessmen or partners.

The cafeteria tables quickly filled up with college students. Some read, and others conversed, played chess or Uno, or finished up class work.

"I couldn't say that I was concerned about college before, but now I want to go," Sean said. "Every Friday, graduates from OHMC come back to speak to us, telling about their experiences in college. If college is how they say it is, then that's the place for me."

"Not to mention Mr. Rinauld, Ms. Harvey, Ms. Allen, and Coach Jones are all graduates of OHMC, and now they're teachers," Vince said, pulling geometry homework out of his book bag. Sean recognized Ms. Schulz's toolkit, a packet of mathematics, because he had one like it.

"That's good and everything," James said, "but if you're going to go to college based on someone else's experiences, then you need to think about college again, Sean."

James, not wanting to be caught sleeping while the others studied, took out a notepad. He made sure he had the long definition of decency, dignity, and diligence for Ms. Stanton's personal development class. "You might have a different college experience, plus you have to stay on top of your *homework.*"

"Hey, guys," a girl shrieked, making them all jump and grimace.

"Hi, Jeanette," Curtis said harshly.

"Hi, Aaron," she said, winking at him.

Jeanette was a freshman pursuing a junior, which normally didn't work out if one of the two was immature. She was cute with a medium-brown face, her hair was always done, and she had a nice, thin figure. When it came to Aaron, she was a stalker. Ever since Aaron had befriended her one time, she wouldn't leave him alone.

"Hi, Jeanette," Aaron said, looking back down at his work.

"Do you want to come upstairs with me?" she asked, walking behind him.

"I have to finish my work, maybe later." Aaron shifted uncomfortably and scribbled in his notebook, pretending she was breaking his concentration.

"I'll be looking forward to it." She rubbed his head and walked out of the room.

"Is she gone?" Aaron asked, his voice cracking.

"Yeah, Man, calm down." Sean burst out laughing. "You should just give up your number."

"She already has it." Aaron lowered his head. "She got it from the front office since she interns there."

"Man! So how many times a day does she call?" Vince asked, scratching his head.

"Enough." Aaron shook his head in disbelief. "My mom and sister are ready to put a serious hurtin' on this girl."

"Just give her some, and act like you're bad at it," Curtis said, shrugging, "Terrible sex is always a turn-off."

Sean laughed. "Are you speaking from experience with Marry?"

"Don't get your face kicked in," Curtis said, lifting his size-thirteen foot toward him.

"You try telling that to Marry. She's trying to live up to the name," Aaron said. The others gasped. "She called me, telling me to make you propose. You know she has all of our phone numbers so she can check up on you."

"You're only a junior in high school and she wants to be your wife!" Sean said.

"Very funny, but yeah, she's pushing for marriage. And guess what?"

They all leaned in.

"I'm not even giving her any," Curtis whispered.

"Wow! You better not ever give her some. She'll lock you down in the basement," Aaron said.

"I liked that other chick better. Ariel. She had more sense," Vince said. "I can't believe you dumped her."

"Well, nothing lasts forever. She was good. We just weren't on the same page. We argued over so much little stuff that I got tired of it," Curtis explained. 'That's a little nonsense that I could live without."

"I don't know, Man, how many girls do you know would wake up in the middle of the night, drive to Burger King, and bring it to your doorstep, just because you said you were hungry?" Vince asked everyone at the table.

"Not anyone I went out with," Aaron replied.

"Me neither," James answered.

"Can't say that I know anyone," Sean added.

"See there, you had a keeper. Someone worth wifey material, and you let her go," Vince said, shaking his head in disbelief.

"It was my choice, just let it go," Curtis pleaded.

There was a long uncomfortable silence at the table as everyone went back to doing their work.

"But Curt, how could you just do that—"

"Come on, Vince, he said drop it." Sean said, holding his forehead as if he had a headache.

Vince laughed. "Okay, I'll drop it but can someone help me with this. It's hard keeping up with this toolkit."

"It's hard doing all those essays for English," Sean added.

"But it's something that both of you will have to work on," James said, closing his book bag, "even if you have to do extra work."

Sean knew what James said was true. His goal was to major in English and theatrical arts. He needed to do extra work to meet his goal: An "A" in each class.

Middle college changed his whole mindset. A few months ago, he didn't think about doing extra work or even making it out of high school. Now he was really looking forward to going to college. If you weren't thinking about going to college, then middle college wasn't the place to be. It was good to hear men talking about college. Nowadays it seemed like the only topics of conversation in regular high schools were music, girls, and smoking weed—only two of which interested Sean.

"Not too many other schools do that. As you can see the middle college has a different way of teaching," Curtis said, taking a break from his work or maybe it was a break from the work to keep from taking a nap. "It's like they gave us a second chance."

"Yeah," Aaron said. "And we have to—"

"Go to class," Mr. Rinauld said as he walked up to the group.

Mr. Rinauld was heavyset with dark-brown skin, low-faded hair and thick, black, square-framed glasses. He dressed in some of the newest street wear, almost like the students, except he didn't let his pants sag around the waist. He proved that a man could have the street look without being sloppy.

Without further prompting they all went to class.

Sean's day was going smoothly and swiftly. Before he knew it, it was noon. He skipped lunch, choosing to go to the computer lab on the second floor instead. His friends, Stracye and Twin, kept the computer lab in order. They were heading toward the door as Sean walked in.

"What's up, Sean?" they asked in unison.

"What's up? You guys leaving already?" Sean asked, tossing a Pepsi can in the blue recycle bin in front of their office.

Stracye patted his denim bag. "Yeah, I have class right now."

"And I'm going to KFC, gotta feed this big ol' thing," Twin said, smacking his stomach. "I'll catch up with you later."

"Okay." Sean looked for an available computer. KFC was good, but it had nothing on his Grandma Celie's chicken, or her mashed potatoes and gravy. The Colonel would have fallen off the map if she had opened her own restaurant.

He spotted a computer in the third row. He put his book bag down on the floor under the desk and reached for the mouse, but a green folder rested on top of it. He turned to ask the person next to him if someone was using the computer. The most beautiful face he had ever seen looked back at him. Her full, glossy lips mesmerized Sean. As she returned his gaze, he looked deep into her almond-shaped, hazel-brown eyes. He heard music, violins, birds.

"Umm—excuse me. Could you move your folder, please? It's on top of my mouse."

"Sure," she said, giving him a mischievous grin. "Have I seen you around here before?"

"I don't think so. Do you go to the middle college?" Sean asked, forgetting all about what he was going to search for on the Internet.

"I just got in about three weeks ago." She ran her fingers through her shoulder-length, light-brown hair, which glimmered with golden highlights. "They changed my schedule; maybe I'm in one of your classes."

"I don't think so. You would never have gotten past me," he said, taking in the scent of her body spray, most likely from Victoria's Secret, which was popular with the girls at school. Sean didn't think she needed to be sexier than she already was.

"Oh, by the way…," he extended his right hand, "I'm Sean Morris."

"I'm Rachel Bennet." She gently shook his hand and he slid his thumb over the back of her hand. "So, do you come to the computer lab a lot?"

"Yeah, I'd say so," he said, finally releasing her soft, gently curved hand.

"Then you wouldn't have a problem meeting me here tomorrow, would you?" Her tone, sensual and sweet, challenged his ability to control himself.

"No, no problem," Sean said, his hormones reacting to the slow rhythm of her voice.

"If you find time tonight, give me a call," Rachel said as she stood. "Write down my number."

Amazed at her voluptuous figure, Sean took out pen and paper. As he wrote the last two numbers, she walked away. "Wait a minute, you don't want mine?" Sean asked.

Her feather soft hair fell forward around her shoulders. "I'll get it, if you call me tonight," she said, winking at him.

Oh boy!

Still grinning, Sean walked out of the computer lab. "Whew! *Scandalous.*" Sean shook the nervous chill off, stomped the marble floor, then fixed his shirt and continued to his sixth-period speech class. He slid into the front row between Aaron and Curtis, who, as usual, were having a lively conversation. Aaron moved back to give Sean a bit more space.

Curtis raised his eyebrows suspiciously. "What are you so happy about?"

"What do you mean?" Sean asked, trying to hold in a laugh.

"Your smile is about to break your face," Curtis replied, poking Sean's cheek. "Unless maybe there's something wrong with your mouth."

Sean swatted his hand away. "It's nothing, Man. Can't I just be happy?" He tried to straighten out his expression, but failed. Rachel had done a number on him.

"Man, usually guys have that smile when they get some. Am I right, Aaron?" Curtis asked.

"Yep," Aaron said. "So unless you tell us something else happened, we're gonna think that you got some between lunch and English in that nasty dressing room on the lower level."

Curtis sniffed Sean, trying to pick up that special scent that normally parents could scout out as soon as a teenager hit the door. Sean's mother did the same thing after she started leaving him at home alone. "What fast-tailed girl did you bring in my house? It smells funny in here." His reply would always be, "I just used the bathroom."

"Think whatever you want," Sean said.

"Come on, Man, what's going on? What'd you do?" Curtis asked, irritated.

"All right, all right. I just met the most beautiful girl. She has the sexiest face, voice, and everything else I've ever seen," Sean said, his words rushing together.

"Man, calm down. We've been here for three months and I've never seen a girl like that," Aaron said, holding Sean in place.

"Rachel Bennet," Sean said, smiling and gazing at the ceiling.

"Rachel?" Curtis asked. His smile instantly disappeared.

Sean's whole mood changed from excited to cautious. "Yeah, you know her?"

"I've met her, and...I'd watch out for her if I were you," Curtis warned him. "Some of the guys around school say that she's a major—um," he cleared his throat, "around-the-way girl." He threw a quick glance at Aaron for backup.

"Yeah, what he said."

"Come on, guys, she seems like a good Christian girl," Sean said, slapping his hand on his knee.

"Based on what I've heard, Rachel is the type of girl that makes *everybody* say, 'Good *Lawd*, have mercy,'" Aaron said, leaning over his desk. "So I don't know about that good, Christian girl thing."

Eyes glowering in disappointment as his buddies shared a laugh, Sean asked, "Do you always listen to what other guys say?"

"No, but I'm just trying to help you out." Aaron said. "Don't say we didn't try to tell you."

"Tell me what? That she's a flirt? If we get together, as long as she's not flirting with someone else, we're cool."

Ms. Harvey, their speech teacher, walked into the class wearing a red and white Delta Sigma Theta Sorority, Inc. sweater and tight-fitting blue jeans. "Good afternoon, scholars." She forced a smile, which told everyone to sit down and shut up.

"We'll talk about this later," Curtis whispered to Sean.

Something about that didn't sit too well with Sean. How could Rachel, that gorgeous young woman walking God's green earth, be on his friends' bad list?

When class ended, Sean grabbed his things and strolled next door for English. Instead of having the seats in rows like other classrooms, Mr. Rinauld preferred them in a large circle in the center of room. He wanted to make eye contact with everyone, while he paced the floor like a jailbird.

"Good afternoon, scholars," Mr. Rinauld said.

There were a few mumbled responses.

"In my class," he said, moving around the circle, "we need lively people. So, once again. Good afternoon, scholars!"

"Good afternoon, Mr. Rinauld!"

Just as Mr. Rinauld began to speak, Rachel walked into the room. Everyone watched her walk toward him. "Is this English Four?"

"Yes it is. May I see your schedule?" he asked, holding his hand out impatiently.

After looking it over, he handed it back to her. "Welcome. You may have a seat."

She took the spot next to Sean. The rest of the guys in the classroom were still staring at her.

"Okay, scholars, please take out your homework. Today we will be discussing your essays on alternative education."

"When did you get into this class?" Sean whispered to Rachel as he searched through his folders.

"Like I said, they just changed my schedule today," Rachel quietly replied. "What did I miss?"

"Nothing much. We just started." Sean held his hand in front of his mouth, hoping Mr. Rinauld wouldn't notice them talking. No such luck.

"Mr. Morris and Ms. Bennet, you're going to talk while I'm talking? When a speaker is speaking, where should your eyes be?"

"On the speaker," came the answer from Sean's classmates.

"So, you two have a choice. You can either close your mouths, be quiet, or shut up," Mr. Rinauld snapped sarcastically.

Wow! Three whole options. Sean would just—uh—be quiet.

Mr. Rinauld didn't joke around. Educating scholars was a serious business. Mr. Rinauld was a graduate of OHMC, and went on to Rust College in Holly Springs, Mississippi. He came back to the middle college to teach. Maybe that's what Sean was meant to do. Go to college then come back to the community and teach students who were like him.

It was near the end of the class by the time the students had finished reading their papers. "Okay, scholars, you have a three-point-five essay on what makes a man a man and what makes a woman a woman. It's due tomorrow. Have a wonderful day."

Sean had noted that a 3.5 essay meant three points on the topic in five paragraphs including the thesis statement and conclusion. As Sean was getting ready to leave with Rachel, Mr. Rinauld asked to speak with him.

Sean approached Mr. Rinauld's desk. "Yes, Sir."

"I can see that you have developed a friendship with Ms. Bennet. However, all sidebar conversations are going to have to wait until after class." Mr. Rinauld looked at Sean over the rim of his glasses and his expression darkened. "Girls are always going to be there, Mr. Morris. Don't let one get in the way of learning."

"Yes, Sir."

Walking out of the classroom, Sean felt fairly confident that Rachel wouldn't stop him from getting his education. He was already getting decent grades. Math was still a struggle, but he was working on that. Ms. Stanton had promised him one thing. "The college tour will change your life."

OHMC was a school of opportunity. Every year students could earn the privilege of going on different study trips. In addition to the college tour, there were trips to places like New York and tours of Harlem, Washington, D.C., Senegal, and Hawaii. That's why it was called the "school without walls"—learning took place outside of the classroom. OHMC was all about getting its scholars ready for the next phase in education.

Ms. Helen Stanton had a vision years ago of taking care of students when schools pushed them out because of little mistakes. It was like a rescue mission. She set up the school on a college campus, which turned out to be a wonderful thing—eighty percent of the scholars went on to attend college. Sean was one of those lucky students her school rescued. Now he was proud of himself. His grandmother, as well as Rick and Chris, were proud of him. But most importantly, Superwoman was proud of him again. Sean thanked God every day that even if she had given out, she hadn't totally given up.

Now he had to keep up. He always got off to a good start but then something would go wrong in his personal life, and things would go downhill. No matter how hard he tried, one thing still plagued him—he had not heard from his father in three years. Not a word. Not a letter. Not a peep. It lingered in the back of his mind like a worm on a hook. Stuck in one place and going nowhere.

This time around, Sean was not going to let anger make him lose focus. He refused to give his father the satisfaction of seeing him fail again. He would not let his pain be the reason he fell down—again. There was too much life going on—too many good things. Being on an actual college campus, Sean was able to talk to many college professors and get the feel of college while still in high school. Would the school be special enough to help overcome that first year and a half? Or was college out of the question?

Chapter 23

Two weeks before the college tour, Sean sensed something was wrong with his mother. Her mood had been as dark as the gray clouds that hovered overhead that afternoon as he walked home. Sean hoped she'd *lighten* up. He could always tell when his mother was angry but keeping it in—she wouldn't say a word.

When Sean reached his street, he saw a black Chevy Blazer parked in front of the house. At first Sean thought it was Chris' truck, but there weren't any gray stripes or a Cryptic Racing decal on the back with a skull and his racing number. *Hmm, must be somebody next door.*

Putting the worn key in the lock, Sean heard two people laughing inside. He knew his mother was home, making up for all the overtime she had been putting in, but he didn't recognize the other voice. It was male but certainly not his dad's. Roberto and Cynthia laughing? *Nah.* That was impossible.

Sean pushed the door open to see his mother and a tall, dark man in an army uniform sitting on the couch. This was scary. Next thing you know Maury was going to come out.

"Sean, this is Jake," Cynthia said. "He's from Job Corps."

"Hi," Sean said.

"It seems, Mr. Morris, that you've broken one of the rules. I got a call yesterday at work from Mr. Robertson. He told me that you didn't turn in one of your assignments," Cynthia said.

Superwoman always told the teachers, "If he messes up, call me and let me know." That was as embarrassing as sending Sean to the store for tampons.

"But Momma—"

"But nothing, Sean. I told you I wasn't playing. I said the first time you messed up, I was going to ship you off. Well, today's that day."

"Momma, please, it was just one assignment," Sean said, kneeling in front of her. He knew Superwoman wasn't playing. "Momma, that will be the last time that happens," he said as he placed his hands on her knees.

"I know it will be, because you're going to the Job Corps," she said.

Jake stood up and said, "Sean, come on. It's time to go."

A tear slid down Sean's cheek. He looked at Superwoman.

"You aren't hurting me with those tears. You're hurting me when you don't do what you're supposed to do," she said.

Sean wasn't able to say anything, because he had turned sixteen. She had the legal right to ship him off. Jake was pulling him away. Sean was holding on to Superwoman's leg. He felt like Nettie in *The Color Purple* when Mister dragged her away from Ms. Celie.

An hour later he was in the car, but not before running around the block a few times. Sean ran his behind off as though the police were after him. Superboy pulled a fast turn around the corner and felt a sharp pain in his leg. *Lord, why did I get a charleyhorse now!* Sean fell to the ground.

While Sean sat in the stale cigarette-smelling car, Jake went inside. *He'd blown it big time. Job Corps meant no college tour. No college tour, no college— period. It was one assignment; why couldn't Momma have cut him some slack?*

Five minutes later Superwoman came to the car shaking her head and laughing. "Boy, you better not ever run away from the police. We already know you'd get caught." Superwoman seemed to be enjoying seeing Sean at his worst. "Get your behind in the house, and I don't want to do this again."

"Yes, Ma'am," Sean said, easing out of the car, relieved that he wasn't really going to Job Corps.

That day was abnormally interesting, but the weekend was even freakier. Jake showed up at the door in a black suit, a dozen pink roses in hand. He was there to take Superwoman on a date. Sean went from scared to confused. His mother going on a date. What was the world coming to?

★★★

The five-thirty a.m. alarm woke Sean. He smacked the off button, slid out of bed, and slipped his feet into his black flip-flops. The college tour started today and he didn't intend to be late. As much time as he spent in the shower every day, six-thirty would be there before he knew it.

Singing and doing the "George Jefferson," to the *Sanford & Son* theme song in his head, he grabbed his royal blue towel and washcloth off the chair.

Three songs later, he only had thirty-seven minutes to get dressed.

Sean wrapped the towel around his body, put some oil on the bristles of his brush and ran it forward through his low, curly fade. Checking out his nicely trimmed sideburns and mustache, he thought he looked pretty good. He completed the rest of his morning bathroom routine, walked back into his room, and pulled out a pair of blue jeans, and a black T-shirt. He finished his look with a pair of white Puma gym shoes. Ms. Stanton had warned him that she was going to walk their behinds off. With as much energy and spunk as she had, Sean believed her.

Remembering the cold that the weather channel had predicted the night before, he pulled out his blue Old Navy fleece pullover and his puffy blue coat. Grabbing his watch, cell phone, iPod, and wallet off the nightstand, he went down the hall to his mother's room. Sean knocked but she didn't answer. A quick peek confirmed she was still asleep. He walked in and gently sat on the edge of her bed.

"Hey, Momma, I'm all set to go."

"Okay, Sean." She yawned and stretched. "Are you sure you packed everything?"

"Yes, Ma'am."

"Do you have your bank card?"

"Yes, Ma'am."

After confirming he had clean underwear, his left leg, clean socks, his right arm, notebooks, all ten toes, deodorant, toothbrush, his behind, and the kitchen sink, the interrogation ended.

"All right, have a good time and be careful."

"Yes, Ma'am," he said, giving his mother a kiss on the cheek before he walked out and closed the door.

"And do your homework. I don't want to have to call Jake again," Superwoman called after him.

The college tour would take Sean away from Chicago and his mom. It wasn't that he didn't love her, but he was eager to explore other places. Now all Superwoman could do was reflect and say the three famous and embarrassing *Oh Boy* statements. "Oh Boy, I remember when you were little," or "Oh Boy, shut up! I was there to wipe your little thing." Or the all time favorite, "Oh Boy, I was in labor with you, and you wouldn't come out with your complicated behind."

Running down the creaky wooden stairs to the living room, he felt his new cell phone vibrate. He flipped it open and put his earpiece in. "Hello."

"I'm outside, hurry up," James said. "It's almost six forty-five and we have to be there at seven." James had gotten up earlier than anyone else on the college tour. He had offered to pick up Sean, Vince, and Aaron to go to the school along with his girlfriend, Sierra. Big mistake! In the morning their names translated to: Sleepy, Lazy, and Dopey, and these dwarfs were going to make James late getting them to school, especially how widespread they lived from each other. And if Sierra didn't get a seat in the car, the BS would hit the fan and one of the boys would end up catching the green limousine—public transportation—back home. Not good.

"I'll be out in a minute. Besides, you know they're not gonna start on time," Sean replied and ended the call.

Sean rolled his blue and black suitcase out into the sunny morning, put it into the trunk of James' new black Ford Taurus, and hopped into the back seat, joining Vince and Aaron. Sierra sat up front, but didn't look up. Sean suspected she was sleep. A little hog call three seconds later confirmed it.

"What's up, people?" Sean asked, closing the door.

"What's up, Superboy?" they responded, calling him by the nickname they'd heard his mom once use.

James sped up to the stop sign at 94th Street and Wentworth Avenue. At the next corner, he turned onto 95th Street.

"Man, I wasn't feeling squished until you got into the car," Aaron complained, shrugging his shoulders to make more space. "You need to drop some pounds instead of trying to stock up on those muscles."

"Well, it would help if your head wasn't so big, taking up fifteen extra feet of space," Sean retorted.

"It would definitely help if you weren't wearing that gigantic coat. That thing could hold two dead bodies," Aaron snapped back.

"You can't talk, with that gorilla-sized coat you're wearing. And speaking of the dead, who killed the squirrels to line your hood?" Sean asked, referring to Aaron's huge black coat with the fur trim.

Vince slammed his ninjitsu study book shut. "Every single time I'm with you two, you're always roastin' each other."

"Sean knows I'm jokin' with him and I know he's jokin' with me," Aaron said.

"Besides the only thing he can be mad at, is that his is fake Burberry," Sean blasted back into it. "What is it, Blueberry or Strawberry?"

"Don't even talk, with those fake Louis Vuitton pants you bought from those boosters in the lobby," Aaron cracked. "More like some Louis Armstrongs."

"And Vince, you're definitely not the one to talk," James said, making a right at 103rd Street and Michigan Avenue. "You're always talking about everyone's shoes, just because yours are Gucci."

"That's because some of them have it coming. They're always trying to hate on mine," Vince responded, proudly popping his collar. "Now, if you would please be quiet, I'm studying,"

"Yeah, right," James said as he turned up the radio. Sierra jerked out of her sleep and scowled.

James hunched down in the seat a little, but a grin escaped before he could cover his face. He turned the music down. Sean knew T-R-O-U-B-L-E was about to follow.

James and Sierra began yelling at each other as he slowed down on 103rd Street.

Sierra was usually nice and quiet, but today was one of those days everything angered her, Sierra only got like this a couple of days a month. Wonder what it could be? Sean should tell James about keeping a calendar. He should've left her home, but who else could James trust to drive his car back to his house, since his mom went to work early every morning?

Sean looked out the window just as James blew through the stop sign across the street from Corliss High School. Sean put on his seat belt. James accelerated with every sentence.

"James, watch the road!" Sean yelled.

He slowed down and came to complete stop at the red light on 103rd Street and Woodlawn.

Sean opened the door and put one foot on the pavement. "Drive like you've got some sense! James, you know she's a loose cannon. Why would you want to make her mad?"

"Whatever, man. You better stop messing with me before I pull off and leave you here. You know I will."

"Okay, I'm back in," Sean said quickly. He remembered the first and only time James pulled off on him, leaving him in the cold. That four-block walk was a long distance as Sean fumed, steam coming from his piping hot head, due to the cold wind. They wouldn't be friends, if James hadn't come back.

When the scholars arrived in front of OHMC, James parked his car in the front lot. Normally filled with cars, the area was relatively empty. The only people there this early were the college tour scholars. They got out of the car, quiet and a little afraid of Sierra, who was still fuming. That girl was hotter than fish grease. Quickly pulling their luggage out of the trunk, they almost ran toward the big black building.

All of the students going on the college tour were standing in the lobby on the first floor. Walking through the door, Sean automatically held up his student ID for the security guard and took his place in line. He prayed Sierra and James wouldn't get into it again. It was a good thing she wasn't going on the college tour. It was a lot less trouble, especially since she was the jealous type.

"I don't see Rachel," Aaron said. "What happened to your girl?"

"Her grades kept her from coming," Sean said, shaking his head. He still couldn't believe she had received Fs on her last report card. "Anyway, I really didn't want her to be here."

"Why?"

"Her attitude is all messed up and her flirting is out of control."

"How so?" Aaron asked, unzipping his coat.

"Her eyes and hormones started drifting elsewhere. She said she was just being friendly, but kissing another guy on the cheek right in front of me was out of order," Sean said, covering his face to erase the image from his mind.

"So what's the status of the relationship?"

"Right now we're separated, until I make a decision. I guess you and Curtis were right about her."

"I swear, boy, you don't listen," Aaron said, patting him on the back. "But I guess that's what happens when you get sprung."

"Yeah, whatever, man." Sean laughed as Jeanette came through the doors with newly done braids. "I see your girl," Sean said.

Aaron swiftly turned to see his nightmare. "What is she doing here?" he asked, looking as if he were about to cry.

"You didn't know she was going?" Sean asked, surprised.

"She said she was, but I thought she was joking," Aaron said, shaking his head.

"Well, if you don't know, now you know," Sean replied, patting Aaron on the shoulder.

"Naw, Sean, she's going on the college tour," Aaron said sarcastically. "Of course I know that!" Aaron roared.

Sean laughed. "Give her a chance, she might put it down on you, and you'll be the one stalking her."

James and Vince popped up behind them scaring Aaron who shrieked. "Man! Don't scare me like that." Aaron leaned over holding on to his knees.

"Calm down," Vince said, backing away from him. "Oh, yeah, we saw your girl, Jeanette."

"Don't make him any more scared or mad than he already is," Sean said.

"Wow! That girl has you strung out," James said. Leaning closer to Aaron he whispered, "Maybe you should take Curtis' advice about that terrible sex stuff."

"No!" Aaron said, standing straight. "She will not mess the trip up for me."

The conversation ended when the teachers called everyone into the middle of the lobby. They formed a circle to listen to the announcements.

Ms. Stanton stepped into the center. "Good morning, scholars," she said jubilantly. "How's everyone feeling today?"

The collective response was "Fine, Chief," the nickname she'd earned because she was the head of their little village on the third floor.

"Okay, I know that we're running late, but we're still waiting for some of the others. While we wait, I'm going to have two of our graduate scholars speak to you. Here's Nia and Andre."

Sean was annoyed. He thought they should leave without the kids who were late, especially since he had busted his tail to get there on time. Everyone rolled their eyes, edgily shifting from side to side. Sean could tell that they were as impatient as he was.

After the stragglers arrived, the scholars held hands and student/pastor, Amelio Williams, prayed for their journey, their quest to find the right institutions for higher learning, and for their safe return.

The female teachers tied different colored yarn on the luggage, according to room assignments. The men loaded the luggage onto the bus. Sean picked a seat all the way in the back next to Aaron. Well, actually, he didn't have a choice; Aaron waved him back to the seat so that Jeanette wouldn't try to sit next to him.

Sean put his travel bag in the overhead space and sat down.

"Whatever you do, please do not get up without making sure I'm up."

"Man, instead of running, just talk to her. What could be so bad? She might not be as crazy as you think."

"Yeah, she's probably as crazy as your girl. She could've gotten expelled for pulling a patch of that girl's hair out," Aaron said, shifting in his seat, trying to get comfortable.

"Yeah well, that's between her and Donna."

"I told you that girl was crazy," Aaron said.

Aaron was telling the truth about Rachel, but Jeanette was a different kind of crazy. She would probably pay someone to switch seats, just to sit next to "her man."

Sean tried to get his mind off Rachel and imagine all of the possibilities that open up by going to college. He suddenly realized that his education was much more important than worrying about things that he couldn't change, like, Rachel, or his father. Visiting the colleges was going to be a lot better than just hearing about them.

The silver and black bus pulled out of the parking lot and headed for Nashville, Tennessee, at nine-thirty, ninety minutes late. CPT (Colored People's Time) was in effect already.

The driver picked up the microphone. "Okay, listen up, people. I'm Mr. Mack, and this is the other driver, Mr. Murray," he said, pointing the mic to his partner.

"We're about to tell you what isn't going to happen on this bus. There will be no sexual engagements of any kind. That goes for you guys in the back, too."

If the bus driver had to say that, then Sean was sitting in the wrong area.

"There's not enough room anyway," yelled one of the guys in the middle.

"No horseplay will be tolerated."

"Well, what about child play?" someone asked.

"That either."

He pointed to the back. "Lastly, you can't use the toilet back there. The smell will linger, and I'm pretty sure none of us wants to smell anything foul."

Can't use the toilet? Then why was it back here? Decoration?

Everyone was confused. Were they supposed to wear diapers on the trip?

As Sean made himself comfortable, he thought about how much his mother had invested in making sure he got a good education. Sean took out his iPod and played "Love and Happiness" by Al Green, tuning out the noise around him, and eventually drifting off into a deep sleep.

The Super Mario ring tone startled Sean out his sleep. Scrambling for his phone, he found it between the seats. Caller ID indicated it was a private number.

"Hello," Sean answered.

The call end sign flashed on his display. That was odd.

The bus parked in front of the La Quinta Inn in Nashville around seven p.m. The students were assigned four to a room, except Sean's, which had five. In addition to himself, James, Aaron, and Martez Henderson, another one of his friends, they shared their room with Lorenzo Amos who was new to the school. Five men and *two* beds. Unfortunately it was going to be that way for the duration of the college tour. Sean slept on the floor that night, which his back said was a bad idea, but he did what he had to do. He was so happy to be on the tour that he would've slept on the roof of the bus if necessary.

Sean picked up his phone and went into the bathroom; it had a funny smell. Vince had started already. He dialed his mother. After two rings the answering machine came on.

"Hey Mom, just calling to let you know that we made it to Nashville, and I was calling to say good-night and I love you," Sean said, kissing into the phone before hanging up.

As he walked out of the bathroom, Aaron teased, "Momma's boy. We could hear through the walls."

"So, what if I am a momma's boy? I just love my momma," Sean said defensively.

"I hope you aren't that way when you get to college," Aaron said, pulling the cover over himself.

Chapter 24

James woke Sean out of a deep sleep. Checking his watch, he saw it was already seven a.m.—he should've been up at six. Sean was surprised he had slept so well in spite of the hard floor and itchy carpet.

"Come on, man, wake up. You're the last one," James said, nudging Sean with his foot. "We leave for Fisk in twenty minutes. You'd better get in the shower before they leave you."

"All right, man, I'm up!" Sean sat up, rubbed his neck, and looked around. Everyone was slipping into something, slipping out of something or spraying something.

"Someone really doesn't like to wake up in the morning," Aaron teased, putting on his white Timberland boots. *White? As much walking as they would be doing, how would he keep those clean?* Sean thought.

Sean cut his eyes at Aaron. "Yeah, well you try sleeping on this hard floor." He got up rubbing his lower back like an old man and walked to the bathroom to take his shower. There were no towels, not even a hand towel. He sighed, walked back to his suitcase, and pulled out his own maroon one. Thank God for Superwoman. They could've at least saved him one lousy towel, but he didn't make a big deal of it. Sean closed the bathroom door, stepped into the cold porcelain tub, turned on the shower, and froze. For real!

Sean stormed out of the bathroom. "There isn't a drop of hot water!" he said, his frustration mounting like the center of a smoldering volcano. He wasn't a morning person, but soap and water hitting his body wasn't something that could wait for nighttime.

"There wasn't that much to begin with," Martez replied, ironing his clothes. "So I don't know what you're getting mad at us for."

"Man, how am I supposed to take a shower?"

James put on a blue South Pole shirt and a pair of Old Navy jeans. "Do what I did, use *cold* water."

"This can't be happening," Sean grumbled, stalking over to the marble sink. He turned the water on and quickly washed up. A cold shower was not something he could face today or any day.

Everyone else was ready to leave but Sean was still getting dressed. He hurried to put on a pair of black Sean John jeans, a light blue T-shirt, and dark Pumas. He splashed on a little cologne, grabbed his green notebook, and put it in his backpack. His iPod barely made it into his pocket before he walked out into the bright sunshine.

From the second-floor balcony, he could see students boarding the bus. He ran to the elevator and pressed the button repeatedly before deciding to take the stairs. He ran past the ballroom, the front desk, and an old lady in a motorized wheelchair who gave him a quick bird. Wiping his face, he slowly climbed into the bus, taking deep breaths, and walked to his seat in the back.

Mr. Jones did a quick roll call before the bus pulled out of the parking lot. Coming up on Donelson Pike and Royal Parkway, Sean could see the big red Shoneys sign. It was home of the best Southern breakfast. Everyone got off the bus, some still groggy, all very hungry. He stood back, allowing all of the girls to enter first.

"You not hungry, Sean?" Vince asked, walking past him.

"It's ladies first, fool." Sean yanked him back.

"My bad," Vince said.

They stood in a single file line, waiting to be counted. As always on school trips, the students gathered in small groups. There was a pretty-girl group that talked about all the girls they thought were ugly or sluts; a video-game group that talked all day about ways to beat "Grand Theft Auto Vice City;" a book worm group (pretty obvious) always reading new books by Zane, Mary B. Morrison, and Naleighna Kai; a pretty-boy group that talked about how many girls they pull a week; and an ideal-gentleman group, always discussing how most mistreat women. They even had a white T-shirt crew, inspired by the rap group Cash Money Millionaires. They were always talking about the latest gym shoes, blue jeans, or other new fashions.

Unfortunately, that group happened to be standing behind Sean. He couldn't believe that all they could talk or think about was clothes. There was so much more to think about than a pair of gym shoes. Sean's group—the smart-guy group—suited him just fine. He couldn't wait to be counted so he could get away from the mindless chatter of the T-shirt crew. The smell of scrambled eggs, sausage, and corned beef hash filled the air and tickled his palate.

Nashville was certainly a different type of city. Even though it was considered a large city, it was relatively small compared with Chicago, where you could get lost in the downtown area even if you'd lived there all your life.

Nashville—Music City—had a great history rich in musical talent. Sean loved the scenery, with Titan's Stadium flashing announcements on the big screen and the Bell South building standing tall, looking like a huge cell phone looming over the city.

Finally, Sean stood in line for the buffet, waiting for Martez to move his slow behind down the line.

"Man, for someone who was so hungry this morning, you sure are moving slow," Sean complained.

"Shut up. You were moving slow this morning yourself," Martez replied, taking his sweet old time putting hash browns on his warm plate.

"But you're moving slower than my grandma," Sean said, finally putting something on his plate. Martez's movement reminded Sean that he hadn't talked to his Grandma Celie in a long time.

As soon as his plate was full, Sean sat down at the table with his friends. He said grace and began eating.

All the girls were seated, some talking about meeting some of those *pretty boys* from Kappa Alpha Psi. Some of the female seniors wanted to meet up with those beautiful women of the Fine Pi chapter of Alpha Kappa Alpha. Some of the guys wanted to meet the men from Omega Psi Phi and the men of Alpha Phi Alpha, Alpha Chi chapter, just to see them step, or look at the branded letters on their arms. Sean wanted to meet them because most of their alumni were known as leaders and intelligent contributors to the world.

"Hey, Superboy, what time are we supposed to be at Fisk?" James asked, biting into a piece of sausage.

"Ten, why?" Sean asked, cutting into his pancakes.

"Just seeing how fast I have to eat."

"You'll scarf that down without a time limit," Sean said as he pointed at James packed mouth.

"They said we were leaving here at eight forty-five," Vince said.

Sean suddenly realized that Aaron wasn't part of the conversation. He looked over at him and noticed he was reading. "Hey, Aaron, what're you reading?" he asked.

Aaron tipped the book up so they could see the cover, and said, *"Every Woman Needs a Wife* by Naleighna Kai."

"See, why can't *everyone* enjoy reading, like my guy Aaron here?" Vince wondered, scratching his pulled-back dreads. "Most of the kids I know from my old school can't even read at their own grade level. I've even noticed some people in our school who don't like to read."

"Well, they probably think if anyone saw them reading, it would destroy their reputation," James suggested.

As the group continued to debate about people not reading, Sean thought about the issue. His mother could read a book in a day. She could get so caught up in a book that she would laugh out loud at funny parts and cry at sad parts. That had made him want to read. Maybe some people didn't read because they weren't brought up around people who read a lot, or at all. Sean felt sorry for them because books open people's minds to different worlds and visions, and also increase vocabulary.

The group was so caught up in its discussion that no one noticed the rest of the students leaving. Sean looked up and realized what was happening.

"Oh, crap, c'mon guys, we gotta run." Leaving their plates half-full, Sean and the rest of the smart-guy group ran for the bus.

As soon as Sean was in his seat, he yanked his phone from his pocket, and dialed his Grandma Celie's number.

"Hello," she answered, sounding as though she just woke up.

"Hey, Grandma," Sean said in an embarrassed tone, because he knew she was going to get on him.

"Oh, what's up, stranger?"

"Come on now, don't be like that, Celie," Sean whined.

"'I will call, I will visit, I promise.'" She mocked his words from the day he moved. Sean had to remember that on her time schedule, a long time meant one or two days. "Now you know I need my attention."

"Yes, Ma'am." He shook his head, laughing, "It will never happen again."

"It better not or your tail is mine," she threatened. "So what's going on with you?"

"On my way to Fisk University," Sean replied, gazing out the window.

"That's right. Your college tour is this week. Time just flies on by me."

"Yep. How's Rick and Aunt Denise?"

"Rick's in bed with a fever. I had to rub him down with alcohol to keep him from really burning up."

"Man, that's terrible!"

"Yeah but he'll live. Aunt Denise is fine. She had to go to work on her day off."

"For what?"

"Someone called in sick or something."

"Hmmm, people always do that. So how are you doing?"

"Can't complain. Just breathing God's air and keeping busy."

"Busy is good," Sean said, popping the mosquito that landed on his forearm.

"Yeah, it's so boring around here."

Sean heard Rick calling her name in the background.

"Guess it's not boring anymore. I gotta go, but call me later."

"Okay, Celie, love you."

"Love you, too."

Maybe it was his imagination, but it seemed like an awfully long ride. Everyone else was half sleep. Sean was reading Travis Hunter's *The Hearts of Men*. He occasionally looked out the window at parts of Nashville. He was just beginning to get lost in his book, when he felt the bus slow down. Looking up, he noticed a sign on a black gate that said Fisk University. The bus parked at the front entrance on Seventeenth Avenue and Jackson Street. His godmother, Beatrice Odom, was an alumnus of Fisk, and had told him to pay special attention to the campus. She said the history was wonderful, but then again she was a little biased.

Everyone got off the bus and headed toward Fisk Memorial Gate. Sean and some of his friends got their cameras out and started taking pictures. He posed for a picture in front of the gate to give to his godmother. They walked all the way to the Fisk Memorial Chapel, which seemed ancient to Sean. It was a unique structure standing tall with a stone and wooden base and a pointed tower.

A brown-skinned, bald-headed man of average height greeted the scholars. "Hi everyone, my name is Chandler Keith and I'd like to welcome you to Fisk University," he said, sounding like a TV history show narrator. "Most of you probably don't know that you're walking on history right now. This school was founded in 1866, and has many prominent alumni that have contributed great things to the world such as politics and the education of more black students. This school has struggled throughout its history just to stay open, but we're still here."

They all walked into the chapel, which was a lot larger than it looked from the outside. Sean sat in the front, next to one of the teachers, Ms. Best.

Mr. Keith began by discussing the requirements to attend Fisk University. As he guided Sean and the other scholars on a walk around campus, he talked about the history of the school. They walked over to Jubilee Hall, an 1870s Victorian Gothic six-story, faded, red-brick building with a bell tower. It is the university's oldest building, constructed with funds raised by the Jubilee Singers during international concerts. When they went inside, Sean noticed a stairwell that was covered in gold carpet, and a velvet rope blocked them from the stairs.

"Mr. Keith, why are the stairs gold?"

"These stairs are special," he replied, turning his attention toward the staircase with blue carpet. "They aren't really gold; they're just painted to look like that. These stairs are only used during a ceremony to mark the fiftieth anniversary of a graduation." The scholars continued walking through the building until they reached a room that contained a huge painting of eleven African-Americans. Mr. Keith gazed at the painting with reverence and explained in a hushed tone, "These are the original, incredible, historic Fisk Jubilee Singers. They sang songs that people called Negro spirituals. In 1871, they sang for Queen Victoria, who was so impressed that she donated to the school on their behalf. Overall they collected one hundred fifty thousand dollars." Sean was impressed.

As the scholars toured the rest of the campus, they felt a strong sense of community. Everyone came over to greet them. Some students stood in the yard and the Alpha Phi Alphas stood by their golden pyramid in their gold and black jackets. The AKAs stood at the bottom of the oval on the spot in front of Shane Hall, a seven-floor, rusted brown brick building.

Although Fisk was a well-kept school, like many HBCUs—Historically Black Colleges and Universities—it was in the heart of the ghetto. Right behind New Livingstone Hall, the freshman dorm, was near the Jo Johnston projects. It reminded him of Princeton Park.

The scholars walked to the statue of W.E.B. DuBois holding his college dissertation. He was an activist and a scholar who graduated from Fisk and helped educate many African-Americans. He was also involved with campus activities like the *Fisk Herald*, the school newspaper, and became an honorary member of Alpha Phi Alpha. His books such as *Souls of Black Folks*, are required reading in many schools. He was only one of the distinguished alumni. Others included Nikki Giovanni, a well-known poet, activist and educator; and James Weldon Johnson, a poet and a statesman who, along with his brother, composed "Lift Every Voice and Sing."

"Hey, Sean wait up." Sean turned as Vince jogged toward him.

"What's up, Vince?"

"Nothing much, just looking around. I think I want to go here," Vince said, trying to catch his breath.

"Man, we've only been to the one college," Sean said, putting his hands on Vince's shoulders and shaking him. "Don't jump the gun."

"You're right, I'm just ready to go to college. I'm tired of staying in Chicago. And seeing how college is the only way out, I'm going to take that road." Vince was one of the smartest young men in school. There was never a day he hadn't done his homework.

"I understand, because I think I'm ready, too, but we have to pick the one that's right for each of us. I don't think you can make a good choice by visiting just one."

As the bus headed for Tennessee State University, Sean looked through his notes. Loud commotion and laughter from the middle of the bus interrupted his thoughts. There was a vibe—words being rhymed to a mouthed beat. It was called free-styling, something that everyone thought started with Black people.

Sean's mother had instilled the knowledge of their culture in him. Unlike a lot of people, she was aware of the things that were going on in America. Things that young people should be paying attention to.

The bus passed the large TSU football field before stopping on John A. Merritt Boulevard in front of the ROTC building, where an Air Force training jet was on display. This tour wasn't just about the colleges, it was about history.

The students followed Ms. Stanton downstairs to an ROTC classroom, where a Caucasian man dressed in a navy blue suit entered and greeted them. He talked about the fourteen Tennessee State requirements. Then he droned on about how Tennessee State was formerly Tennessee Agricultural School. He told them that Jesse Russell, who created the cell phone chip, attended TSU.

Sean wondered how a guy who obviously didn't want to be talking to the group expected to keep the students' interest.

Anybody could talk about acceptance requirements, but Sean was looking for motivation, for a reason to choose TSU. At least the Fiskites talked about more than the entrance requirements. Superwoman had told him to look for something extraordinary in a college, not just a name, to go for quality.

"Man, what is up with this guy?" Vince whispered to Sean.

"I was about to ask you the same thing," Sean replied.

"I'm falling asleep over here," Vince said, laying his head on Sean's shoulder.

"Man! Wake up," he said, shrugging him off.

"Haven't you heard of 'Lean on Me'?"

"Yeah, but you're not falling on hard times. Lean over again, you'll be leaning on the floor."

At one point during the TSU tour, Sean had to use the bathroom something fierce. He didn't bother to ask permission. The need was too great.

When he came out, he didn't see his group. He went through the gymnasium and all the way out toward the dorms, going through the various hallways, following the signs. It reminded him of River North. He wondered how a first-day freshman would ever find his classrooms. Sean normally had a good sense of direction, but this was ridiculous.

Finally, he walked over to a group of students gathered by a dorm that looked like a cleaner version of the Robert Taylor Homes projects in Chicago.

"Excuse me," he said, standing on the second step. "Hi, I'm Sean Morris from Chicago and I'm looking for the college tour group that probably passed this way."

The students seemed surprised to see him.

"What's up, kid? I'm John," said a tall, dark-brown man as he walked down the steps. He extended his hand to Sean, as if to assure him that he wasn't going to get jumped. John could probably tell that Sean was a little uneasy by the way his eyes shifted from side to side. Karate taught him to be watchful and ready to protect himself.

"I'm cool," Sean said, shaking his hand firmly. "Came over partly because I'm lost, but mostly because I'm wondering what it was about this school that made you want to come here. I'm pretty sure it wasn't the tour guides."

John chuckled and leaned on a stone railing in front of a light-skinned guy who was talking on his cell phone, apparently to his girlfriend. "I came to this school because it has a great reputation, both academically and socially, and it has a great business program. At least I *think* it does."

The others nodded.

"If this school is so great, then why didn't our guide seem like he had any pride in the school?" Sean asked.

The students looked at each other. Some shrugged, but one of the girls walked over to Sean. "If you want more information about the school, give me a call. My name is Jessica. I'm an intern in the Office of Admissions," she said, her seductive Asian eyes peering into his, her soft, medium brown hand flowing across his cheek. Sean pulled out his cell phone and put her number in his phonebook. As he was putting it back in his pocket, his cell phone rang.

"Hello."

"Sean, where the hell are you?" James asked.

"Over at the dorms by the gym." Sean grinned sheepishly at the group listening in. "I got lost."

"Whatever. Man, you better get over to the football field," James whispered. "Ms. Stanton doesn't know you're lost, but that's not going to last much longer."

"All right, I'm on my way."

"How do I get to the football field?" Sean asked somewhat frantically, realizing that if he caused problems that Ms. Stanton would ship him back on the first Greyhound headed for Chicago.

"I'll walk you over there. I have band practice anyway," John said, walking past Sean.

Band? "Thanks." The walk to the football field took about ten minutes, giving them the chance to see more of the campus. John talked more about his experiences at the college and about the band. Sean caught up with the tour group just as they were about to leave.

"Hey, take my number down in case you have any more questions about the school," John said as Sean was about to run. Sean typed the number in his cell phone and took. He blended into the rear of the group unnoticed and boarded the bus.

The sun had just set as they pulled up to Meharry Medical College. The bus parked on Eighteenth Avenue, in front of what looked like a hospital across the street from Fisk University.

"Why didn't we just come here when we were done with Fisk?" Sean asked James who was standing in front of him.

James shrugged. "Don't know. Maybe they have a closed campus during the day."

"Guess that's why we're here at night," Sean said, rubbing his arms. "Since Nashville's in the South, I didn't expect it to be this cold."

"You should've worn a jacket. I would give you mine but you're not a *woman.*"

The night orange lights bounced off the tall gray buildings. Campus security patrolled on foot and by car.

"Whatever, James." Sean laughed his comment off, putting his arms inside his shirt.

"It must've been pretty easy for my godmother to get to class," Sean said, looking at the distance between where he was standing and where the Fisk campus stood.

"Why do you say that?" James asked.

"My godmother first went to Fisk University, then right across the street to Meharry. She became a registered nurse, and then opened the first African-American Day Spa in the United States."

"Oh, so your family has some high rollers. Let me get a dollar then." James laughed, holding his hand out.

"Let me think about it." Sean smiled, then took off with James chasing him.

The scholars walked around the campus until they got to the D.T. Rolfe Student Center. They watched a movie on the history of the school. Sean was interested in knowing about the past, but had no interest in the medical field. With all that blood? He almost hurled when he saw too much of his own. And the surgeries? Suppose he went in for a kidney and took out a liver? Then having to tell people that they've lost a loved one…he couldn't do it.

The group strolled around the school, looking at the classrooms and labs, including a place they weren't supposed to be—a room on the lower level where students were working on dead bodies. Sean felt like he had been punched in the stomach. His body was covered in goose bumps. He thought he might vomit and quickly backed out of the room. Sean was ready to go, but others wanted to see more of the campus, so he reluctantly went along. '

"Man! That was horrible," Aaron said as he held his stomach.

"Wasn't it? I forgot people sometimes donated their body to science," Sean replied.

"That was so cool," James said.

"Why are you so happy? What happened to Vince?" Sean asked.

"Um—Vince had to go to the bathroom, after seeing that," James answered. "And I'm happy because I've never seen a dead body up close."

"Go on the West Side. You'll find plenty of them." Sean quivered at the thought of those dead bodies.

"What, a bunch of tricks?" James asked, patting them on the back.

"James, weren't you the one who ran out of the bus terminal when the dog barked at you?" Aaron asked..

"I didn't run, I was speed-walking, I didn't want the security guards to think that I had something on me," James explained.

"Anyway, I'm tired," Sean said. "When do we go back to the hotel?"

"Hopefully soon," James answered.

As promised, Ms. Stanton kept them out until most of the group was exhausted. They boarded the bus and headed to Swett's Restaurant for dinner. Sean's stomach hadn't quite recovered, but he didn't want to be hungry later so he'd just have to suffer and shovel it down.

The restaurant specialized in old-fashioned, home-style Southern food that looked and smelled wonderful. Fried chicken, baked chicken, smothered chicken, collard greens, candied yams, meatloaf, dressing, and peach cobbler. It made Sean miss Grandma Celie. He had visited her a few weeks before the college tour. She told him, "When you go down South, baby, they know how to put their foot in some food. That's the kind of food that can make you say holy...well you know."

Sean had chuckled. "But Grandma, I thought you said only *your* cooking could make me say that."

"Well, there's only two types of great cooks: those Southern folk and me. Now, if I can get you and your momma to do the same, we'll be alright."

The way she described Southern cooking made you believe she was from the South. But Celie had been born, bred, and raised in Chicago. Whenever she talked about the South she added *hmmm* in the middle of her sentence, like a Southern granny.

Sean sat at the table with Vince and James. Aaron went to the bathroom.

"Sean, have you seen Aaron?" Jeanette asked, startling him and making him choke on his greens.

"Cough it up," Vince said as he pounded him on the back.

After a few slaps on the back, Sean managed to gasp, "I'm fine." Then he looked at Jeanette. "I'd appreciate it, if you'd stop sneaking up on us like that. Please."

"Okay, but do you know where Aaron is?" she asked, twirling her thumbs.

Feeling more than a little irritated, Sean snapped, "No, I don't."

"Let me know if you see him," she said as she walked away.

"That girl is going to kill you one day," Vince said.

When they finished eating, the scholars dragged their weary bodies onto the bus. They were anxious to get back to the hotel and into bed—or in Sean's case, the floor.

They would be heading for Alabama in the morning.

Chapter 25

Sean woke from a rough night's sleep at six forty-five a.m., feeling like an old man who had been working the fields all day. As he got up, he held his neck and back as he'd seen his grandma do so many times. No wonder Ms. Stanton wanted them to be *well rested;* she was walking them to death. In order to be well rested, Sean needed a bed. If anyone asked him, he would say "Oh, that square thing in the center of my hotel room, with the pillows and a blanket? Haven't seen it. But when you find it..." Five people to a room meant for four was really getting to him. Some changes were needed—and fast.

Once again, Sean was the last one to shower because he hadn't heard the alarm clock.

"Come on, Sean, hurry up," Aaron said, putting his suitcase next to the door. "We have fifteen minutes."

Getting dressed in gray jogging pants and the Fisk sweater he had bought the day before, Sean sprayed cologne on his chest. He quickly tossed his toiletries into his suitcase, hurried out, and boarded the bus. During breakfast at Shoney's, they talked about career choices and compared Fisk to TSU. Fisk came out on top. Following breakfast, most of the students slept during the three-hour ride to Alabama A&M University.

As the bus slowed, everyone began to wake. Sean grabbed his bag and walked into the bathroom. It smelled like a garbage dump. Someone had probably used it and didn't bother to spray, despite the bus driver's warning. He quickly put in his contacts and changed his clothes.

As he opened the bathroom door, he scanned the bus. Not a soul in sight. Everybody stood in front of the burgundy brick L. R. Patton Building. As he grabbed his backpack and rushed off the bus, he saw the sign— Alabama A&M University. They were in Huntsville-Normal, Alabama. The extremely clean campus environment reminded Sean of those Chicago suburbs populated by picket-fence folks. He didn't see a lick of garbage anywhere.

Sean caught up with the group and stood to the right of Vince. Gazing at the dorms in the distance, he commented, "Man, it must be hard getting to classes here. Look at all the space between the buildings. And since the dorms are all on the top of the hill, I would definitely need a car if I come to this school."

"You ain't lying." Vince shook his head in disbelief. "Walking up and down that thing must be hell."

"Or something close." Sean could only imagine how many pounds he'd lose if he had to walk this campus.

"The academics had better be worth it," Sean said, looking at other parts of the campus. "Where are all the students? It looks a little deserted out here."

"Maybe they're all in classes, at lunch, or sleeping," Vince replied, glancing at his watch.

Despite the inconvenience of getting around, the place appealed to Sean. He knew that it would be on his "I want to go here" list.

Anthony Boyd, Director of Admissions who resembled the comedian George Wallace, greeted the group. He directed them to the cafeteria, which was full of students.

"Man, this looks like the school for me," Sean said, gazing at the students, who were doing everything from playing chess to homework. This was the type of environment Sean needed. Positive people.

"It would be a good school for me, too," Aaron said, scanning the course catalog, "if they had 3D-animation as a major."

"Well, I don't know about that," Vince replied, gazing at a beautiful, light-skinned young woman with a short haircut. She was sitting with a group of other beautiful young ladies. "I'd be willing to change my major, especially if I was going to be around all these lovelies," he said.

"Really? You'd change your major, give up the chance to follow your dream and do something you love, over some booty?" James asked, turning his attention toward the discussion rather than the young lady.

"In all honesty," Vince replied, folding his fingers together, "I wouldn't change it for a piece of tail. But Aaron's major is only going to be offered at either a school on the West Coast or up north where we live." Vince counted the places on his fingers. "I'm just saying that if Aaron wants to go to a Southern school, then he should look into a different major, one in a field *close* to what he wants."

"That makes sense," James agreed.

Vince and James always seemed to debate or philosophize about everything. This was why Vince was on the "Know Your Heritage" team at school and James was on the leadership committee. Sean was too busy catching up from freshman and sophomore year to join anything but the "keep-up-in-school, turn-in-your-homework club."

Superwoman meant business. She was still dating that recruiter guy. (She tried to make out like she wasn't, but Sean was no fool.) He knew why the guy was really still around. *Humph!* No matter what she thought, he was not going to Job Corps or Lincoln's Challenge for a "behavior modification." His "behavior" was just fine, thank you very much!

Sean glanced around the lunchroom as the line moved. A woman who was the definition of beautiful, and nothing short of it, caught his eye. She strolled down the aisle, finally sitting at a table with three other attractive females. They were studying, eating turkey club sandwiches with fries on the side, and drinking what looked like grape pop. He tried not to stare, but he couldn't help it; she was gorgeous. She looked like the type that had kept her head in a book ever since she learned to read, but boy, did the rest of her shout out "Come to me."

As he gazed at her, she looked up at him. Their eyes met and she smiled.

Sean quickly turned away, embarrassed. Holding the image of her light brown, lustrous skin and French-braided hair in his mind, he dared to peek again. He loved voluptuous, Black women with some meat on their bones. Sean took a few deep breaths, trying to calm down. Now he understood why some colleges didn't allow opposite sex visitations—no one would get any work done. But the distractions were lovely!

Standing in line for the soda fountain, he grabbed a red plastic cup from the rack. Holding his glass under the Sierra Mist dispenser, he pressed the button and the clear, fizzy liquid poured in. As he turned to head for the table with his friends, he almost bumped into someone. The French braids gave her away—it was the woman he had been staring at. Only now she was looking back at him.

Sean collected himself. "Excuse me." Where did the base in his voice go? *Man!*

"No problem, as long as you didn't spill on my shirt," she replied, pointing at her pink Baby Phat top, which hugged her jaw-dropping figure. "Are you new to the school?"

"Umm, just visiting. My school's on a college tour from Chicago."

"Chicago? Well, Mr. Chicago, where are you gonna sit?" she asked, looking around.

"Over there." Sean pointed to the table where Aaron, Vince, and James were sitting. They were busy talking, totally ignoring that he was having a conversation with one of the finest women on campus. "And my name's Sean."

"I'm Colleen. Why don't you tell your friends to come over to my table so they can meet some of *my* friends?"

"Sure."

As he reached his table, the guys were still debating how to choose a college. "Guys, why don't you take a trip with me over to another table?" Sean asked, his smile extending from ear to ear.

"Why? We have a table right here," Aaron said with a puzzled look.

"Well, do you see that table over there?" Sean pointed to Colleen and her friends, who waved like the homecoming court in a parade. "I talked to the one second to the right, and she invited us to her table."

"Good going, Superboy. Good way to use those super powers," Vince said.

He didn't have to say it twice. They all stood up, grabbing their book bags and lunch trays. "Sean, you have potential," Aaron said, passing him on the way to Colleen's table.

"I know," Sean said as he laughed and popped his collar before catching up to his friends. They set their trays down and took places between the girls. "Ladies, allow me to introduce my friends, Aaron, Vince, and James." Sean pointed to each of them as he said their names in his most charming voice. He might not know about the campus, but the women were mighty friendly!

As his friends began talking to Colleen's friends, Sean picked up their conversation. "So, what year are you in?" he asked.

"I'm a freshman, majoring in English," Colleen answered. She twirled one of her braids around her slender fingers.

"That's what I want to major in," Sean said, feeling as if Cupid had struck his heart. "But I'm thinking about double majoring in theatrical arts."

She smiled and a warm feeling overtook his mind; a few violins played in the background.

"So, how do you like it here?" he asked, trying to stay on track.

"It's better than I thought it would be. I originally wanted to go to Grambling State University," she said, giving him a sensual, mischievous smile. "And to tell you the truth, I don't regret it one bit. So, are you thinking about coming here?"

"I'm actually kind of impressed with the school. I'm adding it to my list for applications, and if I get in, I get in." His heartbeat escalated when he looked into her dark brown eyes.

Sean glanced away and noticed his group was missing. "It's time for me to go."

"Okay. Try to come to my dorm before you leave," she said in a low, sexy voice.

Dorm? he thought, as his hormones kicked in. "I won't be able to," Sean said regretfully. "We're leaving as soon as we finish our tour of the campus."

Sean suddenly heard Aaliyah's song, "If Your Girl Only Knew," playing in the back of his mind. He pushed himself to tell Colleen the truth. "And actually, I have a girlfriend; I'm still making a decision on whether we're going to stay together."

Her eyes widened. "Well, I guess you can still call me, as a *friend*. Just make sure you keep in touch." She wrote her number down on his black notebook.

"Okay," he said, wondering if the last part of her statement really meant *let me know if you break up with your girlfriend.*

"Go catch up with your group." She smiled, tore off the sheet, and stuffed it in his shirt pocket close to his heart—the place Rachel was supposed to be.

As the scholars filed into the first two rows of a tan-painted, maroon-carpeted auditorium, Mr. Boyd rejoined them. From the oak podium, he explained Alabama A&M in its entirety, from undergraduate programs to the male-to-female ratio, as well as jokes about his experiences with the students. If he missed a detail, Sean couldn't tell. What impressed him most was that Mr. Boyd was excited about education and thrilled to be a part of this particular school.

Sean asked numerous questions and took voluminous notes. The group boarded the bus to tour the rest of the campus, including the dormitories, but he didn't see Colleen. Going up and down hill after hill, Sean felt like he was on a personal roller coaster.

A variety of people were talking in the parking lot, tossing around a football, or getting in their cars. Everybody looked like they belonged to a group. This time there was the cool-car crew, the scholars, and the beautiful-women group, just like high school. But there was a major difference—the various groups hung around each other, like a family would.

This would be a big change for Sean. Southern colleges were very different from colleges in the Northern and Western areas of the country. The North was fast-paced and sometimes competitive, while the South was friendlier and laid-back. Except when it came to parties—Sean had heard about the bangin' parties at Southern colleges. People told him that those college parties, and girls, could trip him up. *Not if you do it in moderation*, he thought. But he had to worry about actually *getting* into a college first, so he wasn't going to concentrate on college women...yet.

Sean's phone rang. It was Superwoman.

"Hey, Momma," Sean answered, glad to hear from her. "What's up?"

"Nothing much, just returning your call."

"That was two days ago."

"But at least I called. Where are you now?"

"Alabama A&M."

"Hmm, sounds like fun. How is it?"

"It's fine, but it's huge. I wouldn't be able to get around without a car."

"Well, I guess you better get your walk on now. I have to get back to work. So be safe and call me tonight."

"Yes, Ma'am, bye."

As the campus tour was ending, Sean walked outside, taking pictures of some of the buildings. He even took a picture with Mr. Boyd, so he'd remember the man's enthusiasm for his school.

Climbing back on the bus, he plopped in his seat, put his book bag underneath, and tilted the chair back. As soon as everyone had boarded, the bus headed for Birmingham, Alabama.

The one-hour drive seemed like a half-hour, Sean thought as he woke up. The bus was parked across the street from a church. Grabbing his book bag, Sean stepped off the bus behind James. Although it was still daylight, Sean noticed the sky turning gray, but he couldn't smell rain. He gazed around at a large park, where four statues of what appeared to be women stood in elegant poses.

"Okay, scholars," Ms. Stanton said. "We are now in Birmingham, Alabama, and we're about to go into the Sixteenth Street Church."

Walking across the street, Sean stared at the large red-brick church, with its three large flights of stairs. Although it wasn't cold, Sean suddenly felt a little shiver when he entered the church. *What's so different about this church?* The lighting was dim, the students' whispers the only sound. Strolling toward the front row, Sean noticed a big-screen television at the front of the church. Suddenly the television came on, startling the scholars. An old man with white hair, wrinkled skin, and a wobbly gait walked in from the back room.

"Sorry, folks, I had to plug the TV into the back outlet," he said, holding a remote and videotape in his hands. "Welcome to the Sixteenth Street Baptist Church. My name is Charles Hampton."

Taking a pen and his black notebook out of his book bag, Sean wrote the information down.

"I'm going to show you a video in a moment," Mr. Hampton said, tapping the tape against his hand. "But first, a quick bit of information that you need. This church was built in 1911. It has survived racism and withstood the test of time. But there's one story that this church will never forget, and that's what's on this tape," he continued, concentrating on getting the tape in the VCR.

It must be a pretty famous story, but if it was, then how come I've never heard about it?

The video started with the faces of four young women. Two of them, Carole Robertson and Cynthia Wesley, looked like they were in their teens. The other two, Addie Mae Collins and Denise McNair, looked no older than twelve.

Sean and the other scholars watched the video in shock, taking in the heartbreaking story unfolding on the screen. On September 15, 1963, the four girls were getting ready for the service in the basement of the Sixteenth Street Baptist Church, when a bomb exploded, killing all four of them. A shudder of terror shook Sean out of a trance. He stared unbelievingly at the images of the damaged church.

Superwoman had always tried to make him aware of the history of being an African-American in the United States, but maybe this was something she didn't know about, either. Maybe that was because public schools hadn't really taught him about Black history. Sure, they taught U.S. history, but Sean wondered why stories like these were never included. This was part of U.S. history, too.

Although Robert Edward Chambliss, a White man, tried to blow up the church, it remained standing. Even though the girls died and other people were injured, what really struck Sean's heart was seeing the stained-glass window image of Jesus with only his face missing. Sean swallowed against his tears. How could someone hate so much that they would want to take away the lives of young children?

As the tape continued, Sean looked around. Some of the girls were crying, and some of the guys weren't too far from tears. Everyone was in shock.

"Now, we will move to the basement," Mr. Hampton said, as he stopped the tape and walked toward the back of the church.

"Those poor little girls," Sean heard someone say.

The students followed Mr. Hampton down the stairs to the basement, which had white tile and wood paneled walls. Mr. Hampton pointed out the section where the bomb had exploded, and where they found the girls' bodies. Next he directed the group toward a small walkway near the back of the basement. There they saw pictures of the girls, the wounded people, and the blown-up portion of the church.

"Man, some of the things that people did because of hatred back in those days was ridiculous, and that's not even describing it fully," Vince said, standing beside Sean as they studied the pictures.

"Back in those days? It still goes on today, even back home in Chicago. It's just the hatred is silent, along with segregation. We live on the South side and Whites live on the North. That's how we got the title: *The Most Segregated City in the United States.*" Sean said, still gazing at the pictures. "If you'd quit sleeping in African-American History class, you'd know all this."

"Do you know about Emmett Till?" Vince asked, inching toward the next row of pictures.

"Never heard of him," Sean replied. "Who is he?"

"Man, you don't know about the things that happened right in your own backyard? Emmett Till was a fourteen-year-old boy who lived in Chicago," Vince said. "He went down to Money, Mississippi, for vacation and supposedly flirted with a White woman in a store. Later on, some men grabbed him in his sleep, beat him, shot him, and dumped him in the Tallahatchie River. He could only be identified by the initialed ring on his finger. At his funeral, his mother had an open casket so that viewers in Chicago would be able to see hate for what it really was. *Jet* magazine published the pictures, but even if you saw them, you probably wouldn't be able to describe it."

Sean realized that even though he'd been catching up lately, he still didn't know a lot of things he should know about African-American history. The focus at Gadson and River North had been on World and European history. Most of the middle college teachers tried to get the students to learn more about Black history. Mr. Rinauld always touched on the struggle that Blacks had faced to get them where they were now.

"People sacrificed their lives to give Blacks the right to an education, for them to have the right to learn about their own culture. To learn about things like what happened to these four girls, how they contributed to the motivation of the Civil Rights Movement. Injustices like the one the girls experienced only serve to prove to America that the racism needs to stop," Sean said, before moving along.

The group walked up the stairs and out into the well-lit streets of Birmingham. They continued down the street to the Civil Rights Institute. There, they got a better understanding of the struggle African-Americans went through in the days of slavery and segregation, which still affect parts of the country.

Sean bought a Booker T. Washington plaque, with his picture and the quotation: "Success is to be measured not so much by the position that one has reached in life as by the obstacles which he has overcome."

They left the museum, cut through the large park, and stopped in front of the four statues that Sean had seen earlier.

"These four statues represent the four girls in the womanhood they never got a chance to experience," Mr. Hampton explained, gazing at the tall, stone statues. Sean snapped a couple of pictures, then walked around the park by himself.

When it was time to board the bus, Sean glanced one last time at the statues before walking back to his seat. He put his book bag in the top storage area, grabbed his pillow, balanced it on the window, and prepared to go to sleep. Those four girls weighed heavily on his heart. The information and insight gained from the museum visit filled his mind. A person could read about those things all day, but seeing them gave them new light and meaning. The same amount of understanding needed to be applied to school, because he still missed an assignment here and there.

Sean's phone rang and the caller ID displayed private.

"Hello?"

Seconds after he picked up, the caller hung up. That was strange. Sean never got calls from anyone who had an unlisted number. Now it had happened twice.

Sean dialed his mother. "Hey, Sean." She sounded thrilled to hear from him.

"Hey, Mom, did you just call me?"

"Nope, I was waiting on you to call me."

"Someone just called me from an unlisted number," Sean said, wanting to dial the number back, but the call-back feature only recognized numbers.

"Someone has been calling here, too," she said in a confused tone.

"Hmmm, can we call the phone company to get the number or block out private calls?" Sean asked, looking for a customer service number for his cell provider.

"I don't know, but I'll check into it. So, how's the trip?"

"It's really fun, learning a lot about colleges and social clubs, and other historical facts along the way," Sean said, puzzled by the loud banging noise in the background. "Mom, what are you messing up over there? Because I cleaned up before I left."

"I'm cooking," she said proudly.

"Really, what made you do that?"

"I have to eat, you know."

"But Grandma said you couldn't cook."

"I can cook. I just don't like to cook, and obviously it's been a couple of months," she said, struggling with something. "Let me call you back. Love you."

Before he could say *love you, too*, she hung up.

The bus pulled out and headed for the next stop, Talladega, Alabama. Two hours later, Sean awoke as they pulled into the parking lot of a

Budget Inn hotel. The boys dragged themselves off the bus and helped unload the girls' luggage as well as their own. Exhausted from the day's activities, everyone seemed to be moving in slow motion.

Sean unlocked the door to the hotel room. He dropped his luggage by the closet, grabbed something out of the top of his bag, stuck it under the pillow, and plopped down on the nearest bed. He didn't even bother to take off his clothes. He didn't even realize he had finally accomplished what had become one of the greatest goals of this trip—to sleep in a nice, warm bed!

Chapter 26

Sean dreamed of being in a snowball fight with Rick, like when they were kids. He was winning until Rick clobbered him in the face with a huge snowball.

Sean felt a cold sensation on his face. Then his nose started to tickle.

He twitched, but the itch didn't go away. *Probably a fly*, he thought, smacking at himself.

Laughter erupted. Sean recognized the mint odor, and felt a sticky, gooey substance on his hand.

Someone had put toothpaste on his hands.

Aaron, Martez, and James stood over him, snapping pictures of his toothpaste-covered face. While they were laughing, Sean slowly reached behind his pillow and grabbed a medium-sized bottle of his mother's lotion. Quickly pulling it out, he squirted the perfumed lotion on all three.

"That's just the beginning of what I'm going to do." He got out of bed and walked into the bathroom. "I suggest you not fall asleep tonight," he continued, blinking hard because the toothpaste burned his eyes.

"C'mon, Sean, it was just a joke," Aaron said.

"I want you to remember your own words," Sean said, grabbing a towel.

James put his hand on Sean's shoulder. "Lighten up, man." Then he snapped another picture.

Sean chuckled, "Maybe after I get you back. You might notice that you smell a little like women. Might want to take another shower."

Those jokers, I can't believe they did that. Sean had learned about practical jokes from his cousins, Richmond and Ariel. One summer night when Richmond was sleeping, Sean walked in with long wet hair and shook his head over Richmond's bed, waking his cousin from a sound sleep. That next day, Richmond and Ariel woke Sean from a nap. "Sean, get up, we're about to go to the store," Ariel said as Richmond grabbed the house keys.

Sean pulled on his socks and then grabbed a shoe and put it on. Sharp pains stabbed the bottom of his foot, and it felt wet. He took off the shoe and turned it upside-down. Kitty litter poured out. One whiff and Sean knew it *wasn't* litter from the bag, but directly from the cat box. Mr. Whickums had done more damage that day than a few showers could fix.

From that day on, he always kept something with him while he slept around any of his friends—call it *survival*.

The next morning, Sean and the others helped the bus driver finish loading the luggage, before departing for their next destination.

Sean closed his eyes, trying to steal a few more winks like the rest of the people on the bus. Each day, the bus seemed quieter and quieter as more and more kids took a sudden interest in cat-naps. *That Ms. Stanton!*

When he opened his eyes, he realized the bus had stopped alongside an old red brick building. Sean looked around, wondering where they were. He saw a sign that said Battle Street. He was almost the last one on the bus. He quickly exchanged his sweaty T-shirt for his clean OHMC one, grabbed his book bag, and rushed off the bus so fast he nearly tripped. He slowed down to collect himself then caught up with his roommates and Vince, who were at the end of the line of scholars following Ms. Stanton.

"Aaron, how come you didn't wake me up?" Sean asked as he tugged on his shirt to straighten it.

"I tried, but you just turned around. You're a hard sleeper," Aaron said, chuckling. "I could thump my music and you still wouldn't wake up. Must be having those wet dreams, boy."

"So, where are we at?" Martez asked, gazing at a long row of houses.

"Behind that preposition," Sean said with a smile, remembering how Superwoman always corrected him when he spoke that way. "Never end a sentence with a preposition. Didn't you learn anything in English class?"

"Anyway, *Mr. Rinauld*, where are we?" Aaron said with a smirk on his square face.

"Talladega College in Talladega, Alabama," James answered, looking over his itinerary.

"It looks like a village," Sean said. The area even had its own corner store and barbershop. He wondered where the classes met.

Checking a campus map, Vince said, "I believe we're here." He pointed first to the map, then to the pink and green stone benches of AKA, then the black and gold stone benches of the Alphas. The purple and gold benches of Omega Psi Phi and red and white benches of Delta Sigma Theta were on the other side of the block. "Evidently, we're in Greek country."

Eventually the scholars came to brick structures that looked more like college buildings. A short, pudgy, dark-skinned man came out one of the buildings and approached them with a bright smile. "Good morning. Welcome to Talladega College. I'm Mr. Powell, and I will be your guide." In spite of the heat, he was wearing a gray suit, white dress shirt and a tie. *He could have at least taken off the jacket.* Sean's back smoldered through his T-shirt thanks to the dark orange sun—he wished he could go without anything over his chest.

Some of the buildings on the campus looked like old three-story mansions. The college was one of the oldest historically Black institutions of higher learning in the United States. Most Southern colleges were old. Some of them started out in small churches after the slaves gained their freedom. They expanded from those humble beginnings into colleges and universities. So now most HBCUs were in the heart of the Black communities, or in ghettos. Higher learning in the center of poverty and high crime. But hadn't Black people always triumphed over apathy to reach their goals?

As the group continued walking along the concrete path, Sean noticed a medium sized white rock, resting on a blue circular platform. The rock was engraved *Talladega College*, founded 1867. An image of an old ship, with a head shaded black at the front of the ship was carved above the inscription. Sean snapped a picture, then caught up with the group as they stopped at the Slavery Library.

"Before we go in, I must inform you that you cannot take pictures of the art inside," Mr. Powell said. "If you do, your camera will be confiscated."

Sean was amazed by what he saw. The paintings on the walls and in the floor of the middle passageway depicted the story of how slave traders brought Blacks to the United States and forced them into years of slavery, hard labor, and separation from their families. There was also an interesting collection of objects relating to African culture, such as Senegalese masks and art.

Next the group moved on to the building's library where they had the opportunity to ask Mr. Powell questions about the college.

"Man, this place is really full of history," Sean said, looking at the architecture.

"Yeah, and you know Mr. Rinauld is going to want us to write a paper on it," Aaron said as he jotted down more notes. "That guy wants us to be historians or something with all the note-taking we do."

"Yep, but it'll be fun to write," Sean said, following Aaron's lead.

"*You're* the journalist, *I'm* the artist. But as long as I learn something and get a grade, I'll do it."

The group walked around the campus a while longer, mingling with the college students. When Sean boarded the bus at one p.m., his feet were in serious need of an appointment with Dr. Scholl's. He could use some of those gel soles.

Riding away from the college, Sean gazed out of the window. Project houses lined the streets. Kids played on the street and others stood outside their homes and waved as the bus passed. Sean wondered why they were waving, but waved back anyway. He soon learned that Southern folk were generally courteous and friendly. In Chicago, somebody would have waved all right, but it might have been one finger—the *wrong* finger.

Most of the students slept as the bus rolled toward ASU. Why had sleep suddenly become the most important thing for the scholars? And why was Ms. Stanton so perky? *It just ain't right, I tell ya!*

Sean's phone rang. Without looking at the display, Sean answered.

"Jerk!" an angry girl snapped and hung up.

Sean didn't recognize the voice and closed his phone.

"Man! Who was that?" Aaron asked. "I could've heard that from the front."

"It's some girl, but before she kept calling and hanging up. Now she actually said a word."

"Is it Rachel?" Aaron asked.

"Probably, but it doesn't sound like her."

"I don't know, man. You should've stayed away from her like Curtis said." Aaron turned back over to go to sleep.

"Yeah, I know."

Sean needed his Aunt Denise to set the mystery caller straight. She knew how to prevent someone from continually calling back. One day when she was home, telemarketers called all day until she'd had enough. The person she snapped on got the message. No one except family or friends called for three months.

The setting sun and darkening blue sky signaled the start of evening. Sean and the rest of the scholars entered the tall reddish-orange brick building on the Alabama State University campus. They filed into a small, dimly lit auditorium with a highly polished, black grand piano on the stage, they filling up the first two rows. A dark-skinned man, standing around five feet nine inches tall, dressed in a black polo shirt and khaki dress pants, walked down the stairs to the front of the stage.

"Good afternoon. I'm Mr. Phillips, the music director here at Alabama State University. I, along with some of our students, welcome you," he said, pointing to the small group to his left. "First off, do we have any musicians in here?"

Sean's hand immediately went up, along with that of his classmate, Leslie Mickel.

"Yes. And your name is?"

"I'm scholar Sean Morris, and I play alto and tenor saxophones." It was still true, although he hadn't touched one in a year.

Mr. Phillips smiled warmly, "And you, the young man in the back, your name is?"

"I'm scholar Leslie Mickel, and I play the piano."

"Would you mind playing a song for us today?" Mr. Phillips asked as he gestured toward the piano.

Leslie walked up to the stage, slid onto the black wooden piano bench, and filled the room with the sounds of Stevie Wonder's "My Cherie Amour." Leslie, a big man, and proud of it, had a great sense of humor and treated people very kindly. He was always able to make the other scholars laugh. He was also the best dressed, with a fitted baseball cap in every color, one for every day. He had on a black and white New York Yankees cap, a black Roca Wear T-shirt and blue jeans, topped off with a pair of black K-Swiss classics. Definitely not the look of a concert pianist, but perfect for the urban maestro.

It took some of the students a minute to figure out what he was playing. Sean knew it after the first three chords. Everyone caught on, then started singing along. Some of the other students definitely wouldn't get a music scholarship.

After Mr. Phillips went over the school's requirements, the scholars had time to walk around. Sean and the fellas went to see what the dorms were like. A fraternity was about to have a party in one of the buildings. The scholars asked a couple of Alpha men about fraternity life.

"I always thought that fraternities just beat pledgees with paddles and made them do ridiculous tasks, then went wild," Sean told the frat group.

"Naw, I mean you will have to do something, but as long as you know you can handle it, you'll be fine," one of them said.

"What about hazing?" Aaron asked, hoping to get the truth. People had died when hazing got out of hand.

"We don't haze."

"Basically what I heard from one of my friends in college," Sean said, "was that you guys are mainly known for your brotherhood, sense of community, and without a doubt, how to throw a party."

"That's true, but we're also known for our principles of fellowship, scholarship, good character, and the uplifting of humanity. Oh yeah and the ability to throw a party," another one of the men replied. "Hazing is only for those who allow themselves to be tortured. You have the right to say no. Don't do anything you think will harm you or your line."

That conversation changed Sean's whole view on fraternities. Aaron tapped his watch. Sean and his friends ran to catch up with the rest of the scholars to board the bus for their next destination.

The next stop was the Dexter Avenue King Memorial Baptist Church. Unfortunately, the building wasn't open so the scholars had to settle for taking pictures of the outside. While pastor at the church, Martin Luther King Jr., led and organized the Montgomery Bus Boycott, people had to walk to work—miles even—for a whole year, but it paid off. Just like Superwoman had led the way to integrate Gadson's teaching staff, and to stop River North from classifying all black boys as remedial. There were people leading "little civil rights" movements every day. Everyone can make a difference— no matter how small the effort.

From the church, the group walked the short distance to the Civil Rights Memorial at the Southern Poverty Law Center. A thin film of water cascaded over a round marble table, shaped like a cone. The names of famous Blacks who had taken a stand during the Civil Rights Era were etched into the table. Martin Luther King Jr.'s inspirational words "...*Until justice rolls down like waters and righteousness like a mighty stream*" provided the inspiration for the memorial design and were engraved into a glossy, black stone wall behind it. Sean's trusty camera and notebook captured it all.

After dinner at Denny's—a serious stray from the Southern meals they'd been having—it was on to Tuskegee, Alabama.

The group arrived at the Tuskegee University Kellogg Conference Center at midnight. As they walked into the lobby, Sean was amazed by the inside of the on-campus hotel. It looked like a luxury hotel, with crystal chandeliers, red carpet that looked like velvet with gold threads for trim, elegantly draped windows, and golden elevators. Old-fashioned paintings of vases and flowers decorated the walls. *Booker T. Washington had class!*

"Man! I've almost had enough of this walking all day long," James complained, plopping on the bed.

"You need the walk, as much as you've eaten on this trip," Sean cracked.

"Shut up, I didn't eat that much," James shot back.

"Um—is it me or was James the guy who had to unbutton his pants at Swett's, Aaron?"

"Sean does have a point. And then you kept farting in your sleep when we got back to the hotel," Aaron said.

"Forget y'all," James said, putting his face in the pillow.

A sudden knock at the door made everyone's head turn. When Sean answered the door, no one was there and the hallway was empty. As he closed the door, the hotel phone rang.

James, answered it.

"What's your favorite scary movie?" the wavering voice asked.

"Your mama in a thong," James replied before hanging up. "I swear people play too much."

"James you do the same thing," Martez said. "What about that time in English class you kept calling the main office and pretended to be someone's mother?"

"Man! Forget you, too," James said, throwing the other pillow at him.

Sean grabbed a towel from the closet and headed for the bathroom.

"Hey, no whacking off in the bathroom," Aaron said.

"If anything, I'll think about your sister while I'm doing it," Sean said, running into the bathroom as Aaron came after him.

"That was a cheap shot," Aaron yelled from the other side of the door.

"Sure was." Sean turned on the water. If Aaron weren't his friend, he would have broken open the door, and beat him down.

"All right I'm out," Sean said, trying to keep his towel in place with one hand and his clothes in his other hand. As Sean laid his clothes on the bed, he heard someone putting a key card in the door.

"Room checks," Sean said automatically.

Major problem for nearly naked guys. Sean quickly dropped his things including his towel and reached the pillow.

"Scholars, we have to do room check," Ms. Stanton said. "Sean, put some clothes on." She covered her eyes.

"Yes, Ma'am," he said, slipping on his blue-striped Calvin Klein pajama pants, bouncing on one leg afraid that the pillow would drop. Thank God for fast reflexes, or Ms. Stanton would've seen a side of Sean she didn't need to see.

"I'm making sure everyone is here because one of the slick scholars just got caught in a girls' room. He's on his way home." She checked her list, looked around the room, in the closet, the bathroom, and under the bed. "Thank you, and Sean, keep that pillow for yourself. No one's head but yours should touch that pillow," she said as she walked out.

"Yes, Ma'am," Sean said turning the pillowcase inside out.

Sean dropped onto to the bed and smiled. Hey! Two nights in a bed! Things were looking up.

Chapter 27

Sean awoke refreshed, for the first time on the trip and got in the shower *before* everyone else. This time *he* used up all of the hot water. *Payback!*

As Sean toweled off, he glanced at the sink and spotted a large can of shaving cream. Sean raised an eyebrow as he looked into the mirror, then silently crept out of the bathroom, can in hand. He grinned at his roommates who were still sleeping. James' mouth hung open. *Tempting!*

Moments later, Sean put James' shoes and pants back in their original spot and scurried into the bathroom. He went straight to his bag, pulled out a toothbrush, toothpaste, and his deodorant that claimed to be *so effective you could skip a day*. Hmmm, nice idea, but Sean wouldn't dream of skipping a day. There were already a couple of people on the bus trying that, but they obviously weren't using the right stuff.

James, Aaron, and Martez woke up and began arguing, each blaming the others for the white foam on their faces. Lorenzo had already left the room before they woke up. Luckily for him he was out of the line of fire.

Sean dressed quickly, crept quietly to the front of the room, and took a seat close to the door.

James got in the shower and reacted immediately. "Aw naw!"

Sean took out one of his magazines and began reading, but couldn't focus on a thing.

Martez, who was brushing his teeth, turned around and looked at Sean. "Why are you so quiet over there?" he asked through his toothpaste-filled mouth.

"I'm reading," Sean replied, trying hard to keep a straight face.

His eyes narrowed. "But you usually *talk* when you read."

Sean shrugged. "There's no one to talk to."

James stepped out of the bathroom steaming mad, or, more accurately, chilled and mad. *I should've put shaving cream on their toothbrushes, too. But that would be too much.*

As the three young men started to get dressed, they paused, one by one. Deafening silence filled the room.

The hair on Sean's arms stood on end.

The three boys looked at each other, then at Sean.

He dropped the magazine, jumped up and was out of the room in three seconds flat.

He made it halfway down the hall—free and clear—before a thought stopped him in his tracks. He forgot his book bag!

Running back to the room, he mumbled. "I'm going to kill them if they put anything in my bag." He couldn't even think about having to replace his iPod and notebook, let alone his homework and college tour notes. That was money and a grade. Mr. Rinauld didn't accept excuses. You either had it or you didn't.

Sean pressed an ear to the door. Not a sound came from the other side. He swiped the key card and slowly opened the door. As he poked his head inside, pillows and shaving cream came from all sides. Sean had gotten his revenge. Now it was their turn.

Revenge: a cycle that never ends; and no one ever wins.

When it was time to leave, Sean was the only one who was dressed. He had left the door open when he returned, hoping to grab his bag and jet.

Some of the girls were walking past and saw everything—well not *everything*. Aaron was finally smart enough to put a sheet up to his naked behind, but one of the giggling girls was sure to have seen something.

Sean walked to the doorway, looked out, and slammed the door. "Clean up, and hurry!" He scrambled to straighten up the room.

"Why?" Aaron asked.

"Mr. Jones is coming."

Those four words made them move. Clothes flew through the air like fighter jets. Sean stuffed a few things under the bed. Aaron kicked things into the bathroom. Straightening up the beds took the longest.

The guys held their breath as Mr. Jones walked into the room. He was a nice guy, and often joked with the scholars. He also had a lot of wisdom to offer. But he wasn't someone to fool with if you were doing something wrong.

"What's going on in here?" he asked in a tone that could start an earthquake.

"Nothing, Dean Jones," they said in unison, fake smiles pasted on their faces.

Mr. Jones glanced around the room, which appeared spotless. Luckily, he couldn't see the clothes stuffed under the bed, or the shaving cream-soaked towel, or inside Sean's possibly devastated book bag. He looked at each of them suspiciously. It was almost time to go and they still weren't ready.

"Okay, I'm trusting your *word.*" Mr. Jones scanned the room one last time before leaving.

As the door closed, the guys released a collective sigh of relief. Sean plopped on the bed. James slumped to the floor. Aaron dropped the sheet.

"Hey, cover that up!" Sean, James, and Martez all said, turning away.

"Don't hate me," Aaron replied on his way to the bathroom. Unfortunately, he didn't cover his backside. That wasn't something Sean wanted to see, either.

It was still early, but the sun already occupied the middle of the sky; Sean walked out of the glass front door toward the bus. The drivers, Mr. Mack and Mr. Murray, must've woken up early. They were already standing by the bus, stretching and fixing their matching black leather vests. Sean put some of his things on the bus, took out his phone, and dialed his mother's number at work.

"This is Cynthia Morris. How may I help you?"

"Hey, Ma, what's up?"

"Nothing, I'm not feeling so good," she said, sounding tired.

"What's wrong?" Sean asked. If he were in town, he would be at her job in a minute to help.

"You don't want to know," she said wearily.

"Mom!" He knew what that meant. Forget about Sean's offer to help—

she needed Jesus and all twelve of his homeboys. Sean checked his calendar on his phone. "You're a week late."

"How do you know?" she asked.

Sean could hear her keyboard go silent in the background. "I still keep tabs on you. You aren't—pregnant are you?" Sean asked, afraid of the answer.

"Boy, quit getting in grown folks' business. No, boy, get off this phone. I have to get back to work," she said, laughing as she hung up.

Maybe Momma and that recruiter guy she kept in the background were finally... Nah!

Sean chuckled and looked at his papers. The itinerary said they would be walking another campus today. Sean knew that meant the *entire* campus.

There was something strange about Tuskegee University. No one was outside. At ten in the morning, it should have been busy. He made his way back to his group. Someone from the school had joined them.

"Good morning. I'm Mr. Hoover from the admissions office and I'll be showing you around today," he said, putting on a hat to shade his face from the sun. No jacket for this guy. It was hot enough to grill a burger on the sidewalk.

The group fell in line behind him. The first stop was The Airplane, a replica symbolizing the airplane of the famed Tuskegee Airmen. They overcame racial boundaries and fulfilled their dreams by getting a chance to fly.

Mr. Hoover gave the group information on each of buildings, along with the school's requirements. Their next stop was the Tuskegee University Chapel, a tall, dark-orange, brick building that had no right angles. Inside, it was dim and...like the ghost town campus...empty.

As they were walking out of the chapel, his phone vibrated. Putting in the earpiece, he looked at the caller ID.

"Hello," he whispered.

"How come you haven't called me to let me know how you're doing?" Rachel yelled at him.

"I've been coming in late," Sean said, covering his mouth. "Ms. Stanton's been keeping us so busy, I'm exhausted when we get back to the room. I don't call anybody. Not even God. He knows how tired I am."

"Well, *Joann's* been calling me, telling me that you've been talking to these college girls. What's that about?"

Sean tried to act like the call didn't bother him. "Of course I'm talking to the girls," he responded, his voice rising. "I'm speaking to the guys, too. How else am I supposed to get real info on the schools? If you want to find out if I'm cheating on you, find some other source. Because in case you haven't noticed, *Joann* has a crush on me, and on top of that *you and I* are separated anyway." Sean hung up the phone.

"Hey, what's wrong with you, Superboy?" Aaron asked.

"Rachel just called me with some mess about Joann telling her that I was talking with some college girls," Sean hissed, keeping his voice low. "I could strangle that girl."

"Alright, man, calm down. You're scaring me," Aaron said as he took a step back. "Of course you were talking to girls, but as long as it wasn't serious, then it's cool."

"Try telling that to Rachel." Sean flashed back to Colleen's beautiful face. "Why would I get serious with a college girl, especially if it's a college I'm not sure I'm going to attend?" His phone vibrated again. "It's my mother."

Aaron stepped away and Sean put his earpiece in. "Hey, Momma," he said, quickly calming down.

"Hey, I'm on my lunch break," she said. "Sean, what's wrong? You sound like me." Concern crept into her soft voice.

"Rachel—Rachel is getting on my nerves."

"Boy, you're too young to say anything about somebody get on *your* nerves." She chuckled. She always knew how to make Sean smile, even when he didn't want to.

"I don't think this thing with Rachel and me is going to work," Sean said, disappointed as he remembered how much he liked Rachel in the beginning..

"Well, as much as I don't like that girl with her fast tail, it's up to you to decide whether she's right in your life. There are a lot of things you have to decide on your own. That's all a part of being a man."

She was going to tell him how a man should grow up? But, then again, she *had* been mother and father ever since he was born, so maybe that did count for something. "Thanks, Momma."

Aaron punched him in the arm to get his attention. They were falling behind the rest of the group.

"Oh, you're welcome. So, how's the college tour going?" she asked, sounding like she was struggling with the phone.

"Good. Right now we're touring Tuskegee University, walking toward the cemetery."

"You *learning* anything?" He didn't miss her sarcastic tone.

"Of course, Mom, I'll tell you all about it when I get home." Sean tried to shade his neck from the sun with his notebook. Boy, was it hot.

"Are you taking good pictures?"

"Momma, I got things covered over here." Falling a couple of steps behind the group, he realized he was missing what Mr. Hoover was saying. He'd have to get notes from Aaron later.

"Good, I want to see them."

"I know, Mom. I have to go," he said, even though he didn't want to end the call.

"Okay, I'll talk to you later. Love you."

"Love you, too. Bye."

Superwoman knew just what to say to comfort him when he was feeling down. She was nothing like the woman he remembered five years ago. Running away from home, butt naked was a thing of the past. Although with Mr. Collins still lurking around, he knew that he might not have a choice in his exit if he screwed up again. *Talk about motivation!*

Sean felt like the negativity Rachel tried to bring in his life was lifted, and it was all because he was making better choices.

The group came to a complete stop at Booker T. Washington's grave and monument, a sculpture of him called "Lifting the Veil," stood out among the other graves. He was the man who founded the institution in order to promote and improve Blacks' education.

When the students visited the George Washington Carver Museum, Sean found out that the faculty member's inventions went far beyond three-hundred uses for peanuts. He also created car paints. Almost everyone driving a car these days should be grateful to George Washington Carver. If not for him, all cars would be black.

Sean turned to the corner of the room and saw Aaron talking to Jeanette. But it didn't look like he was telling her to get lost. They both were laughing. Maybe a friendship would work between them.

Tired from all the walking, the scholars were grateful for the lunch stop. As they neared the cafeteria, Sean heard rap music. The closer they got, the louder it got.

His jaw dropped and eyes widened when he saw a little party going on in front of the cafeteria. There was a DJ and a wild crowd. Everybody was dancing to Sean Paul's "Get Busy." Back in Chicago, people usually waited until night to have a party. This was definitely something new. College would certainly make up for all the parties he missed in high school.

Vince caught up to Sean and grabbed his shoulder, his locks hanging loose. "This is what I want to do when I get to college."

"What, party? You can do that at home."

Vince pointed to the man in a little glass booth. "No, man, I want to be the DJ."

"But you don't have any rhythm."

"Man! I have more rhythm than…the Jackson 5," Vince said, throwing a little spin movement at Sean.

"Yeah—you couldn't touch 'em on their worst day."

The group passed the party and went through the double doors of the old castle-like building. Sean got in line, picked up a plate with two slices of pizza, another full of fries, and a bottle of juice. He sat by himself, since he didn't see any of the smart-guy group. They were probably trying to make time with some of the women.

Sean pulled out his iPod and selected Andre 3000's song "Hey Ya" out of the song bank. He was eating in peace, until one of the guys from the white T-shirt crew threw a piece of ice at his head.

Sean ignored them.

He tossed another one, and Sean glared at them, but still didn't say anything. Maybe they didn't like him because either he wasn't as lame as they were or didn't have a name-brand plain white T-shirt. Sean bet it was both. He got up and moved to another table. The best revenge was success, and since some of them weren't doing so hot in school he'd sail right past them where it counted.

Revenge came sooner than planned. A college girl had seen the whole thing. The T-shirt crew had been eye-balling her ever since she came in. She strutted past them in her red, form-fitting, Delta Sigma Theta sorority skirt, and went straight over to Sean.

His mind was going in every direction but the *right* one. She swished her rear-end over to the table, pulling back her neatly braided hair. Sean whipped his book bag over his lap, asking God to help him get through this.

"Are you okay?" the girl asked, sitting down slowly and crossing her long, shapely legs.

"Yeah, I'm fine," he replied, smiling from ear to ear as the T-shirt crew watched and pointed.

"That was wrong, what they did to you. You look like a *nice* guy." She inched closer. Her voice sounded sweet and seductive.

He inched away from her, because of Rachel and her tell-all friend. "Thanks—and your name is?" He glanced at the T-shirt crew, who stared back at him, whispering to each other.

"Crystal Pryce. And yours?" she asked, scooting closer.

Sean was unable to back away any further. One more inch and he would be on the floor. "Sean Morris."

"Well, Sean, do you want to come outside and dance with me?" she asked in that same soft, seductive voice.

He couldn't say no. How did women always have a way of getting what they wanted? "Sure," he said, gathering his things. *What's one or two songs. About six minutes, right?*

Crystal put on a show with Sean, while the other guys stared. She showed them that they couldn't have her. If anyone was taking notes, Sean would receive the Oscar for best supporting actor. They both threw sly glances in the T-shirt crew's direction. They walked out of the cafeteria arm-in-arm. Sean was pleased to notice the white-T crew's jaws practically touching the floor.

Sean looked at his shirt, then theirs, then back at his and smiled. The message was clear—it's not the shirt, it's the *man* in the shirt. If steam could have come out of their ears, it would have. They were pissed.

After dancing to six songs in a row, Sean's legs were ready to give out. He moved closer to Crystal, whispering. "You want go sit by the courtyard?"

"Sure," she said, looking as if she thought he'd never ask.

Sean took her by the hand and strolled along the pathway to a metal structure in the middle of the courtyard.

Rachel? Rachel could take a walk. She needed an attitude adjustment. On the other hand, Crystal, mature, sexy—college girls were the…well *you know*.

"Whew, those guys were kind of mad."

"Mad ain't even describing it," Sean said, glancing back one more time, as they walked on the grass. "Those guys think they can always get the girl."

Crystal stopped, putting her hands on her hips. "I hope this isn't a bet."

"Why would you think that?" Sean asked.

"Well, I know how sometimes people will do anything to fit in."

Sean knew that while many women are up for a challenge, none liked to be the object of a bet. Crystal's words had him thinking about the time he was nine years old and his mother had taught him that lesson.

He had been dreamy-eyed over a neighborhood girl, Karen. His friend Lamar had bet him a dollar that he would be too chicken to touch her butt. Sean proved him wrong, but the reaction was unexpected.

Karen grabbed him around the neck, punched him in the nose, then ran and told her mom, who told Sean's mother.

Sean had to apologize and was humiliated that his nose was swollen to the size of a toucan beak. It was a hard lesson. Took his nose two weeks to get back to normal.

"This *is* a bet, isn't it?" Crystal repeated, disappointment in her voice.

Sean snapped out of his daydream. "No, it isn't. Having learned from experience, I never bet on anything when it comes to girls. Anyway, why would I bet on someone like you? You're too good for that."

"Aw, that's sweet," she said, kissing him on the cheek. "Even if you don't come here, I still want to keep in touch with you."

Sean glanced at her bashfully, tucking his lips in to keep his smile from stretching to his ears.

He could tell that this girl was from the South, with her incredible hospitality; she was definitely not a city girl, and definitely not the type to pull an easy trick on. Most of Sean's teachers were Deltas, even Ms. Stanton. And all of them followed the stereotype of being smart businesswomen.

Sean's group was leaving the cafeteria, headed in the direction of Booker T. Washington's house for the Oak tour.

"I think it's time for me to go," he said, not really wanting to leave. "But I have a question. Why is it so important to go away to college?"

She thought about her answer and said, "It's mainly for the experience of being away from home, being somewhat on your own, but still having people to look out for you. And you get to meet people from all over the world."

"Like a beautiful woman like you," Sean said.

"Yeah, and since you're leaving me, take my number down," she told him.

He pulled his cell phone from its clip and punched in the number. Boy, he had collected more numbers on this trip than he had all year in Chicago.

She also gave him her e-mail address. "Be sure to call me if you don't see me later," Crystal said, hugging him, as if she'd never see him again. The warmth of her slender body and the scent of watermelon-kiwi body spray washed over Sean. Forget Rachel and her big ugly attitude. Sean would take a hug from a beautiful college girl any day.

"Okay, I'll do that. Bye," he said, running to catch up with his friends.

"Man! Don't run up like that," Vince said.

"My bad." Sean stepped back cautiously. "Why are you so jumpy?"

"I'm not, I just don't like any sudden movements," Vince explained. "Why are you so happy?"

"Boy! I just met this beautiful Delta named Crystal, and she knows how to make a guy jealous. Man, she made the white-shirts feel like gum on the bottom of my shoe."

"What happened?" Vince asked.

Sean explained, with a few exaggerations.

All Vince could do was laugh. "Man! I knew there was another reason I wanted to marry a Delta."

"What were the first reasons?" Sean asked.

"They're highly intelligent—"

"So are AKAs, Zeta Phi Beta, and those women in Sigma Gamma Rho," Sean pointed out. "My aunt's an AKA, and Celie is a Sigma."

"I know, and I'm not done," he said. "I want to be a member of Omega Psi Phi, and my mom is a Delta, so if I bring in anyone else, I'm dead." Vince lowered his head.

"Say no more, man." Sean patted Vince on the shoulder. "My aunt said the same about AKAs. I can't date and possibly marry anyone but an AKA. She'd probably get mad about the connection I just made with Crystal."

Sean loved all the sororities and he didn't want to be limited, but what that Crystal *did*, all while able to remain ladylike? The white-shirts had mud on their faces.

Score one for the smart-guy group!

They passed through a tall, black gate and walked across the street to Booker T. Washington's house. Sean was excited about visiting the home of one of the greatest African-American activists and educators who ever lived. Washington had also been the first principal of Tuskegee Institute. Everything was the same as it was when he was alive. The institute took great pride in maintaining the well-kept, historical house. There wasn't a single speck of dust on anything.

When Sean walked out of the house, he noticed that the sky was about two shades from dark. As they were walking past the cafeteria, Crystal was coming up the hill.

"So, where are you headed now?" she asked, as Sean helped her up the last few steps.

"Atlanta," Sean replied as she walked with him to the bus. "We're going to see some of the colleges down there."

"Hey, remember, even if you don't come here, I still want you to keep in touch with me," she said, stopping on the side of the bus. "Let me know how you're doing."

"I'll do that." He stood in front of her, sadness showing on his face because he had to leave. Then she leaned over and kissed him on the cheek. That made him smile.

As he stepped back to let her pass, Joann glared at him through the bus window. She was talking on her cell phone, more than likely to Rachel. But he wasn't worried. He had already decided to break it off with Rachel for good, the next time she called.

Sean watched Crystal's every move before boarding the bus. On the way back to his seat, he glanced at Joann. She eye-balled him right back, with her mean mug, topped with a uni-brow, light mustache, and an old brown gel-covered blue scarf. No wonder people called her "The Man." Plus she was always up in everyone else's business like a grumpy old woman. Didn't take much to figure out why she couldn't keep a boyfriend. As soon as he sat down, the phone in his pocket vibrated. He looked at the display and grimaced. *Rachel.*

He went into the bathroom to take the call. Sean took a long, slow breath before answering the phone. "Hello," he said calmly.

"Why—why are you letting these college heifers kiss all over you?" she asked. "I've always been faithful to you. What in the world would possess you to cheat on me?"

"Because I know some things about you. Things that I didn't *want* to find out. Things that my friends have been trying to tell me but I've been too stubborn to hear. Besides that, we're separated, so why are you trip-ping," Sean said quietly.

"What do you know about me?" she snapped. "You don't know jack about me!"

"I know that you're sleeping with your sister's boyfriend and that you were still trying to get with Vince. Stupid move since he's my boy, but what could I expect?"

The silence between them stretched out. The bus lurched forward, caus-ing Sean to hold onto the handle by the door.

"Who told you that?" she asked in a deadly tone.

"Vince and Curtis and, oh yeah, your brother Clifton," Sean answered dryly. "I'm ending this conversation now, and I'm pretty sure you know my decision." Sean disconnected the call and stepped out of the restroom.

He slipped into his seat next to the window and turned on his iPod. A song by the Ohio Players came through the headphones, "I Wanna Be Free." Sean immediately thought about Crystal, and began humming the song. He smiled as his mother's words popped in his head: *You'll find the right one. A smart one with her head on straight.*

"Man, if you were in there any longer, Mr. Mack would've thought you were trying to blow up the place," Aaron said, scooting over. "What's wrong, Superboy?"

"It's totally over between Rachel and me," Sean said.

"Oh, we knew that when you first started dating her," Aaron said.

"I just can't believe I wasted my time and my money on that relationship." Sean shook his head. "Trips to the movies, Cheesecake Factory, Navy Pier, the mall, and not to mention, that play—it cost me almost thirty-two dollars a ticket."

"Sean, stop, don't worry. I'll spot you a dollar, when you're down, but you're only making yourself angrier. Besides, you can't be mad right now because we're going to A-town, party city, Hotlanta—Atlanta, Georgia."

"Guess you're right. So what was up with you and Jeanette?"

"She's not as bad as she seems. We talked, and I'm going to give her a chance."

"What!" Sean said, eyes wide with surprise.

Aaron grinned. "I told her that I would go on a date with her. If it goes good I'd take her on another. She said she would stop following me, because she'd only been doing it to get my attention."

"It got everybody's attention, but at least you're trying something new." Sean shook Aaron's hand. "I'm proud of you, son."

"Whatever, man," Aaron said, pushing him away. "You're a fool."

One relationship ends, another begins.

At about three o' clock in the morning the bus ran over a speed bump turning into the parking lot of the Fairfield Inn. Sean's head thumped against the window, waking him.

Sean opened the door to his group's room and unloaded his things. He laid out his clothes for the next day, not really caring whether Aaron and James wanted more revenge. Sean undressed in the bathroom and collapsed on the bed. He was so tired he didn't care if he slept in a bed with someone else, as long as nothing happened to him while he slept. Morning would be ugly if it did!

Chapter 28

Sean woke up early, feeling refreshed and much better than the day before. Even though he had dealt with Rachel, he found he was still thinking about her. He did what most men did to relieve the stress—work out.

One-hundred pushups, one-hundred sit-ups, and fifty leg-lifts later, the fellas were just waking up.

Sean dashed for the bathroom like an action hero. He took a quick shower, trying to be considerate of the time and everyone else's need to have a little hot water in their lives. Sean's mind was clear; he didn't have to think about class work, Rachel or her snooping friend Joanna. He could concentrate on colleges and more historical sites.

He put on his Roca Wear blue jean shorts and an Adidas T-shirt before stepping onto the balcony. The roof hid the sun, but the smooth concrete balcony in front of him mirrored its rays. He could see the Georgia Dome. The sun added an orange tint to the white building.

The students met downstairs and climbed on the bus to go to Shoney's before heading to the four-college campus. Morris Brown College, Clark Atlanta University, Morehouse College, and Spelman College were all across the yard from each other.

They arrived at the entrance of Clark Atlanta University. Of the four schools in the Atlanta University Center complex, it was the only one that granted graduate degrees. The campus was clean, but the area outside the entrance needed work. Maybe there had been some type of party. The group walked in, explored the campus, and mingled with the students.

When it was time to split, the boys went to Morehouse and the girls went to Spelman because neither college was co-ed. Sean and his group walked into a chapel on the Morehouse grounds. There, a younger man named Joshua Gatlin, talked to them while standing in front of a stage, which held a large organ and an empty pulpit.

Sean was considering Morehouse College because his French teacher at OHMC, Mr. Johnson, was always bragging about his great experiences at the college. Joshua Gatlin, however, did little to keep Morehouse on Sean's prospective college list. Many of the scholars were ready to fall asleep.

"Why couldn't we just put on a disguise and roll with the girls?" James asked.

"Because we'd look like fools, but I'm sure the girls are having a better time than we are," Sean answered quietly.

Evidently, Joshua assumed since the college was well known, he didn't have to say much. But that didn't mean that all the *information* about the place was well known. Sean couldn't wait to get out of there. Sean was considering Morehouse because it was Dr. Martin Luther King Jr.'s alma mater.

The group walked around, looking at the different buildings, finally coming to a huge statue of one the greatest civil rights activists who ever lived. Sean joined James on a nearby bench, took out his camera, and snapped a picture of the tribute to Dr. King.

"What's up, Superboy?" James asked, as he put on his blue South Pole cap to shield his face from the burning sun.

"Nothing much. It's just that we're almost at the end of the tour, and the only school I really like is Fisk. I wanted to go home with at least three schools, so I'd have a choice. I wanted to apply to three so I'd get into at least one of them," Sean said, scanning his itinerary.

"Are they that bad?"

"No, not exactly. Some of them seem to have everything that I want, but man, I felt so *connected* at Fisk. But I can't just apply to one school!" Sean said, looking through his pile of half-filled-out applications. "I guess I'll have to pick some others by comparing the social environments and number of graduates out of the English programs."

"Yeah, well you're not alone. I'm still undecided, and my major is harder to find than yours." They got up to rejoin the group.

"Computer engineering is not that hard to find. I think Tuskegee has it."

"Yeah, but that college might be out of my mom's price range right now. It seems like every year the price is going up."

"With your grades, you should be able to get a full scholarship," Sean said as he pulled out the folder with his transcripts. "OHMC is helping me big time. If it wasn't for being there, I'd be screwed out of going to college."

"All right, guys, keep up," Mr. Jones said. James and Sean quickened their pace to match Mr. Jones' downtown-Chicago stride.

The guys rejoined the girls, and prepared to visit the last college on the tour. Morris Brown stood on the east corner of the campus grounds. The school was steeped in history, but had a new feel to it, like the other three schools in the complex. The students who attended this cluster of schools had come from all over the world, adding even more cultural diversity.

Before Sean knew it, two-thirty p.m. rolled around and his stomach reminded him that it was past his usual lunchtime. They were having lunch at Scholar's Restaurant across the street from the football field. He loved the name. As the group walked to the restaurant, the harmonious sounds of percussion, woodwinds, and brass instruments echoed in the vicinity, lifting Sean's spirits.

As Sean approached the field, the marching band's red and white sweatsuits came into focus. Sean smiled as he noticed how the formations resembled those he had once performed at River North High School.

Sean missed his band days. He missed escaping life through his music. But now his mother's words rang in his head: *Just do things right the first time.* Sean had heard what she said, but he hadn't listened. If he'd done his work, he would've had his saxophone, he would've had his band and he would've had that incredible feeling again of playing in front of a large crowd with people cheering him on.

"Hey, Sean, what's wrong?" Aaron asked, looking out at the field as the band formed a big diamond with smaller ones inside.

"Nothing, man. I just wish I was out there right now." He had missed so much by not doing what he was supposed to do. "It's the greatest feeling in the world to know that you're a big part of why the crowds cheer."

"I know," James said, trying to keep up with the walking pace. "Since our school doesn't have a band, I haven't been able to play the trombone."

"You guys'll be able to play with a band again when you get in college," Aaron said, attempting to put Sean in a headlock, but failing. "Down here, it's about culture, and band *is* culture."

The three walked across the street, up several concrete steps, and into the lobby of a building that housed the restaurant. The lobby area resembled every other college cafeteria from the outside—and smelled like it, too. But when they walked to the end of the hall and through the open double doors, the restaurant had a more elegant look. Purple carpet and tables set European style with white tablecloths and purple cloth napkins set this cafeteria apart from the others they had seen.

Walking past the windows dressed with white sheers, they picked a table close to the buffet line. The smell of fried fish, roast beef, and fried chicken filled the air, sailing straight into Sean's nostrils and making his stomach roar louder than a mountain lion. "Man, that smells good. I'm ready to eat," he said. He'd have dived into the food headfirst if allowed.

"Calm down, Sean," Vince said, walking up to an empty seat. "You'll get a chance to eat."

When Ms. Stanton said they could dig in, Sean was first in line, but waited for the girls to pass.

"What's wrong, boy? You ain't hungry?" one of the boys from the white T-shirt crew asked.

"Ladies first, man."

"That ain't got nothing to do with food."

"It has everything to do with manners. Grow up."

"Fool, get out of my way." The boy tried to push Sean out of the way, but the smart-guy group instantly surrounded Sean.

"Ladies first," Aaron repeated. The rest of the white T-shirt crew was nowhere in sight. The boy huffed, but didn't move.

When the last girl got in line, Sean grabbed a plate, all the other boys crowding behind him like a pack of lions. He moved down the line, stacking the plate with greens, fried chicken, crab cakes, rice, candied sweet potatoes, and crab legs. He walked back to his seat, sat down, and said grace. But before his fork could touch his food, his cell phone vibrated.

He hoped it wasn't Rachel. He whipped out his phone, looked at the caller ID, and smiled—Superwoman. "Hey, Mom," he answered as if he hadn't heard from her in years.

"Hi, Sean," she said bitterly.

Sean put his fork down. "What's wrong, Mom?"

"Boy, you sure do know how to pick 'em!" she snapped. "That girl Rachel has been calling my phone every fifteen minutes and hanging up. I'm about to show that girl a side of me even *I* don't like."

Sooner or later if Rachel didn't stop, Superwoman would turn into *Bat*woman and then they'd all have to leave the planet.

Sean felt a headache coming. "Mom, don't trip. I'll talk to her."

"You've done that, already. I'm going over to her house and show her some *act right.*"

"I'll talk to her again and if that doesn't work, we'll report her to the police," Sean pleaded. If his mother went over Rachel's house and clowned, *she'd* be the one leaving in a police car.

"Well, hopefully you'll get through that thick skull of hers, because in a minute I'll do it and she won't like it, and neither will her mama."

"Okay, Mom." Superwoman meant business. Sean wouldn't mind if she did put Rachel in her place, but it would get ugly and he wanted to avoid ugly at all costs. "Calm down."

His mother inhaled and he could imagine her lifting her arms with every breath in, lowering them as she exhaled out. "So, how's the tour going?"

"It's going good. We're done with the colleges now and we're going to the mountains on Sunday."

"Oh great. Have a good time, and don't forget to bundle up. It might get cold."

Cold? In Atlanta? She was joking!

"And call that she-devil before I get a hold of her."

"Yes, Ma'am," he said, eyes looking up to the heavens for help.

"Well, that's all I wanted to call you about, anyway," she said softly. "So I'll talk to you later."

"Okay, bye." Sean turned his attention back to his plate, noticing the other fellas were sucking up their food like vacuums.

"Who was that?" James asked with a mouthful of food.

"Superwoman," Sean replied, after swallowing a small forkful of wonderful collard greens.

Aaron held out his own forkful of greens, blowing on them to cool them off. Sean could have used some of that air to cool off Superwoman. Rachel had made her hot.

"What did she want?" Aaron asked. "I thought she 'wasn't going to call you anymore' since she was going to be so happy that you're out of the house."

"Rachel's been calling the house and hanging up."

James chuckled, almost choking on his food. "Ooooh, your mom's gonna give her the *act right beatdown*."

"Nope, I'm going to call her in a minute, just before we leave," Sean replied. "Momma won't have to do a thing. Rachel doesn't realize that if Momma can pack my bags and have her own child ready to be shipped out, there's no telling what she'll do to someone else's kid."

Walking out of the restaurant a few minutes later, Sean felt as if his stomach was going to explode. He unbuckled his belt. As they landed on the steps, Sean looked to his right, where some of the other students were holding their stomachs and wobbling like ducks as they walked. Grandma Verna was right. Southern cooking was no joke.

As they waited for the rest of the crew to return from the restroom, one of the boys started a house-music beat with his hands on a garbage can. Four of the boys performed a famous Chicago dance called foot-working, which was similar to break-dancing or ticking, except it involved more leg movements than hand movements. The rest of the group watched them jump in the circle one at a time and dance. Sean got up and walked back into the building. Taking out his cell phone, he dialed Rachel's number.

"What do you want, Sean?" Rachel answered abruptly.

Sean kept his composure. Ms. Stanton always said, "Scholars are never out of line." Rachel sometimes had made him break those boundaries, but not today. "I'm calling to ask you to stop calling my house and hanging up."

"Well, I'm sorry, but I don't know what you're talking about, *Mr. Morris.*"

Sean remained calm. "If I get another phone call from my mother about this, I'll mention it to Ms. Stanton. And that may get you put out of school. But that's the least of your worries, 'cause I'm pretty sure my mom will press charges against you."

A week after they started dating, Sean knew Rachel wasn't right for him. Knowing was one thing, but it didn't help since he was thinking with the wrong head in the first place. She could get any guy she wanted. But her attitude was off—way off. And anyone with a bad attitude, no matter how good they looked on the outside, was ugly from head-to-toe. Sean wondered when a good woman would come his way, one that didn't use her looks or manipulate a guy's mind in order to get what she wanted. One with self-respect. Someone just for him. Someone just a little like…the superwomen in his life.

"Do what you want to do." She slammed down the receiver.

"Thank you, Jesus," Sean sighed, not only because she was out of his life, but also because the conversation could have been much worse. All their other arguments had ended terribly. Once she had actually burned his homework because she thought he was flirting with another girl.

Rachel was in need of Ms. Stanton's Personal Development class, a shrink, and the Lord. That girl needed to reassess herself and become a true scholar. Sean had decided to end things some time ago but he didn't know how to say "it's over." If all of the boys at school who she had slept with admitted it—half of them would raise a hand. And he still stuck by her. Now he felt like such a fool.

Sean went to the phonebook on his cell and erased her number. It wouldn't stop her from calling, but she wasn't his concern anymore. He had college to think about. And college girls. And grades. The three went hand in hand.

He stepped back out to the front of the building as the group lined up to walk back to the bus. The sun rested heavy in the western sky, ready to fall below the horizon and take the daylight.

As they reached the bus, Vince walked up to him. "Ever since you came out of the restaurant, you haven't been talking. What's up?"

"Nothing. It's just time for me to concentrate on my own stuff. It seems like no matter who I let in, they're bound to hurt me," Sean replied, leaning against the bus.

"Well, maybe you're falling for girls who aren't your type and not right for you."

Sean wasn't just talking about girls. His father flashed in his face—a relationship that never really existed. It had been years since he'd heard from Roberto.

"Okay, Scholars, we have some time before we have to leave, so you're free to walk around," Ms. Stanton yelled over the noisy conversations. "But please, *do not* go anywhere alone. I need you all to be back here at half-past six because I have us scheduled to go to a play."

Walking toward the bookstore, Sean and Vince picked up their earlier conversation. "Maybe you're right," Sean said, "but how will I be able to tell who is right? Every girl seems sweet as pie when I first meet her, then she turns as sour as old milk—buttermilk at that." Sean crinkled his nose as he remembered the time he took a swig of the bitter stuff, thinking it was good old vitamin D. He couldn't make it to the sink fast enough.

"It'll get better," Vince assured Sean. "You'll find one, and she'll be good to you, not like that backstabbing Rachel. Did you realize she'd been with almost half the guys at school?"

"Please, don't fill my head up with all that. It just makes me think of how she always told me she was innocent," Sean said. "Boy, she could put on an act."

As they reached the campus store on the corner of the hill, Aaron and James were right behind them. Morehouse and Spelman T-shirts, jerseys, jackets, and other athletic apparel filled the racks. What should he get his mother? He searched through the clothes, while the fellas looked at fraternity and sorority license plates and fitted caps. Then he saw it. A Morehouse shirt with the saying, "Hated by many, respected by all," under a bottle that said Haterade instead of Gatorade. He looked for the right size and bought it for his mother, then waited on the guys, even though they weren't buying anything.

They walked around campus a little more, seeing the tall brick dorms, all the students, and hearing cars blasting their speakers.

"Oh boy, I'm going to get me one of those cars," Aaron said, pointing at an old candy-red, two-door Chevy Impala, with red lights blinking under and inside the car. It also had three TVs, two in the front and one big one in the back.

"And you'll just waste your money, and add another bill to your mom's name," Sean said, nodding his head in time to Ludacris' "Southern Hospitality." "Your job couldn't pay for that."

"Sean, you can't tell me you don't want those sounds." James shoved Sean.

"I'm okay with the sounds, but there's no reason for all those lights."

"Well, we can see why he has those red lights," Vince said. The driver got out of the car with a red and white cane in his hand and blended in with the men of Kappa Alpha Psi and Phi Nu Pi who were doing their stroll.

"I wonder who those guys are," James said, pointing at two groups with jackets they'd never seen before. "Sean, what do their letters say? You're the only one here that knows the Greek alphabet," he said sarcastically.

Straining to see, Sean said, "Alpha Phi Omega and Phi Mu Alpha. *Hmmm*...never heard of them before. Let's go talk to them."

Grabbing Sean by the collar, Aaron said, "No, boy, you don't just walk up on people like that; you have to blend in with the crowd."

"That's nice and all, but everyone over there has jackets with letters and we don't," Sean reminded them.

"I have an idea, let's leave, just to be safe," Vince added. "Y'all must've forgotten this is Atlanta. They get buck down here."

"Stop being wimps. They aren't going to hurt us unless we try to act like we're one of them. And it's in front of the dorm so we have to go back this way anyway." Sean led the way, as the others followed hesitantly.

Although Aaron was right—you can't just walk up to folks—Sean wanted to find out about those organizations. *How would he play it off?* Sean and the fellas posted up on the steps with some of the men. He found himself next to an Asian guy with spiked, black hair and a black Alpha Phi Omega jacket with royal blue letters and the number six on the back.

Hesitantly, Sean asked, "Do you guys have a lot of parties out here?"

The Asian guy looked at Sean for a second, then shrugged. "Sometimes. Let me guess...freshman."

"No. I'm a junior in high school," Sean replied.

"I'm Alex, I go to Clark Atlanta," he said, shaking Sean's hand.

"I'm Sean and that's James, Aaron, and Vince." Sean introduced each person as they waved, trying to look natural. "What is Alpha Phi Omega?"

"It's a National Service Fraternity. We do things like blood drives, AIDS walks, campus clean-up. We basically give service to the nation, community, campus, and the fraternity."

"Oh," Sean said, looking at some of the girls. "If this is a fraternity, then why do the girls have jackets?"

"This is a *co-ed* fraternity. Women and men can become members."

"That's cool, I've never heard of that before—" Before Sean could finish his sentence a tall, dark guy in black dress pants, and a gray polo shirt with a Phi Mu Alpha jacket towered above Sean. "What's up, Alex?" he said in a deep tone.

"What's up, Brent?" Alex asked, shaking his hand. "Oh, this is—I forgot your name."

"Sean, from Chicago," he said, extending his hand.

Brent gripped Sean's hand in his huge one. "Chicago? What are you doing out here?"

"I'm on a college tour with my high school," Sean said, noticing the Kappa playing R. Kelly's "Twista." Finally some Chicago music.

Alex jumped back in the conversation. "Brent here belongs to every fraternity in the parking lot."

"So you're a Nupe *and a* member of Alpha Phi Omega, and Phi Mu Alpha?" Sean asked.

"Yep," Brent said.

"What is Phi Mu Alpha?" Sean asked, looking at his black jacket with red and gold letters.

"It's a music fraternity," Brent said, leaning against the railing.

"Really?" Sean was blown away; he didn't know there was one for music.

"But how are you able to join more than one fraternity?" Sean asked as his interest peaked.

Alex cut in. "These fraternities are not one of the Divine Nine," he said.

"What's the Divine Nine?" Sean asked.

"The five major Black fraternities and the four major Black sororities, like Kappas, Alphas, Omegas, Sigmas, and Iotas, then you have the AKAs, Deltas, Zetas, and S. G. Rho," Brent said.

"So your fraternities allow you to be members of their fraternity or sorority and also be a member of the Divine Nine. But you just can't be an Alpha and a Kappa at the same time?" Sean asked, making sure he understood.

"That's right," Alex replied.

"Hmm, that's interesting," Sean said, checking his watch. "Well, it was nice meeting y'all, but our bus will be leaving us soon and I don't want to get left." Sean shook their hands.

"It's cool. You just make sure you see all you can see at these colleges, and know that they have a fraternity and sorority for everything, even your major," Brent said.

"Okay," Sean said before he and the guys headed back to the group.

The bus took off, but stopped a short distance away as they had reached a side street too narrow for the bus. The rest of the way was on foot. The walk seemed like a five-mile hike. Cars honked behind them because some of the scholars had to walk in the street. They finally reached the theater and grabbed their seats.

The play was ninety minutes. The actors made the play come alive, speaking in '60s slang, calling each other "cat daddy" or "cool moves daddio" and wearing clothes from that time period. Some of the humorous parts probably weren't even in the script, and the actors outdid themselves in a play. Sean enjoyed a good production once in a while, especially if it was one he could picture himself acting in.

The group walked out of the theater, back through the narrow street, laughing and reciting the lines they liked most.

After dinner at Paschal's Restaurant, they finally arrived back at the hotel.

Two boys from the room next door came over and started a pillow fight. Sean sat on the floor and wrote notes about his day as the fight went full force. But when a pillow hit him in the head, he stood. Leslie "Big Fella" Mickel had thrown the pillow.

Sean grabbed a pillow and joined his roommates in attacking Leslie.

The guys from across the hall picked up all two hundred-twelve pounds of Sean, and body slammed him on the bed like WWE Monday night wrestling. Aaron, James, and Martez were next. Leslie was strong and remained unconquered until Vincent tossed a quilt over his head and got him on the back of the head with the pillow. Laughter filled the room.

After beating each other for about thirty minutes they all collapsed on the floor, exhausted, but ready to go on if someone started up again.

The eight guys pooled their money and wound up with around ten dollars, so they ordered the movie *Austin Powers: Goldmember* with Mike Myers and Beyoncé.

Other people decided to get buck wild. The fellas heard a lot of running and giggling in the hallway.

"You guys want to go out there?" Sean asked as he heard the toilet flush. "We can still cancel the movie."

"I'm going to pass. Let them get in trouble," Aaron said, leaning over the bed. James came out the bathroom spraying his travel-sized Lysol can and fanning the smell back into the bathroom.

"James, you want to go out with everybody else?" Sean asked as he held his nose.

"Well, we're going to have to go outside; we need to get a plunger," James said with an embarrassed smile.

"Man! You clogged up the toilet?" Martez complained with great reason. He was in there most of the time. "James, close the door before the smell hangs around."

"Too late, Sosa," Leslie said, as he moved to the other side of the room.

"Sean, you coming?" James asked as he held open the room door.

"I guess," Sean said, putting on his house shoes.

"Wait for me. I want to see what's going on outside," Aaron said, pulling his shorts up from around his thighs.

"Oh, *now* you want go," Sean said.

"Yeah. I wasn't going to go out there by myself, sounds like they're having too much fun." Just as Aaron said that, Sean stepped one foot outside the door and into a puddle.

"What the—" Sean said, looking down at the water.

The laughter gradually became louder, but he couldn't see who it was because it came from around the corner.

"What's wrong? What's the hold-up?" James asked impatiently.

"I don't know. Wait a minute," Sean said, scanning the hallway. He heard quick footsteps, like someone was being chased. A girl screamed and laughed.

As the laughter died down, they all walked around the corner to the elevator. As they waited, Sean heard shoes scrapping the ground. Just as Sean turned around, a girl pelted him with six water balloons as James and Aaron dove out of the way. Standing at the elevator, soaking wet, Sean laughed.

"Don't worry, I'm getting all of you," Sean said as the doors opened and they got in. A beautiful Asian woman, whose name tag read, Karen, was at the desk.

"How may I help you?" she asked, with a light voice.

"May I have a plunger?" James whispered. "And an extra towel for my friend."

"Yes, Sir," Karen whispered. She chuckled as she went to the back room.

"Very funny," Sean said, shivering a little.

"Just here to help," James smiled mockingly.

"Here's your plunger and towel," she said. "Have a nice night."

"Thank you," James said, throwing the white towel at Sean.

Sean thought nothing else could go wrong that night.

He was wrong.

They boarded the elevator, and pressed the third-floor button. Waiting for the door to close, they heard a guy shout, "Hold that elevator, please." A white man and woman entered. Sean scooted over to the other side by Aaron and James. The woman had on a blue, glittery dress and a lot of makeup. Something wasn't quite right. What was a woman doing with an Adam's apple?

The boys stared at her from time to time. The woman finally spoke. "Hey, guys, how are you?" She spoke in a deep, Ving Rhames voice, as the fellas scrunched together in the corner of the elevator. Sean would never be able erase that voice out of his mind.

As soon as the doors opened, they ran off the elevator and all the way to their room without a look back. They rushed in the door out of breath, and flipped the extra lock.

"What's wrong with y'all?" Martez asked.

"A woman who wasn't a woman," James said between gasps.

"What?" Vince asked.

"We saw a drag queen on the elevator," Sean explained.

Silence filled the room, then a burst of laughter. "I hope you guys aren't feeling a little conflicted," Vince said.

"That isn't funny," Aaron said.

"Sit down, the movie is starting," Leslie told the rest of them.

When the movie ended, Leslie and the rest of his people went back to their room. Sean fell asleep and hoped there wouldn't be any more surprises.

Chapter 29

For the first time on the trip, they were allowed to sleep in. Sean woke at three o' clock for lunch, got dressed, and packed. They had a big game to attend—Morehouse College Maroon Tigers versus Clark Atlanta University Panthers.

Sean, the second one to get up and take a shower, didn't have any pranks for anyone. He put on his blue and white Adidas snap jogging pants with a blue T-shirt and sneakers. He retrieved his book bag from under the bed where he had kicked it the night before so no one would step on it. He jogged around the block and took some pictures.

Within an hour, they had all gathered in the hotel lobby, boarded the bus, and driven to IHOP—food of the world.

Sean already knew what he was getting—country fried steak and eggs, which came with three pancakes. He ordered that all the time back home.

"Man, the tour is almost over," Aaron commented, glancing at his itinerary. "How did that happen so fast?"

"I don't know, man, but I'm not ready to go back yet," Vince replied, setting down his menu. "I'm having too much fun."

"And we're learning something," James said, still scanning his menu.

"So, what are your choices for college?" Sean asked.

"Well, I liked Tuskegee and some of the schools here," James replied.

Vince scratched his head. "I'm undecided as far as an HBCU is concerned. I'm also thinking of going to Columbia in Chicago, then transferring to Howard University in D.C."

"There haven't been any schools on this trip that offer my major, so I might apply to the Academy of Arts in San Francisco," Aaron said. "So, what about you, Sean?"

"My choices are Fisk, Alabama A&M, and Tuskegee, in that order," Sean said, reading from his list. "But I don't see how I'm going to get into any of these schools, with my grades from River North and all. I really messed up freshman year and part of my sophomore year, too."

"Isn't there a way you can work it out?" Vince asked.

"Yeah, I have to get straight A's the rest of the semester," Sean replied. "And next year, too."

"We can help you. That's what friends are for," Aaron offered. "It's nice to have people you can count on, because nowadays they're hard to find."

Boy, did Sean know that firsthand.

After the meal, the bus headed for the football field. The students got off the bus and darted for the gate because the game was about to start. Fortunately, Ms. Stanton had their tickets and handed them out at the gate.

Walking into the stadium, Sean could feel the excitement. As the lively Atlanta crowd cheered at the kick-off, Sean searched for a place to sit.

A small section of seats across from Clark Atlanta's marching band was empty. Sean darted over and saved seats for the fellas who were making a trip to the concession stand. *Didn't they just finish eating?* Sean stared, amazed at how many musicians were in the marching band. He didn't even need to see the game; watching them perform made Sean's day. Sean loved football, but couldn't wait until half-time when the bands threw down on the field. The guys found Sean, and Aaron handed him a hotdog.

At the end of the first half, the team headed for the locker rooms. The band had done a great job playing on the sidelines, but now came the big show.

The announcer said, "It's halftime, y'all know what time it is. It's time to hear some *real* music."

Clark Atlanta's band, tall and straight, marched out onto the green field, in perfect time with the drumbeats. The drum majors sounded their whistles and marched to the front. The band began playing the Jackson 5 song, "I Wanna Be Where You Are." As soon as Aaron heard that, he grabbed the hand of the girl standing next to him and started stepping with her.

Superwoman had taught Sean how to do the Chicago-style dance that smoothly blended the two-step with be-bop and a bit of ballroom dancing. Judging by the sulk on the face of the girl to his right, Sean guessed that she wasn't in a dancing mood. The girl didn't crack a smile even when the band played an old classic by Earth, Wind and Fire, "Let's Groove Tonight." Sean danced by himself.

"See, that's why I joined band in the first place," he said to the fellas. "I love music and I want to entertain."

"No doubt! That was cool," Aaron said, still dancing with the girl next to him as the band neared the end of their song.

The sky had turned orange and the hot and humid breeze had been replaced by a cool one by the end of the game. Clark Atlanta's victory party took place after the game and everyone rushed out of the stadium.

The bus took off for the nearby Marta train station. Their next stop was the Underground mall of Atlanta on Alabama Street.

Entering the subway station, Ms. Stanton gathered up money for their transfers. When he stepped on the train, Sean noticed the size, shape, and interior differed from the CTA trains. The train was a little smaller, carpeted, and the ride was a little smoother. No one walked from car to car selling scented oils, CDs, chews, or anything else. Chicago trains were more like a rolling shopping center. People even sold batteries, cameras, and lighters.

They got off the train at the mall stop. When they reached street level, Sean saw a huge marketplace that sold T-shirts and other souvenirs. A short distance away, they went down another flight of stairs and followed signs to the Underground. When they reached the mall area, which was a long, tall tunnel with stores and carts that sold puppets, colored crystals, and jewelry boxes, Sean walked around looking at the souvenirs, trying to decide what to get his mother.

As he reached the end of the mall, Sean approached a small circle of people surrounding someone. It turned out to be Aaron, getting an airbrushed picture of himself. Sean decided to get one, too.

Every few minutes, Sean asked Aaron, "How's it looking?"

"You're looking good," he replied with a sly smile.

The "artist" made Sean look like he had swollen eyebrows, lips twice the normal size and a droopy expression. *Can you say—refund, please?* Other people in the group walked away after taking a look at what the artist did to Sean.

Sean stopped at Footlocker and bought a Tracy McGrady basketball jersey, then walked through the mall and found a cart with Atlanta shirts, hats, and visors. Sean bought two Atlanta T-shirts, one for her and one for him and a hat for her, completing his shopping. The group met at the front of the mall to go to dinner at TGI Friday's. They were straying from the formula. First IHOP and now this? Where was the Southern cooking at a chain restaurant?

When they finished eating, the group headed back to the hotel.

Sean and the fellas entered the room, tired and ready to plop down wherever they could. They all got their church clothes ready for the next day as Ms. Stanton had requested, and went to bed. No pillow fight tonight.

Chapter 30

"Come on, Martez, get out of there already!"

James, banging his fist on the bathroom door and yelling woke Sean. He noticed that Aaron was already dressed in a black pin-striped suit with a white shirt, black and silver-striped tie, and black Stacy Adams dress shoes. Black sunglasses completed his GQ Chicago Style look.

Sean was puzzled for a moment because he had a suit identical to Aaron's laid out to wear. Then he realized that Aaron's jacket was longer. Sean stepped up to the sink and washed up, then got into his suit.

"Just gotta look good as me, huh?" Aaron teased.

"Boy, you couldn't look good as me on my dress-down day," Sean snapped back with a grin.

Luckily, his suit had a black shirt and gold-striped tie, so he and Aaron wouldn't look like twins. Sean added black sunglasses, and he and Aaron stepped out of the room, checking the temperature. A bit warm, but not enough to make him sweat.

They lugged their suitcases toward the bus. Mr. Mack had the storage doors open. In order to speed up the process, Sean and Aaron went to some of the girls' rooms to pick up their luggage. Some of the girls invited them inside.

No can do. If the teachers caught them, they would be sent home on the Greyhound bus and kicked out of school. Neither would be able to handle that. They smiled and kept moving as they took one room's set of bags at a time down to the bus.

The day's activities included a stop at Ebenezer Baptist Church, and visits to Stone Mountain in Georgia and Lookout Mountain in Chattanooga, Tennessee, mountains made famous by Dr. Martin Luther King Jr. in his "I Have a Dream" speech.

The bus parked along the street in front of a tall, chalky-brown brick church. It was triangular in structure, with stained-glass windows. They made their way into the church, walking through the glass double doors. Music from the organ signaled that the service had already started. Taking a seat in one of the maroon pews, Sean glanced at the all-woman choir, wearing black shirts and skirts, singing "Total Praise."

Being in Dr. King's old church was an honor, but Sean was so tired he couldn't appreciate it. And he wasn't the only one. The whole group had trouble staying awake. Some of them, Sean included, dozed off. He jerked awake every few minutes, aware that if Ms. Stanton caught one of them sleeping, they were in for it when they got out of church.

Two hours later, they walked to a yellow and brown house on the corner of the same street.

"Do you all know whose house this is?" Ms. Stanton asked as she stood on the wooden stairs.

"It's Dr. Martin Luther King, Jr.'s house!" Vince said.

"Yes it is."

A couple snapshots later, they boarded the bus and drove toward Stone Mountain. Waking up from a deep sleep, Sean was looking at the tallest mountain he'd ever seen in person.

Sean was still in his church clothes, but had packed a few things for the hike. Dragging his carry-on bag into the bathroom, he changed into gray jogging pants, a black T-shirt, and red and white sneakers. When he came out, most of the group was still asleep. The bus came to an abrupt stop, jerking Sean three steps forward and waking most of the scholars.

Looking up at the mountain as they got off the bus, most of the group appeared discouraged as the mountain looked very steep with the low clouds hiding the top of it.

"The bathrooms are over by the concession stand," Ms. Stanton said. "Please hurry and change and meet back here."

Having already changed, Vince and Sean had a headstart and stared at the mountain. "I really don't think Dr. King climbed that," Vince said.

"If he was able to take on something hard like the racial troubles of the United States, getting rocks thrown at him, and live life like nothing happened, he was able to climb this mountain," Sean replied, wondering what was going on in King's head when he took these steps. He also wondered about more of his own life. It had been an uphill journey, with a few tumbles into valleys, sometimes one right after another. Now it was time to reach the top and stay there.

When the group had reassembled at the bus, Ms. Stanton spoke to the group. "Okay, scholars, for the past seventeen years, the college tour group climbed this mountain, so I don't want to hear any complaining. And I don't want to hear about anyone not going on this hike unless something is broken or falling off. Since I haven't heard anything about that, let's get started."

Taking his first step on the hiking trail, Sean felt raindrops on his head. Thank God he wore his windbreaker. More than one mile, thirty minutes, and a couple stops and slips later, the group finally made it to the top. Stone Mountain was so tall that you could see three different states from the top. He took in the scenery, the sky starting to tinge orange as the sun peeking between the mist began its descent toward the end of the horizon. Rainy clouds slowly broke up, moving along to another area. "Man! I must be out of shape," Aaron puffed as he kneeled to catch his breath. He was closely followed by Vince and James.

"Sean, look," James said.

His gaze turned to where his friend pointed.

"You've got to be kidding me." Sean's eyes widened. There was a cable car on the other side of the mountain. "Why didn't we just take that up here?"

"Guess Ms. Stanton wanted us to have the same experience as Dr. King when he climbed up here," Vince said as he stood up.

"Good job, Scholars. Now, since everyone came all the way to the top, we'll take the Skyride down," she said. They all clapped, celebrating their accomplishment—and the respite for their legs, too. The group strolled over to the Skyride rest area. Sean saw a pay phone and called Superwoman. She didn't pick up, so he left a brief message.

"Hey, Ma, it's Sean and I'm calling from the top of Stone Mountain. It was hard for me to get up here, so I need set up a work-out plan when I get home. It's was raining up here which made it worse, but the scenery is beautiful. Oh yeah, this mountain is the same one Dr. King climbed. I don't see how he did it. Anyway we're about to get on the cable car to go down. So I'll talk to you later. Love you, bye."

The ride down the Skyride was scary because of the rain and lightning, but they made it to ground level safely, boarded the bus, and headed toward their last stop: Lookout Mountain in Chattanooga, Tennessee.

The hour drive to Lookout Mountain seemed like only minutes. This time the group would be taking the Incline Railway both ways. Sean was glad. Hiking another mountain was not in his plans. Boarding the yellow-slanted car, Sean sat in the rear, facing back the way they had come.

Making their way to the top, Sean's eyes widened as he looked out at the city of Chattanooga as the sun still hung in view just above the horizon. Getting off the railway car, Sean saw nothing but mansions and a little village on top of a mountain. When Sean was younger and studying mountains for a report in sixth grade, Superwoman told him that the top of Lookout Mountain was a place where the Ku Klux Klan met. So while he understood the trek up Stone Mountain, he still didn't know why they visited Lookout Mountain. After walking around the top of the mountain, Sean walked back to the Incline Railway. Once at the bus, the group formed a circle to say a prayer for the trip home.

Chapter 31

S ean walked into OHMC at eight o' clock the next morning but wanted to turn around and go back home. The bus had arrived at the school at six, giving him only an hour to sleep before he had to be up and in school. It had felt more like a one-minute nap. Even though he had the diligence of a scholar, he didn't look like one. His eyes were bloodshot, his clothes wrinkled. He didn't even bring his book bag. And Ms. Stanton had nerve enough to be perky and lively. *What was she taking? Why didn't she share it with the class?*

Sean walked up the stairs to his division, which was pretty much like a study hall in the morning. He went in, hung his coat on the hook, and went to his usual seat in the front row. Looking around at the empty room, he wondered if he was going to be the only one from the college tour in school. Just as Sean was about to put his head down on the desk, Mr. Miles walked in with Curtis. Mr. Miles walked up to the desk.

"Mr. Morris, I see you're back from the college tour," he said, his voice echoing in the room. "How was it?"

"It was great. I learned a lot, but I'm tired," Sean said, wiping the crust from the corner of his eyes.

"When did you guys get back?" Curtis asked, sitting next to Sean.

"Six o' clock this morning," Sean said, checking his watch.

"Why did you even come to school?"

"Ms. Stanton told us to come, if we were *real* scholars," Sean explained. He hoped Curtis would shut up and let him get some sleep.

"The real question is, did the college tour help you decide which college you want to attend?" Mr. Miles asked, adjusting his Malcolm X-type glasses.

"It helped me a great deal. I saw a number of colleges I want to apply to like Fisk, Tuskegee, and Alabama A&M."

Students began entering the classroom, some well rested and others looking like they hadn't slept in ages. As they came in, Sean could tell that Aaron, James, and Vince wanted to go home and sleep for a couple of days as badly as he did.

"Man, can you please tell me how I ended up here?" Aaron asked as he took his seat behind Sean.

"You ended up here because you take learning seriously," Vince replied drowsily, slumping into the seat next to Curtis.

"Well, I'm sorry, but I could've held on to the bed a little bit longer, even if it was just five minutes," James said, tossing his book bag in front of the seat next to Aaron.

"Even if it was five more minutes, you still wouldn't want to get up, and would have wanted five more minutes after that," Curtis said, getting up to sign the attendance sheet.

"True, but I needed to come today so I wouldn't miss out on any work," James said, preparing to sign in after Curtis. "You understand more when the teacher explains it than when it comes from another student. Y'all take terrible notes."

"I'm here because I don't need to fall behind again. Playing catch-up is some serious work," Vince said, picking his book bag off the floor.

Sean's smile vanished as he laid his head down on the desk and closed his eyes. He'd been playing catch-up ever since freshman year. Even though he was enthusiastic about being in this school, he knew he still wasn't doing as well as he could in some of his classes. Despite his efforts with his math and test prep homework every night, his grades slipped. Math was his biggest challenge.

Only God and his mother knew his struggle. His mother knew that he could do better than what he was doing. Although his mother would help him do anything, he was too afraid to ask. Even she admitted that she wasn't very patient. He was getting help from the two math whizzes, Ms.

Schulz and Ms. Wallace. But it still seemed that when he went home, he forgot how to follow all the steps to solve a problem, even if he had written it all down. He had problems in other classes, too, but those could be worked out.

"Mr. Morris," Mr. Miles said loudly, "It's time to go to first period." When Sean opened his eyes, they were red and burning.

If Ms. Stanton saw him with his head down, he'd be in big trouble. No one was supposed to sleep in her school. He rushed to Mr. Miles' desk, signed in, then hurried out of the classroom, heading straight for Ms. Schulz's algebra class.

He walked into class and dropped into a seat in the front row with only thirty seconds to spare.

"Okay, take out yesterday's math homework, day seven," Ms. Schulz said, taking a sip of water out of her dark pink mug. "Does anyone have any questions on the homework?"

Hesitantly, Sean raised his hand, "Yes, I have a question on problem number 36a," he said, looking at his syllabus to make sure he was on the right day, especially since he had to do his homework on the trip. Sean always hesitated to raise his hand to ask questions. He worried people would think he was a slow learner. "Would you use the quadratic formula for this kind of problem?"

While Ms. Schulz was working the problem on the blackboard, Aaron walked in the door with a pass from the office. He set it on her desk and signed in.

"What did I miss?" Aaron asked Sean, sitting next to him.

"Nothing much, she's going over the homework from last night," Sean answered, copying notes from the chalkboard.

"Cool. Oh yeah, I saw your ex-girlfriend Rachel. She's taking the break-up pretty hard."

"Yeah, well, she should've never cheated on me. She's been doing it for a while with Clifton and Raymond and Smitty. She's going to end up catching and spreading something," Sean said.

With all the problems Sean was having, he didn't need to have one from Rachel. If they'd had sex and she gave him AIDS, his mother would've strangled him before the disease took his life. God already had a time limit on people's lives. STDs sped up that process, especially in the Black community.

"I understand—"

"Mr. Hester and Mr. Morris, would you like to explain to the class how to do the problem?" Ms. Schulz asked.

"No, Ma'am," they said in unison with small, embarrassed smiles.

"Then pay attention," she said, turning back to the board. "Mr. Morris, you asked me to do this problem, so *you* definitely need to pay attention." Ms. Schulz snapped with a little "Sista Girl" attitude for a White woman. Guess being around all those Black folks could change anyone.

When the class ended, Sean collected his things and started to talk to Aaron.

"Mr. Morris, may I have a word with you?" Ms. Schulz asked. "Mr. Hester can talk to you later."

"Sure."

"We have a serious problem on our hands. You aren't doing as well in this class as you were in the beginning of the semester."

"I know, I've just had a lot of things on my mind," Sean said, lowering his head.

"Well, as we always say, excuses are monuments of nothingness. You have to pick up this grade. Otherwise, I'll have to make a phone call to your mother, and we don't want that to happen."

"No, Ma'am." His packed bags and Job Corps recruiter flashed through his mind.

"We also have to discuss your grades in general," She looked through her notes. "You have two other low grades. What's the problem?"

"I'm having a hard time with this work. It's a struggle not knowing the material you should've learned in eighth grade."

"Well, instead of going straight home after school, why don't you meet me and Ms. Wallace in room 3305 to get help?"

Sean was interested, but had other responsibilities to consider, like pulling his weight around the house. "From what time to what time?"

"Three to five," Ms. Schulz said, pushing her glasses up on her nose.

"I have to check with my mom to see if I can make it tomorrow," Sean said gratefully.

"You do that. Remember, I can only help those who want to be helped."

"Yes, Ms. Schulz, thanks." That's why he loved this school; the teachers and staff were all very caring and willing to work with them, but a scholar had to be willing to help himself.

Aaron had waited outside for him.

"Man, what were you guys talking about?" Aaron asked.

"Even with all the studying and turning in my assignments, I'm still not doing well in some of my classes," Sean said as they walked toward Mr. Green's classroom.

"For real, man? So what are you going to do about it?"

"Anything I need to. I have to bring up my grades. Superwoman isn't playing about shipping me off this time. You're doing well in Ms. Schulz's class, aren't you, Aaron?" Sean asked as Vince and James approached.

"Yeah."

"You think you could help me out with my work?"

"Now, you know I got you," Aaron said, smiling.

Overhearing the conversation, Vince asked, "What do you need help with?"

"Math, test prep, French," Sean admitted, with an insecure smile.

Vince put a hand on his shoulder. "James and I can help you with that, too."

"Every day, starting tomorrow, meet us in the library during your lunch instead of going to the computer lab," James suggested. "We're in there all period."

"Cool, thanks," Sean said. His friends were proving to be exactly that. They had lifted a weight off his shoulders.

Mr. Green came out into the hallway. "Okay, Scholars, time to get to class."

When Sean's last class let out, he went straight downstairs to the first floor, hoping to hit the bus and make it home for a serious snooze. As he walked through the main entrance, he froze. Rachel was outside with her friends. She was perched on the black seat in front of the building. It didn't look like she was taking the break-up hard, but she always put on a show in front of her friends.

Sean pretended not to see her.

When Rachel saw him, she immediately got up and walked over to him, smiling as if nothing was wrong. "Hey, Baby, I haven't seen you all day." She batted her eyelashes. "Where have you been?"

"Maybe I was trying to stay away from you," Sean replied, forcing a smile on his face.

"Why?" she asked, pouting.

"You know why, so don't play stupid. I don't know why I'm even talking to you."

"Because you know that you're not going to give up all of this," Rachel replied, putting a hand on her hip, giving him that sista-girl confident look.

"I don't get you. You cheat on me and then expect me to just forget about it? Act like it never happened? Well, it doesn't work like that!" Sean said. Some students in the crowd looked at them. He lowered his voice. "And I'm not giving up anything important. What you think was *special* for me, you gave to everyone and anyone else. So it was more like the special of the day."

The students started to laugh at Rachel.

"So I'm not *giving up* anything; I'm kicking it to the curb." Walking past Rachel, Sean looked around at the crowd. Their laughter had left Rachel speechless.

When Sean's bus pulled up, he boarded, put his bus pass in the card machine, and moved to the back. He felt better than he had in a long time because he knew he had done the right thing. Sean had learned a valuable lesson. If he was going to have a young lady in his life, she would have to support him, not set him up for failure. She had to know how to be a friend. Sean remembered Mr. Rinauld's advice: "Friends are like elevators, they can either bring you up or bring you down." He realized that a young man had to be selective about his friends because bad habits would rub off.

There would be plenty of time for him to find the right girl. For now, he just wanted to concentrate on doing well in school and getting into college.

Chapter 32

After another week filled with mostly sleepless nights on the floor, Sean finally voiced his opinion about Princeton Park. The neighbors were going at it even more and the gunshots hadn't stopped.

"Mom, I'm not hitting the floor anymore. If it's my time, that bullet's gonna hit me right there on the floor, too. But I'm not sleeping at night, I'm laying awake waiting for the gunfire to start. We can't live like this."

The next day they started packing as she looked for a new place to live. Someone told her about Oglesby Towers; his mother was geeked about moving there. The place was expensive, so they would be moving to a one bedroom and Sean would have the living room for sleeping quarters. He didn't care as long as he *could* sleep and study.

That past Sunday in church Sesvalah had said, "Take God out of the box. You want a Mercedes then look at your paycheck and ask for a Hyundai. You want a mansion but only ask for a two-room shack. The same energy it takes for God to provide you with that Hyundai or that shack is the same energy it takes to give you the Mercedes and the mansion. He will also provide ways for you to keep it."

Did that work for apartments, too? They needed a two bedroom, but could only afford a one.

Sean said to his Mom, "Hey, why don't we start thanking God for our new two-bedroom apartment?"

His mother looked at him like he was crazy at first, but she did it anyway.

On Wednesday, Sean caught the No. 26 bus in front of his school going north on Stony Island Avenue.

He got off at Sixty-Seventh Street and ran for the No. 6 bus as it was about to pull off. The bus driver must've been having a good day because she stopped. It was normal for bus drivers to pull away. They didn't discriminate, either—old, young, Black, White, male, female—it didn't matter, if you weren't at that bus stop, you were out of luck.

"Thank you so much," Sean said, catching his breath and slinging the book bag on his shoulder.

"You're welcome, Honey," the woman said. She looked no more than forty-five, with black and gray hair pulled back into a braided ponytail.

Sean made his way to the back of the bus.

Sean got off twenty minutes later, looking up at the tall, tan brick apartment building with white patios on each floor facing downtown Chicago. He walked up the stairs under the shaded driveway to the glass double doors. Sean stood in the forest-green, marble entrance as the security guard opened the door. Security? Definitely a step up. The lyrics from the Jeffersons' theme song, *Movin' on up to the East Side. To a deluxe apartment in the sky-hi-hi...* rolled through his mind. And if,—no, not if—*when* they got the apartment, that's exactly what would happen.

Sean glanced at the man's nametag—Walter—and noticed he kept smiling like nothing was ever wrong for him. Things were starting to look good already.

"Hey, what can I do for you, Sir?" he asked, letting Sean pass through to the lobby.

"I'm looking for Ms. Fountain so I can take a look at the apartment."

"She's straight to the back." Walter pointed toward the wide window where a lady with light skin and short, golden-brown hair sat behind a desk.

"Thank you, Sir." Sean shook his hand and walked past the three silver elevator doors to her office.

Sean knocked on the door and peeked into the open office. "Come in." Ms. Fountain looked up and smiled. "You must be Sean Morris," she said as she took off her bifocals and put them on the desk.

"Yes, Ma'am," he said, shaking her hand. He detected a whiff of cigarette smoke, but this lady didn't look like she smoked.

"It so nice to meet you. Cynthia has told me so much about you." She rose and grabbed her keys. "Let's go look at the empty apartments." Ms. Fountain couldn't stop smiling. Guess she knew she had a certain sale.

They walked into the lobby and waited for the elevator. Sean knew that's what his mother wanted—the perfect view and she loved water.

"So how do you like them so far?" She asked thirty minutes later, analyzing his facial expression, which probably showed that he wasn't impressed.

"They were okay, but I didn't really like them," Sean said as they walked to the elevator. They were studios and one-bedrooms. No place for him in either spot. Sofa beds were fine for guests, but a nice solid bed to stretch out in was the best.

"I'll show you one more; I'm sure you'll like this one," she said as they got on the elevator. Sean wondered how she could be so sure.

She was right. It had the perfect view: the Chicago skyline and Lake Michigan, which looked cleaner and calmer than usual. The apartment also had a patio so Sean would be able to feel the Eastside breeze. Sean was afraid of heights but the patio had high railings. He knew the view would be incredible at nighttime.

Sean walked through the rest of the apartment by himself as Ms. Fountain allowed him to take in the feel of the rooms.

The walls were white and carpet was brown. Cynthia didn't like carpet but she was going to have to make an exception. The living room was connected to the dining room; both were very spacious. The kitchen area was small, but well equipped with Sean's favorite appliance—the dishwasher. It nearly brought him to tears. In his previous residences, *he* was Kenmore.

He walked into the first bedroom. It was airy with two huge closets and windows that would allow the rising sun to shine in. "This is my room," Sean claimed, imagining what he could do to it.

Two long hallway closets were big enough to store anything, like eight of those big Rubbermaid storage bins. The bathroom had brown ceramic tile, a tan bathtub, and sink. It wasn't his favorite color, but Sean could live with it. Then he entered the master bedroom, which of course, would be Cynthia's room. It had closet space fit for a woman, and enough room for her king-size, Palladian bed and frame. She even had her own bathroom, with seafoam-green ceramic tile. Overall, Sean loved the apartment and the area. They *had* to get this apartment.

Sean walked back to "his room" and whispered, "God, I'd like to move in this Saturday. We have all of our stuff packed. It's getting warmer and the gunshots are getting closer and closer to our house. My mother's already been through a lot, and she hasn't asked for much. So please, give her this, for me. Please…"

When they went back to the office, Ms. Fountain called his mother.

"You know, I was thinking, I know your income qualified you for a one bedroom, but a two bedroom just became available. We'll work out something. If you want it, it's yours."

Princeton Park let them out of their lease by backdating a letter for thirty days so that Cynthia could get her security deposit right away. This was Wednesday, three days after Sesvalah's sermon about taking "God out of the box."

His godmother pitched in and they lined up the movers. Then they found out they couldn't move in until a week later because the elevators would be tied up with two move-ins that Saturday.

Sean sent up another prayer. Thursday Ms. Fountain called and said one of the move-ins had canceled. Sean and Superwoman moved into the two-bedroom apartment with a view and a patio that very weekend.

Maybe he should take "God out of the box" again so he could help with school. And maybe it would help him get to college, too. Sean began to say a prayer every day. "Thank you, Lord, for expanding my ability to grow and understand. School isn't easy for me and you will send me people to help me and to guide me."

A year later, he was a senior, and Sean was getting closer to his last days at OHMC. Through prayer and meditation, and his affirmations of "Thank you, God, for my great year and keeping me healthy and wealthy," and "Thank you, God, that all my college costs are paid in full at little or no costs to me or my mother," had brought astounding results.

Even though he had done poorly his freshman year, it didn't seem to matter. His drastic turnaround at OHMC, going from a C student to mostly A's and B's, proved he had changed and was worthy of a spot in college.

He had also written a short story for English that was so good Ms. Stanton submitted it to a small publishing house in Chicago, and they wanted to publish his book. Every one of his teachers, including science, math and history teachers, took out their pens and became editors. He would write a chapter and submit it to them. Not only would they edit it, but they'd give him a grade. How cool was that?

When he submitted his application and a copy of his book of short stories to Fisk and Alabama A&M, he was accepted at both places.

Fisk offered a great scholarship and that—along with the fact that he loved the place—was the deciding factor. Cynthia was trying not to let it go to her head, but she bragged. And when she bragged—she bragged to everyone, anywhere—work, the beauty salon, grocery store, it didn't matter. "My baby's going to college." She did the same little dance he had done with his grandma—hip movements and everything.

Chapter 33

Senior prom night! He rushed into his room, took off his clothes, and paused to gaze at the picture of his girlfriend, Elise.

Sean would never forget how they met when he was a junior, and not just because his mother wouldn't let him. It was more than a year ago, during one of the most stressful but rewarding times in his life. When he was a junior, he enrolled in the Chicago Urban League's youth program to learn about stocks, managing corporate finances, and being an entrepreneur.

One spring day, Sean arrived at the Chicago Urban League's building so early the place was practically empty—except for Mrs. Jiles. She was a sweet woman who loved helping students with problems, but anyone caught talking while she was trying to teach, was in for a wake-up call.

"Good morning, Mrs. Jiles," Sean said.

She slid the sign-in sheet his way. "Well, hello, Mr. Morris. How are you doing this morning?"

"I'm doing all right, but I still can't get used to waking up this early, especially on a Saturday," he said, yawning, to make his point.

"I have to get up even earlier to be here in time to let you guys in."

"Yeah, but you should be used to it by now, right?"

She shrugged. "You'd think so, but I'm still having a hard time. I made a commitment, though, so I'll do what I have to do."

"Yeah, I guess I made the same commitment," he said dryly, wishing he were home, curled up in his bed.

Sean walked through the cramped computer lab and found his assigned station. The only other students in the lab so far were his teammates,

Deandrew Johnson and a girl they called AJ. Originally, the students were in four-member teams, but as the demands of the class became more complicated, some of them dropped out, including one in Sean's group.

"What's up, guys?" Sean asked, taking a seat next to them.

"Nothing much, just checking my e-mail before we start class," Deandrew said, clicking away on the keyboard.

"I'm trying to figure out what questions we're going to ask for our survey," AJ said, as she scrawled some ideas in her spiral notebook.

"I'll help you with that in a minute." Sean logged onto his computer.

AJ was playful, but knew how to get serious when it was time to work. She had a great personality and was quick to smile.

As Sean settled in to get to work, another classmate, Satara, walked up. The first time Sean heard Satara speak, he laughed. She sounded like a six-year-old with her high-pitched, happy voice.

"What's happening?" she asked, leaning on his desk. "Can I speak with you for a minute?"

They walked over to her station in the corner of the room where it was relatively quiet. "Would you take one of my friends to prom?"

Sean shrugged. "Who is she?"

"Elise. She doesn't want to go to prom, but I want her to go, so I'm asking if you would take her."

"Why me?" Sean asked, folding his arms across his chest.

"Because you're respectful, handsome, and you're different from other guys; you make people laugh," she said smiling. How could he say no after she'd said all those nice things about him?

"Sure, I'll take her—but this isn't a *real* date, is it?" Sean asked.

"No," Satara said, shooting down his hopes with a single word.

Sean walked back to his desk, then turned back to Satara. "Wait, does she know about this? You finding her an escort?"

"Not yet, but I'm going to call her tonight."

"Then tell her to give *me* a call tonight," Sean said, writing his number in her purple notebook.

"You're sure you're willing to take her to prom, even though you don't know her and have never even seen her?" Satara asked in a cautious tone.

Sean nodded.

"I was right about you. You *are* a nice guy." She gave him a quick hug before she sat down at her computer.

Sean walked back to his seat, thinking about what he had done. Satara's words echoed in his head: *you don't know her and have never even seen her face.* The old Sean would have made a big deal of wanting to see a picture or something. The new Sean wasn't worried about how she looked. As long as she had common sense, a good personality, and a sense of humor to match his, he was cool.

When he got home that day, he went straight to his room. He dropped his stuff in the blue dish chair and jumped on the computer to check his messages. He deleted all the junk mail and read through his other messages, mostly from AJ, Deandrew, and another classmate, Reggie Henderson. He picked up the phone to call Deandrew and had it about halfway to his ear when the other line beeped. He took a quick peek at the caller ID to make sure it wasn't a telemarketer. He didn't recognize the number, but answered anyway.

"Hello," Sean answered.

"Hi, Sean," Satara replied, in a soft, casual voice.

"Oh, hey," he said, relieved that he had ignored the little voice that said, "sales call."

"I have Elise on the line."

"Oh really," he said, sitting up. "Hello, Elise."

"Hello, Sean," Elise said in a soft, sweet voice.

When he heard that voice, he was *kind of* drawn to her, but it would take more than a phone call to know for sure.

"How are you doing?" Sean asked, immediately kicking himself for such a lame response.

"I'm fine. Just wondering why Satara did this."

"Well, I believe she said it's because *she* wants you to go to the prom."

"I'm also wondering why you said yes. You've never even met me."

"I guess I'm taking a chance, but Satara thinks you're worth it," Sean said, trying not to sound too harsh.

"Interesting."

"Well, I want to find out more about you," he said smoothly.

Sean and Elise talked on the phone for three hours. Somewhere in the first thirty minutes, Satara hung up. He wanted to meet Elise face to face, but with his hectic schedule, it would be difficult to find the time. Sean would have to get to know her by phone until he had a free day.

May 17th was that free day—a day that Sean would never forget. Satara, Elise, and Sean met at Chicago Ridge Mall. The plan was to look for a tuxedo at Desmond's and then see *Matrix Reloaded*.

As Elise gave Satara a hug, Sean felt an immediate attraction, but he held off. He had been attracted to Rachel, too, and she turned out to be a psycho. He walked toward her and everything slowed down as Kem's "Love Calls Your Name" played through his mind. She had already won him over with her personality and her sense of humor, but her looks were incredible. She was a full-figured young lady with a beautiful round face, full lips, and amazing hazel eyes. Her golden skin was different from that of the dark brown girls that usually caught Sean's eye.

Obviously she'd noticed something, too. As the girls walked out of the building, they dropped back, letting Sean walk by himself.

Elise whispered, "He's not Mexican."

"He's *half* Mexican," Satara said simply. "Can't you tell by his hair?"

"Hmmm, a little."

Elise didn't sound too thrilled to be dating him because he wasn't Mexican?

"What does it matter?" Satara said. "You liked him over the phone and it's not like you *must* go to prom with a Mexican."

Elise couldn't really argue with that, and the girls quickened their pace to catch up with Sean.

Despite the rocky start to the face-to-face meeting, the couple clicked almost instantly, thanks to their previous phone conversations. They had a lot in common: they liked the same kind of movies and music—until Elise, he thought only James and Vince liked Linkin Park. Both were outgoing, creative, single, and planned to be prosperous. Elise was a straight-A student, which meant she took school seriously; that was another plus in Sean's mind.

Inside Desmond's, they paged through the catalog for a burgundy vest and garter to match Elise's dress. The whole time, Sean was picturing how they would look at prom, concentrating only on her.

"What do you think of this?" Elise said, pointing at the bandana pattern for his vest.

"It's nice, but it doesn't match your dress," Sean replied, holding both material patterns together.

"Yes it does," Satara said, watching the men at the counter. "Men are soooo color-blind."

"That's the truth!" Elise added.

"Oh, I see, y'all gonna get on me like that," Sean said, leaning back in his seat. "Elise, just because you're an artist and know all the colors in the world, doesn't mean that I can't tell that one is darker than the other. And Satara, you couldn't tell whether one of those vests over there were purple or brown."

"Well, Mr. Big Shot," Satara said, tearing her eyes away from the man walking to the register. "What color is my shirt?

"Orange."

"I tell ya guys only know the *primary* colors," Elise said, folding her arms with a sly grin on her lips. "Her shirt is tangerine."

"What's the difference, Mrs. Michelangelo?" Sean asked.

"A tangerine is darker than an orange," Satara informed him.

"It's still orange," he said shaking his head. "Women!"

After finding what they needed at Desmond's, they went to the food court to eat and hung out until a few minutes before the movie. Sean might as well have stayed in the lobby. The only thing he could concentrate on was Elise and how gorgeous she was.

As they were leaving the mall, he stopped her. "Elise, will you be my girlfriend?" he asked, feeling as though he had just proposed. It was sudden, but he knew it was right.

She hesitated a little, then said, "Yes."

Walking into his home that evening, his mother was sitting at the computer desk next to the entertainment center in the living room. She was listening to El Debarge's "Somebody Loves You." And he began to sing along.

"Are you supposed to be going to prom this year with some girl named Elise?" his mother asked without turning to look at him.

He froze as he replied, "Yes, Ma'am." How did she know *before* he gave her the news?

"I don't think so." She turned and he saw the anger in her face. "I talked to your teachers on Friday and you're behind in some of your classes. You're lucky I'm not calling Jake."

"I know, Mom, I'm really working on that. I'm trying to get my work in on time but it keeps on backing up," Sean said, looking at the hardwood floor. *Man!* With all the social stuff and the Saturday classes and church stuff, he had forgotten to do a few things. He found this girl and now Superwoman wanted to take her away. Why did this have to happen now?

"Well, don't talk about it. *Do* it! Because as of right now, you're not going to anybody's prom," she said, raising her voice.

Sean's heart dropped. He had two options—do the work, finish, and turn it into the teachers, or don't do it and lose Elise before they even had a chance to get something started.

Sean busted his butt, staying after school and doing homework late into the night, sometimes having to do it over repeatedly to get it right. Although he did it to keep his promise to Elise, he also did it for himself. His future was on the line—bad grades wouldn't look good on his transcript.

Sean had been so busy, that prom day seemed to arrive in the blink of an eye. He hadn't been sure he could get his grades turned around in time. It had been close—Superwoman didn't tell him until eight a.m. prom day that he could go to the dance. Per her request, Ms. Schulz, Mr. Green, and Mr. Miles had called her from the school office to verify that Sean had turned in all of his assignments.

When he got to Elise's house, he was as nervous as a groom standing at the altar, and it showed.

Elise's father tried to calm him down. "Sean, what's wrong?" he asked, setting up his video camera.

"What are you talking about?" Sean fidgeted with his hands.

"Well, you seem a bit on the uneasy side."

"That's because I'm nervous," Sean said, trying to keep his voice down.

"There's nothing to be nervous about *yet,*" Elise's father said with a sly grin.

"'Yet'? What do you mean, 'yet'?" Sean asked as he paced nervously.

"You haven't met the rest of the family." He patted Sean on the back in mock sympathy.

"What do you mean, the 'rest of the family? There's more'?" Sean asked, his black dress shoes squeaking on the linoleum floor.

"You haven't even met a quarter of the family. They're all coming over to meet you."

Sean's heart started beating even faster. *Are they going to like me? Did I forget to put on deodorant? Is my breath funky?* How could a man this cool be this nervous?

It had taken a while for Sean to feel moderately comfortable around Elise's dad. He was cool with her mom, but her big, tall daddio, with his deep James Earl Jones voice, had Sean spooked. *Was the rest of the family that tall and serious?*

Pacing around the kitchen, he heard the doorbell ring, and rushed to the bathroom to splash water on his face in an effort to pull himself together. *Why are you overreacting? You get along with her grandmother, mother, and father. So you should be able to get along with anyone in her family.*

He was suddenly startled by his cell phone ringing, "Hello," Sean answered, hoping it was Superwoman.

"Hey, Sean, it's Chris. How's it going?" Well, if not Superwoman, who better than his Big Brother to help calm him?

Sean let out a breath of relief. "Not too good. I'm about to go to prom *after* I meet the rest of Elise's family."

"Oh, you'll be fine. You just have to get rid of the idea that things are going to go wrong."

"I'm freaking out, that's what's going wrong," Sean whispered as he paced around the bathroom. "I don't have a big family and Elise has met the only four people that I wouldn't be embarrassed for her to meet: Momma, Denise, Rick, and Grandma Celie."

"Sean, every teenager goes through this. It's like a rite of passage. I even went through it. My date's dad had a shotgun in his closet—"

"Chris! You're not helping."

"Just calm down and take everything slow. You'll be fine."

Sean walked out of the bathroom and toward the living room. As he walked in, everyone was looking in the opposite direction. Sean turned to see what held their attention. The moment he caught sight of Elise, his tongue stuck in the back of his throat.

She was an elegant, curvaceous masterpiece. Her form-fitting burgundy dress hugged her beautiful body and flared slightly at the bottom, barely touching the floor. He walked over to her with a bright smile that no one could wipe off his face. "You look beautiful," he whispered in her ear.

"Thank you," she said, blushing as everybody whistled and clapped.

Now the only thing Sean had to worry about was not tripping or falling, especially since her father held the video camera.

A Lincoln Navigator, their "Limo" for the evening, was parked in front of the house. Sean took a deep breath and escorted Elise toward the door. As they stepped onto the porch, Sean looked down the eight steps between him and level ground. Her father was taping the whole "Walking down the stairs to prom" ceremony.

Okay, Sean, take one step at a time, and you'll be fine. If you fall, go solo, let her arm go. As they stepped onto the first step, he had a vision of Elise's father recording the fall in slow motion and replaying it for the whole family. They made it down safely. Sean wiped a thin layer of sweat from his forehead before helping Elise into the car.

To Sean's surprise, the limo pulled to the curb a few blocks away. Elise explained that the driver was her uncle and their chaperone. Others were riding with them. Her friends took their time coming to the car as a man stood off to the side, recording that ceremony, too. Finally, they pulled off.

Elise introduced them. "Sean, this is my friend Mickey and her date, Kevin."

"Pleased to meet you guys," Sean said.

Sean liked her company. He couldn't understand why someone would brush past her and not ask her to the prom.

Once there, it was hard to get her up to dance. She was shy when it came to that. Sean wasn't one to force anyone into anything he or she didn't want to do. (His mother had several talks with him about that, and it didn't just apply to sex.) He sat next to her and talked until she was ready.

Sean was talking to Elise about graduation plans when someone tapped him on the shoulder. He turned around to see a young lady, with a blinding silver dress and a royal blue sheer shawl covering her shoulders. Her make-up was caked on and she wore her hair in a fountain bun, obviously held in place with gel. Gems sparkled in her hair and on her long fingernails. *Was she auditioning for a play or something?*

"Excuse me, are you doing anything?" *Didn't she see him talking to Elise?*

"Yes, I am." Sean said. The girl looked at Elise and crinkled her nose in distaste.

"Well, I want to dance," she said, putting her hands on his shoulders, lightly massaging them.

Sean shrugged her off. "My date isn't ready to dance yet."

"Sorry, little boys don't know what's good when it's in front of them," she said, storming away.

Eventually Sean coaxed Elise on the dance floor and enjoyed every step.

Turning away from the picture of Elise, Sean checked out his reflection in the bedroom mirror. Brushing off his senior tux, he laughed, thinking of all the fun he had at prom in his junior year. This time, instead of burgundy and black, their colors were royal blue and champagne.

"Hmm—it's this day all over again, huh?" Sean's mother asked. She was still dressed in her work clothes, and looked exhausted from her 9-to-5 job.

"Mom, what are you doing home so early?"

"I'm just here to see you off to prom, make sure you're okay with the limousine driver, and to make sure I don't get a phone call from school telling me that you haven't been turning in your work." She grinned.

"Mom, why do you have to bring up old stuff?" Sean complained, grabbing a green towel and brushing it over his already shiny shoes.

"You can't tell me that last year's prom situation wasn't funny. Boy, those teachers weren't letting up off your butt."

"That's not funny, Momma. I worked my butt off. Then Mr. Robertson was messed up over the fact that I missed *one* of the French speaking-countries in my photo album." He looked over to his mother. "And it took me a really long time to get those math problems right."

"Well, I'm proud of you for turning things around this year so we didn't have a repeat of that whole mess."

Sean was happy this year. The situation was completely different. He didn't have to rush and do anything at the last minute. He wasn't as nervous and his relationship with Elise had blossomed.

Sean's phone rang—his cousin Richmond's number popped up on the display. "What's good?"

"We're waiting in the limo downstairs," Richmond replied.

"I'm on my way," Sean said fixing his suit.

He gave his mom a quick kiss on the cheek, and rushed out, stumbling over the phone book that someone had left in the middle of the floor.

Sean didn't break stride, just kept on walking out into the night with his newfound confidence, anxious to see Elise and to enjoy another prom with great dancing and food that was barely touched.

Chapter 34

S ean had faith that he would make it to this day—graduation day.
It had taken a lot of hard work, several ultimatums, a few threats,
restrictions, missed parties, prayers, and consistent affirmations.
Today wouldn't be possible without God. God, who'd answered his mother's
prayer and sent the right people into Sean's life to help him succeed.
God, who'd answered his prayer to move them to a safe place. God, who
had given him all the Superwomen in his life—and the Supermen.

Sean and the other students, wearing green caps and gowns with gold
cords draped over the shoulders, gathered nervously behind the stage,
waiting to march into the auditorium.

As the commencement began, a sense of accomplishment washed over
Sean.

Ms. Stanton finally started calling out the names of the class of 2004.
Walking into the auditorium behind the members of his class, Sean saw
his mother, Aunt Denise, Grandmother Celie and Grandma Linda (who
had yards of food waiting for everyone back home), his godmother Beatrice,
Elise, and her mother, Mrs. Pryor. They were all in their seats, ready to
cheer him on. Chris and Rick were on the other side of the auditorium
taping the ceremony. Amazingly, he didn't miss his father. Sean had finally
realized that there was nothing wrong with him—there was something
wrong with a man who didn't want to have anything to do with his son.

Why had it taken him so long for him to realize that?

His mother and grandmother were crying. Superwoman had stuck with her son, her baby boy, through a lot; it finally paid off. Though she would say that she did get something out of it—Jake, the recruiter, who actually had turned out to be a pretty decent guy once Sean realized he was also on his side.

As Sean stood across the platform from the golden-skinned young woman with long, flowing, dark brown hair, he smiled. Sandy smiled back. As the marching music played, and Sean stepped onto the platform, he did a little shake of his shoulders. So did Sandy. He did it again. So did she. This time they kept it going. The audience clapped and laughed as Sean and Sandy danced and smiled their way to the stage. Sean felt like rejoicing. He hugged the young woman as they met in the center, then turned and bowed. She curtsied. Nothing wrong with spicing things up a little.

Sean took his seat in the third row next to Aaron, James, Vince, and his cousin Richmond.

"Dag! A three-hour graduation," Aaron grumbled, slumping in his seat, gripping his always empty stomach. "Whose *bright idea* was that?"

"This is *our* day! And compared to what I've heard about other schools' graduations, this is nothing," Vince replied. "Besides, Ms. Stanton will be calling us one day, asking us to come back and speak to the new scholars coming in. At least we'll have something to talk about." Then he scanned the crowd looking for some of his other friends were supposed to be there, but didn't find them. "Some of our classmates aren't even here, because they slacked off and didn't graduate. I'm happy to be here no matter how long the ceremony lasts."

Sean looked at his program and anxiously waited for his turn to introduce the keynote speaker. Listening distractedly to Aaron, Vince, and James talking, Sean thought back over his senior year at Olive-Harvey Middle College High School. It had been his greatest year of high school. All of his teachers helped him with his studies and made sure he stayed on top of his game—even when he was trying to slip back into his old patterns. They didn't give up on him and they wouldn't let him give up on himself.

After the second college tour, he had been more focused. His attitude changed for the better since now he had a clear goal—college. He had seen firsthand how much people enjoyed being there. He had even spent the whole summer in school, retaking four of his classes in order to get passing grades. Ms. Schulz and Ms. Wallace helped Sean out tremendously with his math- ematics problems. He wouldn't forget Ms. Schulz's words, "Stay organized and keep a planner so you can know when your work is due, and do your assignments ahead of time. Stop doing everything at the last minute. Anything could happen."

Sean's attention returned to the stage just in time to hear his name. "For our next speaker, I would like to introduce to you a young man who has turned his life around," Ms. Stanton said, her voice full of pride. "He is definitely a man who I know is a scholar. Ladies and gentlemen, I give you Sean Morris."

Loud applause filled the auditorium as Sean stood and walked to the stage. Stopping to give Ms. Stanton a big hug, he took his place in front of the podium. The applause slowly died down as Sean stood ready to introduce Nicole Durham, an OHMC alumni and recent graduate of Tougaloo University, in Tougaloo, Mississippi. He kept it short and sweet.

After Ms. Durham's speech, the class rose to sing two songs: an African song entitled "Nkosi Sikeleli Africa," which translated to "Lord Bless Africa," and another gospel song, Hezikiah Walker's "I Need You to Survive."

Next, the graduating class had to dedicate their light of learning. Sean walked up to the podium, proud to take his white candle. "I'd like to dedicate my light of learning to God; my ancestors; my mother and Superwoman, Cynthia Morris; my Grandmother Celie; Aunt Denise; and Grandma Linda." Sean looked at his mother as she wiped her tears. He walked across the stage and down the other side, where he received his diploma and certificates of achievement.

Sean was then recognized and given awards as the most energetic, most creative writer, and most professional scholar. When the test scores were announced—15.8 in reading, 13.2 in math, and 25 on the ACT, his mother jumped from her seat and said, "That's my baby!"

Grandma Celie yanked her back down in the seat as everyone laughed.

Sean was grinning too much to be embarrassed. The scores of the other students—students that other schools, teachers, and parents had given up on—were also high. When the scores weren't above the 12.9 range, Ms. Stanton told how many grade levels the scholar had improved. Everyone had something to be proud of.

The class sang one more song, "If We Never Pass This Way Again."

Finally, it was time for the scholars to flip the tassels on their caps from left to right, signifying they were now graduates. Sean's eyes filled with tears as he looked out on his family members who each gave him a wave, a nod, or a big smile.

One last time, each scholar walked up to the podium, this time to announce the college or university he or she would be attending.

Sean approached the microphone, smiling with pride as he said, "I'm scholar Sean Morris and I will be attending Fisk University on a Dean's Scholarship." The audience applauded as he left the stage.

"That's my baby!" Superwoman yelled again at the top of her lungs. The audience applauded even louder.

Sean was the only one in his class going to Fisk. Mr. Keith in Admissions had walked him and his mother through the process. Sean's friend Marsha, who attended Saturday class with him at the Chicago Urban League, had just finished her freshman year at Fisk, and offered to take care of him and show him the campus ropes. Mr. Robertson, his French teacher and mentor, would check on him daily.

Aaron was going to the Academy of Arts. James was going to Tuskegee University, His cousin Richmond was on his way to Tougaloo College and Vince had chosen to go to Columbia University for a year and then transfer to Howard University. Curtis went to Southern Illinois University. The Smart Guy Group was living up to its name.

Going up the stairs, Sean's high spirits fell for a minute when it hit him that he and his friends were going their separate ways. But Sean had made some life-long friendships in high school and he was sure to make even more in college.

After the ceremony, everyone shifted to the lobby area outside the auditorium. There his father stood blocking the bathroom door and Sean had to *go*. Sean walked toward the other bathroom in an effort to avoid him. However, Roberto raised his voice to cover the distance. "Sean, come here."

Sean's eyes widened. The only person allowed to talk to him like that was his momma, who was standing off to the side, watching. She looked like she wanted to step in and embarrass Roberto in front of all the women in the lobby, but Grandma Celie and Elise's mother held her back.

"What can I do for you?" Sean asked, already knowing it was too late.

Robert looked over at Cynthia, then cast a quick glance to the bathroom. "Can we talk for a minute?"

"For what, *Dad?*" Sean said, a little quieter. "You haven't spoken to me since seventh grade I almost had to go through a paternity test to prove that I was your son. Your time to talk has passed," Sean said, and turned to walk away.

"But, Sean—" Roberto said, grabbing Sean's arm.

"Let go of my arm." Sean shrugged loose. His eyes watered. God, he didn't want to cry. Not today. Today was *his* day! "You *will not* disrespect me on the happiest day of my life. You had a chance to be a part of it, but you chose another route. I love you, Dad. And I've already forgiven you for everything, but if you didn't want to be in my life when I needed you most, then stay out," he said, storming into the bathroom.

When Sean came back out, his father was gone. Sean was glad he got that off his chest, but furious that his dad could make him so angry. Sean shook off the bad feelings as he saw his friends outside and joined them. "What's going on?"

"Just getting ready to toss our caps," Aaron said, holding his cap.

"Yeah, we couldn't do it inside since Ms. Stanton got hit with them at last year's graduation," Vince said with a laugh.

"Guys, move in for a picture," Sean's mother said, holding a disposable camera.

Sean nodded and she smiled.

The Smart Guy group posed for several shots, and for the last one they threw their caps in the air.

Chapter 35

As much as Sean Morris wanted to get out of his mother's house and into his dorm at Fisk, college still came too fast for him.

His silver radio-alarm clock blasted the sound of Bone Crusher's "Never Scared" in his ear. He fell out of his queen-size bed, frightened by the rapper's loud call for "Attention!" Sean landed on the brown carpeting with a loud thump and lay there for a couple of moments.

He heard footsteps pounding down the hallway toward his door. His mother slammed through the door, carrying an old black, cast-iron skillet in one hand and a brown leather belt in the other. She saw him on the ground and the window wide open.

"Baby, who knocked you out of the bed?" she asked, eyes wide, alert for someone to jump out at her.

"Bone Crusher," he replied, slowly getting up from the floor.

"You've got company up in here?" she asked, running to the closet. "You didn't say anything about someone spending the night."

Realizing what Sean had just said, and what song was on the radio, she snapped the belt playfully toward his muscular, slightly hairy thigh.

"Ouch, Mama, stop hitting me," he said with a laugh, as he crawled under his baby blue covers.

"Boy, do you know you almost gave me a heart attack *and* a stroke. I have high blood pressure. I can't take all this. Thank God I won't have to go through any more of this, *Mr. Fisk University Scholar.*"

"Oh don't worry, I'll be back for the holidays," Sean said, sitting up and giving her a hug.

"I can't believe this is your last day. I'm so proud of you," she said. A single tear slid down her cheek.

"Thanks, Mom, thanks for being the best."

"Oh, baby, get out of my face before I have your transcript pulled," she teased as she walked out of his room.

Sean jumped out of bed, grabbed his orange and blue Fighting Illini towel and threw it over his body. Elise had bought it for him last year, during her freshman year at the University of Illinois in Urbana-Champaign. She would be returning for the sophomore year in a couple of days. He kissed his mother on the cheek and ran into the bathroom. He adjusted the shower temperature, stripped, and stepped in. No naps this time.

Stepping out, Sean wiped the steam off the mirror. Looking at his reflection, he saw himself as he looked when he was eight years old, without the mustache or thin goatee and sculpted muscles. Only a soft curly afro, small teeth, small gap, and a baby face that a woman couldn't say no to. Well, women who weren't related to him. And his teachers. And his girlfriend. He smiled, put in his contacts, and finished up his morning bathroom routine.

Walking out of the bathroom with the towel riding low on his waist, he could smell turkey sausage and eggs cooking. His mouth was watering and he decided to speed things up so he'd have time to enjoy breakfast. The loud ringing of his phone interrupted his thoughts. The towel nearly fell off as he ran into the bedroom. He looked at the caller ID on the cordless phone. "What's up, Vince?" Sean asked, walking over to his dresser, pulling out a pair of gray Calvin Klein boxers and putting them on.

"What's up, Sean? You packed?"

"Yeah, you and Aaron need to get over here before I leave you both and you'll have to find your own way to Nashville."

"All right, man. Aren't you the pushy one, considering *we're* the ones making sure *you* get to Fisk and get settled in," Vince replied with a chuckle.

"Well, don't mess with the driver."

"Ever since you bought that used Envoy, you've been tripping. I'll be there in a sec."

"Hey, a beat-up ride is—"

"Yeah—yeah, is better than a dressed-up walk," Vince finished. "But yours isn't beat up."

"That's true," Sean replied.

"Well anyway, I'll be there in five minutes."

"Okay. Hey, I thought you were at home."

"Nope, bye."

Sean put the phone back in the cradle, and it rang again. "What's up, Aaron?" he asked after looking at the caller ID.

"What's up, Superboy? Just checking to see if you were up."

"Of course I'm up. We have to be on the road in an hour. So get moving," Sean said.

"Oh, I'm moving all right. As a matter of fact, I'm walking up to your front door now. I smell sausage and eggs, so you better hurry up before I eat your plate."

"You touch my plate and your butt is walking to school."

Sean slipped on his Old Navy blue jean shorts and a light blue Enyce shirt and stepped into his new all-time favorite shoes, white Pumas. He quickly made the bed and picked up the mess on his floor. He put all of his CDs in his black carrying case, then turned off his radio. As he walked toward the kitchen, he heard two voices: one tired, the other soft and sweet, saying hello to his mother. Peeking around the corner, he saw his Grandmother Celie and Elise.

"Come on over here, number one grandson, and give me a hug," Celie said, opening her arms wide. "You know you're a leader, right? You don't have to compare yourself to anyone else. *You* are who counts. What you do with your life is what counts."

"Yes, Grandma Celie," Sean said as he walked over and wrapped his arms around her wide frame. He then took her hand and led her to her favorite soft white chair in the living room.

As soon as Sean had her seated, he turned to Elise. "Hey, baby, how are you?" he asked, giving her a long hug.

"I'm fine and I'm proud of you," she whispered in his ear. They went to the couch and sat down.

Aaron was sitting in the yellow chair and looking out the window. "Hey, Man, where's Vince?" Sean asked.

Moments later, Vince came in through the half-opened door, looking very tired. "What's up? Is it time to eat?"

"Long walk?" Sean asked playfully.

"Man, forget you," Vince said, holding his back. "Just because you don't have to walk anywhere, anymore. The transmission went out on my ride."

"Come on in and take a seat, Vince," Celie said, looking at all three boys. "Let me talk to you guys for a minute."

The three looked at each other before moving in closer.

"Boys, when you go away from home, don't let anyone manipulate your mind. You know what you are destined for in life," she said as Vince shifted in the chair. "Don't worry about those girls; they will always be here. You guys have made it, and unfortunately not a lot of Black men can say that nowadays. But this is only the beginning. You don't want to get to be my age and think, what happened to my life?"

"Yes, Ma'am," they said in unison. Sean helped her get up and the trio followed her into the kitchen.

Elise didn't seem hungry. She barely let Sean eat because she wanted to hold his hand.

"Either you pick up a fork and help me out, or you're going to have to let my hand go so I can eat."

Time passed quickly as the college-bound scholars sat around chatting and sharing a laugh over things that had happened to them during the past year.

Celie looked at her watch. "It's almost time for you to get going."

"Rick's waiting for you to get to the campus so he can drive the car back, seeing how you can't have one down there your freshman year," Superwoman said softly as she walked toward them with an armful of Zip-Loc bags. "I made you guys some sausage and egg sandwiches for the road."

"Thanks. Hey, Sean, who's Rick? I thought you were an only child," Aaron asked.

"Rick's my play brother, but he's been like a real brother ever since I was little."

"Before you go, let's hold hands and pray," Grandma Celie said.

Superwoman's Child

They formed a circle and held hands as Celie said a quick prayer for a safe trip and for prosperity and for wisdom and guidance. They hugged each other and Sean gave Elise a kiss that was so long, Celie yanked his shirt to pull him back to reality.

Everyone walked out to the middle of the circular driveway and exchanged more hugs. The boys walked to the black SUV with its tinted windows.

"You better go to church while you're down there, Sean," Superwoman yelled, tears drying on her face.

Sean looked back and waved at the Superwomen in his life, then put on his black sunglasses as the bright sun crawled up in the early morning sky.

The women watched Sean get in the car and drive off to the next level of higher learning.

"Man, it's a brand-new day for all of us. We're heading off to the land of delicious Southern-fried women," Aaron said, rubbing his hands together before turning to Vince. "This might be a place where they will accept you with your locks," he added, messing with Vince's hair.

"Whatever, Aaron, my locks look a lot better than that fifteen-week-old haircut of yours."

Sean looked at himself in the rearview mirror, glad that his hair was in place. "Both of your heads are jacked up," Sean said, laughing. "Besides, you're not staying that long. Rick said you can bunk in his hotel room before y'all make the trip back to Chicago tomorrow."

As Sean turned off Sixty-Seventh Street onto South Shore Drive, heading toward I-57, he looked over his shoulder. "Yo, Vince, hand me that pack of gum in my bag."

Vince unzipped the bag. "What's this red cloth?" Vince asked, holding up a piece of bright red material. "It looks like some kind of cape. And what's that it says there on the back? S-W-C."

Sean thought for a moment, then laughed. *SWC—Superwoman's Child*.

Sean was a lot like his mother. Both had overcome challenges. And like his mother, Sean had to keep moving forward.

He pulled the cape over the seat, and looked at the bright white letters. He understood his mother's message more than she could know.

"Yes, Momma, I *am* Superwoman's Child."

241

Author's Note

To single mothers a/k/a Superwomen:

No matter what, there's always a way to get through the hard times—especially when it comes to your children. Prayer and the power of the spoken word (affirmations) are what helped me the most. If **you** believe, then everything will fall in line (no matter how bad the grades look or what anyone else says—YOU know what your child is capable of.) With your support, the possibility for your child's future is endless. Allowing them to give up will only put that future on hold. If my mother had totally given up on me (and at times I know she did want to), there's no telling what would have happened. So make sure that YOU hold tight and keep steering them in the right direction. They will eventually become one of the future leaders and will have their own story to tell.

To the sons and daughters of Superwomen everywhere:

Learn to follow the positive examples of superwomen and supermen (role models/mentors if dad doesn't seem to be around). Trust that they are in your corner and there to help you. **No one who loves you wants you to fail.** Though I was faced with some serious academic challenges, and at times that report card looked like I had become an "international citizen" (a few F's—flags as we call them), they did not stop me when I made up my mind to do better and go beyond even my teachers' expectations. No one can do it for you. Make your own clean slate and a new set of goals. You'll be amazed at how much easier things will be when you **take responsibility**

for your life. Don't hold yourself back by being bitter towards people who *should* be in your life, but are not around. **God put the people in place to help you, mentor you, guide you, love you. They're already there. No need to look any further.**

Here's hoping we meet somewhere in the friendly skies of infinite possibilities; and that you, too, will *Circle Until You Land...*

Peace,

J. L. Woodson
Superwoman's Child: Son of a Single Mother

Author Bio

J.L. Woodson, a sophomore at Fisk University, is also the author of *The Things I Could Tell You!* He is a contributing author to Zane's NAACP Image Award-winning *Breaking the Cycle* anthology, and coauthor of *How to Win the Publishing Game*. His debut novel was published when he was sixteen. He is a Chicago native and resides in Nashville, where he is working on his third novel, *Circle Until You Land*.

Visit the author at www.jlwoodson.com

EXCERPT FROM ZANE'S "BREAKING THE CYCLE" ANTHOLOGY, AVAILABLE FROM STREBOR BOOKS INTERNATIONAL:

GOD DOES ANSWER PRAYERS

J.L. WOODSON

The beeping noise hummed under the sound of frantic voices. Consistent, like a dripping faucet, it wore on Steven's nerves.

What is that noise? Steven opened his eyes. People in green, blood-covered hospital suits stood over him with surgical tools, preparing to do something to his body, but he didn't know what. He could hear them faintly, and their faces were covered with bright white masks so he couldn't tell male from female, or doctor from nurse.

All he could really hear was that consistent beeping noise from the heart monitor. And then it happened. The beeps became slower, slower, slooooooower. His twelve-year-old heart was slowing by the second.

Steven still hadn't realized that, somehow, he could see everything perched from his spot right above the operating table. How did he get there?

"What are they doing?"

It looked like they were trying to save his life or something, but he wondered how that could be when he felt fine. "He's bleeding out. Get the clamps," one of the nurses yelled.

He scanned the room—green tiled walls, bright white lights, and extra surgical equipment stood near the bed where his body lay on the white sheets. A flutter of activity took place near the upper part of his body as nurses passed tools, followed quick commands, and overall moved in synchronization as though this entire act were a dance.

For some strange reason, they were still trying to save his life, but they actually walked straight past the "real" him. A glance to his left found his mother and father both crying behind a large plate-glass window. His father's face radiated shame, while his mother kept on banging on the glass, mouthing the words, "Save…him…please."

Who was she talking about? She couldn't have been talking about him. He was sitting up, feeling fine, and watching everything. Steven's face wrinkled in confusion, until one of the doctors lowered the window shade, blocking out the view of his parents. Steven slowly glanced behind him, and shock exploded from every corner of his mind. His own reflection glared back at him. He looked exactly like the Steven he remembered and, at the same time, looked nothing like the Steven he had been for twelve years.

Jumping further away from the table, he soon hovered in the upper corner of the room as questions whirled in his mind. How could that be me? I'm standing right here. It was painful to see himself lying on an emergency room table as doctors feverishly worked on his body, trying to get his heart back to a normal speed. Now he knew the reason for his parents' tears. But how did he get like this? How did Steven end up on that table? Steven wasn't in a gang, so that couldn't have been it. There were no accidental shootings at school that day, so that was out of the question.

Steven was startled by the loud beeping sound, which suddenly switched from a beep to a flat, solid tone.

"He's flat lining. Get the paddles."

A nurse disappeared and a few seconds later, a loud bursting noise came from behind him. He turned around and quickly moved out of the way as a nurse rolled in the cart with electric shock paddles. The nurse splattered liquid on the paddles and placed them on his chest. "Clear." She paused, then added, "No pulse, Doctor."

"I need more. Give me three cc's of—"

Steven hovered there, witnessing how fast everything was flashing before his eyes. "Ouch, what the—" Although Steven wasn't connected to his body anymore, he could still feel the shock every time the jolt of electricity passed through his body. He also felt weak, as though he were fading, drifting away.

"Clear."

Steven lowered to the ground.

"We're losing him…" one of the nurses screamed.

What happened to me?

"Clear!"

"Run!"

That one word would keep Steven up all night.

"If he somehow gets into the house tonight," his mother said softly while stroking his head, "I want you to run. Run as fast as you can, as far as you can. Just get away this time."

She had said those words some thirty minutes before he brushed his teeth, slipped on his green and blue plaid pajamas, and went to bed. Her full lips trailed a tender kiss on his forehead, leaving a thin print of burgundy lipstick as a reminder of a goodnight. The goodnight that happened right before he saw the flowered robe covering her full figure disappear from his bedroom into the dimly lit hallway. Right before the fear in her tear-filled, dark brown eyes could strike worry in Steven's heart. She didn't have to say who "he" was. In Steven's mind, "he" was synonymous with evil. And evil, at least in their house, was synonymous with "Dad."

But Steven hadn't listened to his mother. He lay in bed, wide-awake, eyes shifting swiftly in each direction, waiting for something to jump out. In his heart, Steven realized that he couldn't leave anymore than she could; anymore than she had ever tried. Who would protect her if he left her alone?

Steven was stronger now, almost as tall as his dad. He'd even taken karate classes and definitely knew how to take a man down. So why hadn't he lifted a finger when Hector came bursting through the door? Why was he trembling in the corner of the living room like the last leaf on a snow-frosted tree, watching an instant replay of another world champion Southside of Chicago fight? Why? He'd stepped in front of his mother once before and it didn't matter. It would only happen again tomorrow. Or the next day.

Or the next. Watching didn't matter. Watching was normal. Steven had heard the second verse of the same song so many times. And by now, he could definitely sing it from memory.

Angry blows rained down on his mother's body, purple bruises welling up where smooth, dark brown skin should be. As the living room became another battleground of curses and screams, Steven now understood exactly what his Aunt Vinah meant when she said, "When the shit hits the fan, you don't want to be standing downwind." Steven, at twelve years old, could tell anyone that upwind wasn't all that great either.

As his parents fought, every bitter word, every single blow, was like they were aimed directly at him, hurting him worse than any whippings his mother had every given him. It was always about money. Always about responsibility. Always about the fact that drugs were more important to Hector than his family. If Steven had never been born, maybe…things would've been different? At least, he wouldn't be around to see whether or not that was the truth. He couldn't stand to see this happen to them. Mainly, it was painful for him to watch bad things happen to his mother. But, staying in a bedroom listening wasn't much better.

Steven sunk down even further into the corner, under the painting of Lake Michigan and the portrait of silver-haired Grandma Mildred, hoping that she was able to see and hear from her place in heaven, the torturing words slicing and stabbing the soul of a twelve-year-old boy. He always picked the corner of a room to keep safe. And so far it had worked. He had learned from experience that flying objects didn't land in corners. No way! They whipped in and out like a boomerang and either landed on the floor near his feet, or sailed back into reach of one of his parents. Watching his parents fight was as unreal as a video game or an action movie. Only this was one episode he couldn't turn off and didn't want to watch. And, oh, how he wished he could simply change the channel. How he prayed that he could.

Did God listen to anyone anymore? Maybe all along, the answer to "Please God, keep me and my mother safe and help my father to leave the drugs alone," was a big fat, "No!" While Steven couldn't understand that, he did understand that God helps those who help themselves. The only thing he could see was that his dad—angry, high, or drunk—helped himself to giving out an order of ass-whipping. And his mother helped herself to an order of take one, take two, why not take three. Steven could only help himself to a ringside seat in his favorite corner, and there is where the family togetherness ended. Another blow made Steven wince. Tears welled up in his eyes, blurring his vision. At one time, he had loved his dad. At one time, he had felt his mother was the strongest woman on the planet. Each fight proved him wrong and with each fight he felt more alone.

Fear kept Steven's behind planted on the plush carpet. A carpet that barely hid the blood stains from the previous fights. A living room that had been almost spotless two hours ago, now looked like the before pictures in a home makeover series. Drugs had taken over what was left of his dad's mind. But deep down Steven knew that drugs weren't the real cause of his father's anger. The one night when he yelled at the top of his lungs, "I gave up my hopes and dreams to support this family!" was closer to the truth. Hopelessness. Dreamlessness. They wouldn't even have a family, if Steven weren't there. Steven knew then that the fighting was his fault, but what could he do about it now. He was already there.

What was Mom's excuse for staying? Of course it couldn't be because Dad was so good to her or that he took care of their family. Well, to let Aunt Vinah tell it, at one time he was good to her. But as far as Steven could remember, that hadn't been the case. Maybe someone had fast-forwarded through that scene before he could catch a glimpse. But God made other men, good men. Like his karate instructor. And his gym teacher! Good men. Kind men. Didn't God give mothers a second chance when the first husband broke down like a used car in the middle of rush-hour traffic? Couldn't they be traded in like cars? Or toys? Or refrigerators? Mom took that Kenmore back and got a new one—a better one with an icemaker, too. Didn't that say something?

Mom was superwoman. Mom could make a week's worth of groceries last a month. She could juggle bills like a pro. Mom could somehow pay for Steven to attend private school on a salary that said public school would do just fine. Mom could put a smile on even the meanest police officer's face by making small talk. And Steven had seen that many times as she drove away without a ticket. Even he had known that speeding down Lake Shore Drive like an Indy 500 driver was against the law. He never complained because he enjoyed it. Yes, Mom could do all that and more. Well, except one thing. Leave! Yes, just one thing—leave and take him with her. Why did she stay with Dad when all he could do was hurt her? She was strong. Everyone knew that. Superwoman was always strong, right? She was superwoman. But how could she rescue Steven if she couldn't even rescue herself?

The front door wasn't made of kryptonite. It didn't even have bars or a screen door. A few simple steps forward and both of them could run. Hide. Live. Smile. Dream. That's all it would take, right? Just the two of them. Yes, that would be an answer to a prayer. But deep down, he loved his dad, too. Didn't they have places for him to get well? Yes, rehab or detox, or something like that. But by looking at the rage in his father's eyes, as sick as it sounded, it looked like he enjoyed fighting. There was no help for that; not even counseling. Steven could also see hatred. Not just hatred for his family, but hatred for life in its entirety, like life had done him wrong. If anything, Hector wasn't getting it any worse than anyone else. He was learning life's lesson, but he chose to learn the hard way. Even though Steven's mother was his superwoman, he had been waiting on his father to become Superman. Steven could bet that it wouldn't happen anytime soon, though.

The sudden stillness in the room made Steven hold his breath. Something had changed. The fighting had ended, but not the normal way—with doors slamming and sobs and swiping alcohol over blood-crusted bruises.

No, they were still standing. Facing each other. Oh yes, this time was different. Dad had changed the game. He held a small silver gun in his hands. Mom's hands had yanked upward like a criminal when the police say, "Put 'em up."

"Where's the money, Bitch?" That voice, although spilling from his dad's lips, did not belong to the man Steven once knew. And who was he calling a bitch?

Steven could barely recognize his mother's voice, which came out as a frightened whisper, "It's gone. I had to pay bills. We have to eat. We have to …live!"

Sweat and blood poured from Dad's forehead as though a faucet had been installed at the hairline. "You're lying. I want that money. You got paid today."

What money? Her money? Mom was the only one who worked. Dad never had any money. Dad didn't have a job anymore—thanks to his best friends—cocaine and crack. Now this scene was new—the gun and Dad hitting Mom up for cash? Or was it an old thing, and Steven didn't know about it? If Steven had any respect left for his dad, he would've lost it at that moment. But Dad had a head start on that a year ago, and had done nothing to gain it back. Steven wasn't sure the man even cared.

"You're lying, Bitch. You always take care of that brat. You've got some money."

Brat? When did Steven become a brat? And who gave his dad a gun? Who in their right, or even their terrible mind, would trust his dad with a gun?

"Hector, put the gun down and leave. Or just leave. I don't have anything. You've been through my purse; you've been through all my hiding places. You've seen there's nothing there."

The gun lifted until he connected with the frightened woman's temple.

Fear was instantly swept aside as Steven scrambled to his feet, leaving the safety of the corner. "Here, Dad," Steven said, stuffing a trembling hand into his jeans' pocket. "This is my allowance. You can have it. I—"

The sudden movement caused his father, and the gun, to swing in his direction.

Powwwwwwwwwwwwww!!!!!!

White heat flooded Steven's body. Pain spread from his chest to his toes and bounced back up to start all over again. Standing became impossible. Against his wishes, Steven lowered to his knees, barely seeing the stunned expression on his father's face. But he could see that his mother had reached out for him, trying to catch him before he landed totally on the floor. She was too late.

"Oh God. Oh God. Oh God," he faintly heard his dad say over and over again as he hit his fists on the side of his head. See? He said God! The man did actually know Him!

"Steven. Ohhhhhh, my baby." Mom's sobs made her body tremble as she pulled Steven's head into the soft curve of her breasts. Soft. Comfort. The living room swam in and out of focus. The world was fading. Slowly. Slowly. Who knew that at twelve years of age, Steven would lay there in his mother's arms wanting more time to live, but not sure whether time was on his side or not.

He remembered his mother telling him, "Before we are born and come onto Earth we choose our parents, our life, and our death." Steven didn't believe it then, but he understood now.

She reached out, yanked the phone from the cradle, frantically dialing for help. His dad sank down to the floor by his side. Both of them looked down on him. The fight was forgotten and something else was more important than money, or pain. Steven. Finally, they saw him. Finally, they had stopped fighting enough to see him. See, God does answer prayers. God does listen to children's prayers.

Know ye not that ye are Gods? He'd read that in the Bible. And if that were true, if Steven was God, he would give anything, everything, to see his parents as they were right now. Hands by their sides, his father concerned with someone other than himself, his next hit, his next high—they were together in at least this one thing.

"I love you, Mom," Steven said softly to the woman whose hands trailed a painful path near his wound. Then he turned to the man whose pale skin, thin lips, and wavy hair were a perfect reminder of his Mexican heritage. Steven struggled for breath, but did the one thing that God would want him to do. "I forgive you, Dad. And . . . if you love me . . . you'll get some help. Get some—"

A single nod from his dad, followed by another, then another, needed no words to explain. With that, Steven Santos closed his eyes and prayed. The soft hum of his mother's voice echoed in his heart and mind as he drifted into a peaceful sleep, hoping to awake and see that his dad's promises were kept and his mother had become Superwoman again.

Steven opened his eyes halfway, then fully. The operating room had disappeared. He was asleep in a comfortable green chair, but noticed "the other Steven" still lying on a hospital bed in a coma. His reflection was on life support—several different machines kept tabs on how close he was to death.

Though he remembered how it all happened, the question now was how could it be reversed? And why was he hanging around like a shadow, a ghost, or something.

His attention was drawn away from his body to his parents talking just inside the entrance. For the first time in a long time, it looked like a civil conversation. No yelling, flying objects, or people getting hurt. He was surprised that they couldn't see him; he wasn't gone but he wasn't necessarily "there" either. Somehow, someone would have to explain that to him and fast.

"How could I have been so stupid?" Steven's mother said as he listened in. "I should've left when I had the chance. This is all my fault."

"Where would you go?" Steven's father said angrily, trying to keep his voice down as though he knew that the "other" Steven could hear. "You don't have any family."

"Any place would've been better than staying with you," his mother shot back. "Especially, if I would've known you were going to shoot my son."

"It was an accident!" Hector said, his brow furrowed in frustration. He glanced over to the hospital bed. "He's my son, too."

"You sure have a wonderful way of showing that he's your son," Mom said through clenched teeth.

Hector got up and walked over to the window, looking out at the gray sky.

Mom, sporting a dark blue overcoat and clutching a worn handbag, followed him, saying, "Ever since you got hooked on those drugs, you've paid attention to nothing else. Not your son, and not me. I guess family doesn't really mean anything to you anymore." She grabbed him, whirling him to face her. "The only family you think about are those people that got you hooked on that stuff."

"I don't need to deal with this right now," Hector said, brushing past her, trying to walk out of the room.

Sprinting, Mom made it to the door and blocked his path. "Yes, you do, Hector. If you don't deal with this now, I know for a fact that you won't deal with it later." Dark brown eyes watered with tears that splattered onto her coat. "When are you going to stop running away from your problems and confront them?"

"I am confronting them," he said, running a pale hand through his straight, jet-black hair. "I'm going to get help for my drug problem."

There was an uncomfortable pause in the room. Both of them knew it was a lie—a lie he told often, and a lie she had believed far too many times to count.

"You almost killed your son," she said softly, her gaze landing on the machines standing guard next to Steven. "Your own flesh and blood, your seed, and there's no telling whether he will survive." She faced Hector, glaring at him. "You don't think there's a problem? I know there's a problem. The fact that you pulled a gun on me—a gun for Christ's sake!—says there's a problem. The fact that we're here says there's a problem. You should be praying and asking for forgiveness."

"Heather, didn't you hear him? Steven already forgave me for that," Hector said, lacing his hands on top of his head, as though trying to block out one memory or another.

She glared angrily at him and her voice became icy. "I'm talking about God—forgiveness from God."

Hector grimaced, inching away from Heather's anger. "God can't do anything for me," he growled. "He didn't do anything for me when I was Steven's age and He sure as hell hasn't done much for me lately."

Dad began pacing the room.

"Hector," Mom began softly, placing a single hand on his shoulder. "I know that your mother was abused by your father, but you—"

"Don't even say it." Hector shrugged, removing her hand from his body. "I already know what you're going to say."

"What?"

Hector turned to look at her. "I'm going to have to forgive him. But why should I, after all that he did to my family?"

Steven's mother looked up at Hector. "For the same reason Steven forgave you…it's the right thing to do. When will this vicious cycle end? It should've ended with you!" She stepped out, covering the distance between them. "You swore that you would be a better man than your father. A better husband. A better father. But you've tried so hard not to be like him, you've become worse than he ever was."

Hector whirled to face her, parting his mouth to speak.

She held up a single hand to silence him. "I've taken a lot from you, things that will take time for me to forgive, but I didn't want Steven to experience this. I don't want him to grow up and continue this thing. If he lives." At that moment, Mom broke down in tears. "No, I mean—when, when he wakes up."

But the words were out. If. If Steven lived. Was this the price he had to pay for his mom's inability to leave a bad situation? Was this the price for Dad's love of drugs—things that took him away from reality and into a land that had nothing to do with responsibility? Why did Steven have to pay the price? He'd been the innocent one in all this.

Hector crossed the room, touching the face of the Steven lying on the bed. "How are we going to be able to say that we have a family? More than likely, I'll be in jail."

"I really don't know how that will work out, but you should try to work things out while you can. This is something you're going to have to do on your own. The only reason I'm talking to you now is because I know Steven would want that. Otherwise, I would've had you shipped out of here the moment we came through the hospital doors, so you wouldn't be able to have any contact with me or my son."

Hector's gaze fell to the white tiled floor. Mom was right; Dad was going to have to do it on his own. Could he? Would he?

Small delicate fingers curled around the lifeless one with an IV sticking out of the back side. The sound of a chair scraping across the tile took over all other sounds in the room for a moment. Hector placed the wide, tan leather chair right behind Mom. She sat down, still keeping Steven's hand in hers. Watching for signs of life—any life—any movement. She bowed her head, and Steven knew at once that she was praying.

"Pssssst. Hey, Kid."

Steven looked to the left of his space in the upper corner of the room. Another kid, about his age, with dark brown skin and a low-cut fade perched next to him. He wore a red and white striped shirt, jeans, and Air Force One sneakers. Steven wasn't frightened. Somehow Steven knew that this "kid" was just like him—in between living and dying.

"What's up?" Steven asked.

"Those your parents?"

"Yep. If you could call them that." Steven forced a laugh of disappointment. "What are you doing here?"

"I'm supposed to keep you company," the boy said, punching Steven in the arm playfully.

"Company? I'm not alone; my parents are here." Steven directed his focus back to his parents.

"No, your parents are there. They can't even see you."

"Am I fully dead?" Steven asked, confused by that one statement.

"Nope, you're just like you thought—in between."

"Whew—cool. So why else are you here?"

"I'm just like you. My parents were domvies, too."

"Dummies?"

"No, domvies—domestic violence parents."

"So you're in a coma, too?"

"Nope, I wasn't so lucky," he said, sadly walking to the window, waiting for Steven to follow. "I'm all the way dead."

"Your dad?"

The boy shook his head slowly. "Mom's aim was a little off with the knife. It slipped past Dad and landed right here," he said, pointing to his chest. "She was trying to protect herself from him."

"Wow, my dad had a gun tonight. It was an accident also."

"Yeah, I know all about it. There are a lot of us floating around here." Michael frowned. "My mama had an order of protection and everything, but that was just a piece of paper. We should've gone to one of those shelters or something."

"Was your dad on drugs?"

"Naw, he was just…mean," the boy said, hesitating, trying to find a polite way to put it.

"Well, at least my dad had an excuse," Steven said proudly. "He was on drugs."

The boy chuckled, his hazel eyes twinkling. "Doesn't make you any less half-dead now, does it?"

Steven winced, realizing the boy had a point. "What's your name?"

"Michael," he said, extending his hand. "Michael Roberts."

"I'm Steven Santos," he said, shaking it. "So, how long do I hang around up here?"

"Depends on you. Just like your parents are making choices, you're supposed to make some also. You can stay here for a while or you can go back when you're called."

Actually, the more he thought about it, Steven didn't want to go back—in between was safe.

"How many are there like you?"

Michael frowned, his mind winding with confusion. "Like me?"

"You know, kids that were killed in domestic violence accidents."

"Oh, domvie kids?"

"Yeah. That's what they're called."

"Lots of us, Man. Used to be diseases and gangs took us out. Now it's parents, or when we simply happen to be in the wrong place at the wrong time." Michael shrugged at the thought. "Just like you tonight. It's happening a lot more now than before," Michael said in a somber tone, reaching to grab two Sprites out of the cabinet behind him, handing Steven one.

"I thought we couldn't taste things here," Steven said, wondering whether he should waste time opening the pop.

"You have a lot to learn." Michael took a long sip of pop.

"Do you…get to see your parents?"

"I check on my mama sometimes." An awful stillness came over the room. "She's not doing so good. Killing me really sent her over the edge. Now they've got her on drugs—the legal kind—but she's no better than some street drug addicts I've seen. I think I'll be running into her pretty soon on this side."

"Will I be able to—"

"We all can. Some do, some don't. It depends," Michael said, gazing over at Steven's parents. "Some of the guys just can't go back, because they feel that they'll make matters worse."

"Aren't you supposed to have, you know, like wings or something?" Steven asked with uneasy sarcasm.

Michael laughed, slapping Steven on the back. "That's a myth—we don't need wings to travel—we just go from place to place. Now you see us." Michael slowly faded from view, leaving only the Sprite can behind. "Now you don't."

"Hey! Come back here," Steven said, realizing he was, in fact, a lot less lonely with Michael around to explain things.

Michael reappeared, a smile on his thick lips.

"Do you think my dad will get help?" Steven walked over to Hector, waving a hand in front of his face. Of course, he didn't notice.

"If I were you, I'd be more worried about your mama," Michael said, directing his attention toward the woman crying into her hands.

"Why?"

"Mamas have it hard. Guilt can kill 'em."

Steven's gaze landed on his mother; a small pain flashed over his heart. "Yeah, she's blaming herself right now."

"They all do." A disappointed frown spread across Michael's face. "But women have to be real smart."

Steven's attention was directed toward the nurse wearing a white uniform; her brunette hair was tied back into a ponytail. She checked his vital signs. "What do you mean?" he asked, turning to Michael.

"When they leave, they have to really leave. They can't just say it and stick around hoping things will get better. Sometimes it never gets better without outside help, and that might not always work," Michael replied, staring at both Steven's mother and father. "Sometimes that means they can't tell their families where they're going, or it means leaving the state. Sometimes, it means pressing charges and putting the man in jail." Steven stared at Michael as though he wasn't quite sure he'd heard right. "My mama had a chance to do that and didn't. And here I am." Michael's hands spread out as though presenting himself for an Army inspection.

"Yes," Steven said slowly, feeling the pain in his heart increase as he watched his mom's tears fall. "Here we are."